ML

5C

A Dangerous Charade

HER FOOLISH HEART

The Earl of Marchford brought his hands to Alison's shoulders. His gaze was hot and golden as it sank into hers, and an unthinking response flowered from deep within her. Without preamble, his mouth came down on hers, hard and urgent and demanding. Alison met his kiss with a fierce acceptance that shocked her. Her lips opened willingly for him, and when his hands slid down her back, pressing her along the length of him, she arched against him.

Marchford's fingers fumbled impatiently with the laces at the neck of her gown and Alison lifted her own to help him. But when he pushed aside the thin fabric of her shift to press his hand within, she stilled suddenly. No! a voice cried inside her. This was wrong! This was terribly wrong!

But how could she heed this voice of virtue when it was so faint beneath the pounding of her heart? Especially when the Earl of Marchford clearly did not hear it at all. . . .

By the same author

Miss Prestwick's Crusade

A Dangerous Charade

Anne Barbour

ROBERT HALE · LONDON

© Barbara Yirka, 1995, 2008
First published in Great Britain 2008

ISBN 978-0-7090-8465-5

Robert Hale Limited
Clerkenwell House
Clerkenwell Green
London EC1R 0HT

www.halebooks.com

2 4 6 8 10 9 7 5 3 1

Typeset in 11/14pt Palatino
by Derek Doyle & Associates, Shaw Heath
Printed and bound in Great Britain
by Biddles Limited, King's Lynn

CHAPTER 1

'Dammit, Toby, throw them a couple of shillings and let's be on our way.' The long-limbed gentleman, having momentarily vented his irritation, settled back in his curricle and waited as his tiger, a tousle-haired elf of some fourteen summers, rummaged in a capacious pocket for the specified gratuity.

'Good God,' continued the gentleman, his light brown eyes narrowing in bored exasperation, 'that infernal bleating is enough to make one avoid the city of Bath altogether. I thought the custom of tootling fanfares for every approaching visitor had died an unmourned death long ago. Listen to that fellow! He ought to be tarred and feathered and stuffed into his own trumpet!'

As the curricle sped away, the tiger glanced over his shoulder at the small group of musicians crouched near the tollgate that marked the entrance to Bath on the London Road. An uncertain shower of notes burst from them like spray from a leaking fireman's pipe in hopeful welcome for another equipage just rattling into the city. Toby shrugged his slight shoulders as the sound faded in the distance behind them. 'Everybody's got t'earn a livin' someways, me lord.'

Anthony Brent, the Earl of Marchford, bent a frown on the boy, and easing his vehicle through the increasingly congested streets of the city, turned to his own thoughts. Yes, indeed, he reflected morosely, everyone had to earn a living; unfortunately, some chose to earn it at the expense of others. Swerving to avoid a cart headed for market, he cursed again the summons that had wrenched him from his pleasant existence in London. He did not want to be here. He wished to be amid the familiar bustle of the city, ensconced in his comfortable life, and he most especially wished to be with the woman whose hand he had planned to ask of her father this week.

He could feel the letter that had brought him here crackling in his waistcoat pocket.

'Tony, you must do something!' had been the opening line of a missive crossed and recrossed until it was well nigh illegible. The earl sighed. How many times had he heard those words from Eleanor? She was a good sort, as sisters went, but she seemed to regard him as a combination barrister, wizard, and general dogsbody.

However, it did sound as though this time she had reason for her alarm. Aunt Edith was a very wealthy woman, and living alone as she did, without benefit of masculine counsel, she presented a ripe target for every confidence trickster within sniffing distance of her fortune. Apparently the most recent of this despicable breed was a woman – the most pernicious of the species, he reflected grimly. To make matters worse, the woman was currently residing with his aunt as her companion.

According to Eleanor, this female adder had so completely ingratiated herself with her employer that Aunt Edith was talking of making a sizeable bequest to her in her will. Steps must be taken, his sister had declared ringingly in her letter, and the threat to the family's peace of mind dispatched without delay.

For years the old lady had vigorously denied the need for a companion at all, insisting that she could make do with her abigail, an admittedly formidable personage named Granditch. In recent years, however, her abilities and, seemingly, her zest for life, had diminished dramatically. She spent too much time alone in her grand town house, sometimes even refusing to come down for dinner. Eleanor had finally made her see that she needed someone in whom she could place more authority for her well-being. Someone who could oversee her domestic arrangements and be trusted to provide her with congenial companionship.

Eleanor had offered to procure such an individual, but when Aunt Edith insisted on her own choice, an impoverished gentle-woman recommended by an old friend, March had irritatedly called his sister off. 'You're making a great deal of botheration over nothing, El,' he had written hurriedly. 'If she wants this spinster, let her have her way.'

That seemed to be the story of his life, March mused bitterly. He had apparently been blessed with a knack for being absent when his family needed him most, and now he was reaping the consequences.

At least this time he was on hand to deal with the situation before any serious damage was done. He turned off the London Road into Guinea Lane and then into the street leading toward his aunt's residence. He should have things under control in short order, and by the end of the week the adventuress would be on her way. He only hoped that her demands would not be exorbitant, though, he admitted to himself, he was prepared to part with whatever it would take to get rid of her. He'd a great deal rather see that she was tarred and feathered. At any rate, he was determined that his family would not again fall prey to a scheming harpy.

God, he wondered, would he ever discover the identity of that other? The one whose greed had cause his family such grief? It was an incantation he had repeated many times in the last several years.

Sunk in his own thoughts, the earl negotiated the long curve of Cottles Lane before swinging down Rivers Street, where he was struck suddenly by a glimmer of light in his gloomy fog. Well, two spots actually. He looked forward to his visit with his aunt, for she was the favorite among his older relatives. And then there was Meg or, Margaret, as she was more properly known, his young sister. Meggie was about to be decanted from the select seminary for young ladies in Bath she'd been attend-ing for the last few years and would be in residence with Lady Edith for some weeks before setting out for Eleanor's home to make preparations for her first Season.

The earl smiled. A week in Meggie's company would be just

recompense for the unpleasant task that lay before him, for she was flighty, volatile, and utterly lovable. Thus, it was with more anticipation than he would have believed possible a few moments before that he swung finally into the breezy expanse of Royal Crescent. Putting a hand to his curly-brimmed beaver hat to prevent its being taken by the wind that swirled about him in fierce eddies, he perused the sweep of town houses before him, often called the most elegant in Europe.

Moving briskly toward the one among them that belonged to his aunt, he was brought up short as his outside horse reared unexpectedly, throwing the beast's four-footed partner into some confusion. Having with little difficulty subdued the team, the earl immediately discerned the cause of the momentary upheaval. A small dog had scampered into the street from the park side of the Crescent, apparently under the impression that the horses had been placed in the street for his express amusement, and was now barking vociferously at finding himself surrounded by large, hooved feet.

'Honey! Honey, come back this instant!' Lord Marchford glanced up to see a young woman run into the street after the dog, directly into the path of the curricle. She was tall and plainly dressed and seemed oblivious of the peril she courted as she scooped the little dog into her arms.

Cursing, the earl wrenched on the reins once more and flung them into the hands of a startled Toby. He leapt into the street and, grasping the young woman, drew her urgently away from the curricle.

'Have you no sense?' snapped the earl. 'You could have got yourself killed – or maimed the horses!'

'I'm sorry,' she gasped. 'I – I didn't realize. . . .'

'Obviously.' He released her and stepped back for a brief appraisal. She was not precisely a dowd. Her serviceable ensemble of dove gray merino was not in the first stare of fashion, but was of an elegant design. Her features, except for a glimpse of white skin and a slice of dark hair, were hidden by a bonnet of truly profound grayness, so that altogether he thought he had never beheld such a totally colorless individual. As he pulled her away from the still skittish horses, he half expected her to dissolve in his arms like a column of smoke.

'I do apologize, sir,' she said softly, her eyes cast down in becoming modesty at the spaniel squirming in her arms. 'Honey is as charming as she can hold together, but she hasn't an ounce of sense, and I thought she was about to be crushed.'

Her tone was lamentably lacking in anything resembling an apology, and the earl bristled. 'If we are to talk of a lack of sense, madam—' he began, but the woman had already bent her attention to the little dog, murmuring a gentle scold.

Observing that they stood almost in front of his aunt's house, he issued a curt order to Toby to bring the curricle around to the stables and followed the woman to the sidewalk. Turning once more, she glanced up at him.

'You have every right to be annoyed, sir,' she said with a soothing smile that reminded him of those bestowed on him long ago by his nanny when he was being particularly bad-tempered. 'But no harm was done, after all.'

A suitable retort died on his lips as he observed in some surprise that the young woman had begun to ascend the same steps to which he himself had just set his foot. She was unaccompanied and was neither of an age nor, he thought, of the social status to be paying a social call on Lady Edith Brent.

'Are you here to visit Lady Edith?' he asked in some puzzlement.

'No,' she answered with another serene smile. 'I live here. I am Lady Edith's companion. My name is Alison Fox. And you, sir, are. . . ?'

Lord Marchford stiffened. My God, was this gray nonentity the dangerous predator he had come to vanquish?

'Anthony Brent, the Earl of Marchford,' he said sharply. The woman's pale cheeks had been faintly tinged with pink, brought about by the brisk weather and her exertions, and he watched with some satisfaction as the color drained from her face. She clutched at the wrought-iron railing surrounding the shallow flight of stairs that led to the doorway of the house, and for a moment he thought she was going to faint.

9

After a moment, however, she drew a deep breath, and straightened her shoulders before speaking again.

'I—' she began. 'That is, I have heard Lady Edith speak of you often, my lord. I did not realize she was expecting you.'

They had by now reached the front door, and Miss Fox swung about to open it. The earl allowed her to precede him into the house.

'My visit was unplanned,' he replied smoothly, his eyes seeking hers in open irony. 'I trust my coming is not inconvenient?'

Miss Fox put a slender hand to her throat. 'Of course not,' she said in a low voice. 'I know your aunt will be delighted to—'

'March!' The word was spoken in warm feminine tones, and the earl turned to see a slight figure approaching him from the floor above. A crown of snowy white hair proclaimed her advanced years, but her step was sprightly as she hurried down the stairs, and her carriage was graceful. 'March, dearest! Why did you not send to us that you were coming?'

Lady Edith Brent flew into her nephew's arms and her fragile laughter rang out as she was quite lifted from her feet in his embrace.

He released her gently and stepped back to look at her in some amazement. Why, she looked ten years younger than the last time he had seen her. She had gained a little weight, and her eyes fairly sparkled with vivacity. Was it the little nonentity who had wrought such a change? The little adventuress?

'I thought to surprise you, Aunt,' he replied, returning her laughter.

'Wretch,' Lady Edith scolded gently. 'You would be well served if you had come and found us elsewhere. We have become great gadabouts, you know. Oh' – she suddenly bethought herself – 'but you have not yet met Alison – Miss Fox.' She turned to the young woman. 'My dear, come meet my scapegrace nephew.'

The smiled dropped from the earl's lips as he bent a grim nod on Miss Fox. Her gaze dropped before his, and the hand she offered was icy. 'We have met, Aunt. We, er, encountered each other outside.'

Miss Fox paused in the act of removing her pelisse and for the first time lifted her eyes to look directly at the earl. He almost gasped aloud as he was pierced by a gaze from eyes that were an astonishing, electric blue. The air around him seemed unaccountably heated, as though warmed by a boundless tropical sky. He stood transfixed for a long moment, frozen in bemusement, watching as she lifted her bonnet to reveal a thick mane of lustrous black hair. How could he have thought her colorless?

'Outside?' Lady Edith queried, 'Oh dear, don't tell me, Alison, that you've been out with Honey. I've told you many times to leave that chore to one of the footmen. She is such a naughty little dog, after all.'

Miss Fox's lips curved in a rigid smile that was not reflected in those startling eyes.

'The – the park across the street is quite secure, my lady. It is fenced in so that Honey cannot escape.'

Her voice, noted the earl, was quiet and melodious, and, if he was not mistaken, contained the veriest touch of panic. Had she anticipated the advent of one of Aunt Edith's relatives – a spoke at the ready to be thrust into her grand plans?

'Do let us go in and sit down, then.' Lady Edith shepherded her nephew out of the entrance hall and into a large, pleasant chamber. Miss Fox hung back, looking flushed and uncomfortable.

'Please excuse me, my lady,' she said, backing away. 'You and his lordship will want to be. . . .'

'Nonsense,' was the brisk response. 'I have long been wanting to introduce you to my favorite nephew.'

She smiled up into the young man's face, which lightened with warmth and laughter.

'Do not be plying me with Spanish coin, Aunt. I am your only nephew, after all.' Abruptly, the laughter vanished and the earl's features hardened.

Instantly Lady Edith was at his side. Taking one of his hands in hers, she said quickly, 'Yes, my dear. But do come in and sit down.'

'Please ring for tea, Alison.' This to Miss Fox, whose face was once more tinged with a delicate rose. 'Come sit here by me, March' – Lady Edith settled herself on a sofa by the fireplace and patted the seat next to her – 'and tell me what brings you to Bath. Is your man bringing your things in?'

The earl lowered himself gracefully onto the spot indicated. 'No, Aunt, I would not dream of disrupting your household. I plan to be here a week or so only and have made arrangements at York House. I am just stopping to say hello before I make my way there.'

'But . . .' began Lady Edith. 'Oh, very well,' she concluded, throwing her hands in the air in a fluttering gesture. 'You will return for dinner this evening, though, won't you? And then later you can accompany us to the Upper Rooms. The town is a little thin of company at present, but I'm sure there will be many familiar faces there.'

'It will be my great pleasure, ma'am,' replied Lord Marchford smoothly, noting with some interest that Miss Fox stiffened at his acceptance of the invitation.

'Oh!' Lady Edith clapped her hands together. 'And Meggie will be here tomorrow! She will be quite in alt when she discovers you here, March.'

'Yes.' The earl's face lit with warmth and amusement. 'She has always felt that a brother residing in London lends her an immense cachet among her schoolfellows, and I am prepared for an exhaustive grilling on the doings of the Regent's set. However, Prinny and I do not often inhabit the same space, for which I thank God daily, so I shan't have much to report this time.'

The conversation was general after that, as tea was presented with a flourish by Masters, Lady Edith's longtime butler. Lord Marchford regaled the ladies – or at least one of them – with the latest *on-dits* of the *ton*, and confided his plans to ask for the hand of the Honorable Frances Milford, daughter of the Viscount Briscombe.

'I should not be discussing this delicate matter with you before the engagement is a fait accompli, but I'm sure Eleanor has already apprised you of the situation. She's been at my back for the past month, urging me to do my duty.'

'Well,' said his aunt, nibbling delicately on a poppyseed cake, 'she did write to tell me that you seemed to be showing a marked preference for the gel, but I was not aware that matters had progressed so far. If that is the case' – Lady Edith brushed the corner of her mouth with her napkin – 'what are you doing here? Shouldn't you be down on bended knee in the Milford morning room?'

Lord Marchford experienced an unexpected tightening in his stomach. Surely his aunt did not suppose that in coming to visit her at this time, he was postponing an unpleasant task. Not that he particularly looked forward to the moment of his official declaration, but he had assured himself that once the ritual was concluded, his life would progress once more in its orderly path. After an extended tour of duty as one of the most sought-after bachelors in the polite world's marriage sweeps, he had at last been brought to a sense of what was due his position. Subsequently, it had taken him little time to settle upon the maiden of his choice. Frances Milford, he told himself with some complacency, would make an admirable countess, which was not surprising, since she had been bred to this position – or one like it. From the top of her elegantly coifed head to the tip of her exquisitely slippered toes, she was a model of propriety and good *ton*. She was not one of your simpering misses. On the contrary, without being insufferably high in the instep, she was quite well aware of her own consequence and the respect due her position. She knew as well how to manage a noble establishment as she did to depress the pretensions of an encroaching mushroom. But of what the earl was most blessedly aware was the implicit acknowledgment on her part that she would never interfere with the even tenor of his life. He could spend uncounted hours making duty appearances at his club or at the gaming establishments he favored – although he never permitted himself to wager beyond what was circumspect. He could even choose a mistress with no fear of recrimination, though he was unlikely to do so, since he considered such behavior unbecoming to one of his position. Frances would be his hostess, the mother of his children, and the reflection of his station in life. In short, she would be a comfortable wife, and he was, of course, anxious to conclude this unpleasant business in Bath and repair to her side.

He smiled into Lady Edith's eyes. 'All in good time, Aunt,' he said, affixing what he hoped was a pleasant smile on his lips. He glanced at Miss Fox, who seemed to be suffering some embarrassment at being included in a discussion of such intimate family details. The blue eyes were shuttered as she gazed down at the teacup she held in her lap. It seemed to the earl that it trembled just a little. He smiled.

'Tell me something of yourself, Miss Fox.'

The woman started, and the flush in her cheeks became more pronounced. She bent an anxious gaze upon him and the earl was conscious of a curious stirring in his belly as he found himself sinking into those incredible eyes. He shook himself slightly, annoyed at his unexpected and unwonted susceptibility. He forced his mind along a more austere path. The blush was most becoming, he mused, welcoming the cynical thought. Was she able to accomplish it at will, a knack learned by many courtesans, or was she truly ill at ease? He sincerely hoped it was the latter.

However, her reply was given calmly. 'There is not much to tell, my lord. I am from Hertfordshire. I am the only daughter of the vicar of Ridstowe. Upon his death some three years ago, I was retained as companion to Lady Strangeways. When she passed away, I came to Lady Edith.'

'Augusta Strangeways was a dear friend of mine,' added Lady Edith with a twinkle. 'She was the flightiest creature imaginable in her youth, but as she grew older and was widowed, she became a veritable recluse. She told me many times, however, after Alison came to her, of how fond she had become of the dear child, so of course, I was delighted to welcome her into my home. And I have not regretted it for a moment. She has brought me such enjoyment. . . !' She reached over to pat Alison's hand as the girl smiled fondly at her. The earl's stomach clenched.

'How extremely, er, fortuitous, to be sure,' he murmured, casting Miss Fox a sardonic glance.

In another few moments, Lord Marchford drained the last of his tea and rose to his feet. Pronouncing himself eager to return later in the evening, he took his leave with an elegant bow and a flourish of the curly-brimmed beaver presented to him by Masters.

'Well!' exclaimed Lady Edith, as she turned to reenter the morning room. 'What a lovely surprise. Now, I want you to wear the blue lutestring tonight, with the— Why, my dear, whatever is the matter?'

For upon the closing of the door behind Lord Marchford, Miss Fox had sunk upon a nearby bench, where she remained, rigid and trembling.

'Lady Edith!' whispered the girl through bloodless lips. 'He has come after me – just as I knew he would. Lord Marchford has come to ruin me!'

CHAPTER 2

How was it possible, wondered Alison numbly, for one's world to crumble in such a short space of time – almost from one heartbeat to the next. She had been expecting it, of course. From the moment she learned that the nephew of her employer was none other than the man she knew to be her dedicated enemy, she had waited for this moment. She gazed up at Lady Edith with wide, opaque eyes.

'I must leave here, my lady!' she said firmly. 'If – if you would be so kind as to give me a character—'

'What in the world are you talking about, Alison?' Lady Edith sank onto the bench beside the girl. 'Leave? I won't hear of it!'

'But, your nephew! My lady, did you see the way he looked at me? He knows! He knows who I am!'

'And who does he believe you to be, my dear?'

'Why, the wicked female who caused the death of his brother – and his brother's wife.'

As she finished, tears gathered in her great blue eyes and she groped in the pocket of her skirt for a handkerchief.

'To be sure,' replied the older woman with a wry smile. 'I'm sure he believes you to be an adventuress, but not the particular adventuress he has been seeking for four years.'

Alison gaped at her uncomprehendingly.

'You see,' continued Lady Edith dryly, 'I know my family rather well. Eleanor, March's sister, will have informed him of my wish to bequeath to you a substantial amount of money in my will. She has concluded that you are a scheming fortune hunter who has cleverly wormed your way into my affection.

She will have had no difficulty in bringing her brother to her way of thinking, jaded as he is. March, my dear, is here to buy you off.'

She sat back and observed with twinkling eyes Alison's reaction to this statement, chuckling as the girl sought to give utterance to at least one of the furious thoughts so obviously bubbling on her lips. The old lady rose and extended her hand.

'Come, let us return to the library. I could use another cup of tea, and so, I daresay, could you.'

Alison rose mindlessly and followed her employer in a seething fog of desperation. Could Lady Edith be right? Was Lord Marchford here merely to rid his aunt of what he perceived as a threat to her wealth and well-being? She bristled at the thought, considering the hours she had spent trying to dissuade Lady Edith from making that bequest. And now, for heaven's sake, Lady Edith was talking about giving her an additional, munificent sum outright. Alison smiled bitterly to herself. That would truly fling the cat among the pigeons. The smile faded. Her thoughts had failed to erase her true concern. Lord Marchford, though he had never met her, had vowed her ruin, and now that he was on the scene, she very much feared the day of reckoning was at hand. A familiar, sickening sense of rage, frustration, and shame roiled in the pit of her stomach as she took the chair indicated by a wave of Lady Edith's hand.

When a fresh pot of tea had been provided by a respectful footman, the older woman spoke again.

'Now, Alison, we have been over this a hundred times. What happened to you in London four years ago is over and done with. You did nothing whatsoever of which to be ashamed, and I simply will not have you beating yourself with the dead past. I do believe March's spur-of-the-moment visit is providential. For it is high time to cease those flying visits to relatives every time March informs us he will be coming to see me.'

Alison stared down at the teacup she held in a death grip.

'That is very kind of you, my lady, but—'

'But nothing. It is not your fault that Susannah lost more than she could afford at cards, or that—'

17

'Yes, but it was to me that she lost. And now, she is dead. Dear God, Lady Edith, I drove her to – to—'

Lady Edith laid a hand gently on Alison's arm.

'Susannah was responsible for her own fate, my dear, and for her decision to take her own life. To be sure, her husband bore his share of responsibility for her unhappiness. How ironic that his one act of devotion to his wife led to his own death.'

'Oh God!' cried Alison again. 'If only I had never gone to London!'

'You were there very much against your inclination, were you not? In fact, your only purpose in carrying out your charade was to help a friend.'

'Yes, poor Bethie came to me in desperation. She said I was her only recourse. We had been friends since school and she knew of my – talent at cards. I could not refuse her, for she needed the money to keep her husband out of jail, but—'

'There, you see? Despite what March believes, you did nothing dishonorable. I wish you would talk to him, Alison. Tell him who you are, as you did me, and why you found it necessary to live under a false name. Tell him how you came by your skill with the pasteboards. He will understand your motivation. You learned to play from your uncle, did you not?'

Alison smiled reluctantly. 'Yes. I used to visit my Aunt and Uncle Matchingham when I was a girl. When he discovered my, er, unusual aptitude, he took great pains to induct me into the mysteries of piquet, ecarte, basset, and all the other games of chance at which fortunes are won and lost in polite society. I wish you could have seen how pleased he was when I was at last able to beat him soundly every time we sat down to the table.

' "Allie, m'dear," he said, beaming proudly, "it's too bad you're not a man. You could make an excellent living at the tables." '

'There,' said Lady Edith, 'it is as I said. You could not have refused your friend in her distress. Just tell March, my dear, and—'

'No!' Alison fairly shouted the word, and Honey, curled in Lady Edith's lap, uttered a sharp bark. Alison, embarrassed, continued in a quieter tone. 'He would never believe me. All the world believes I cheated Susannah Brent out of thousands of pounds. You must not tell him, my lady! You promised—'

'Yes, yes,' replied Lady Edith soothingly. 'I gave you my word, and I shall stand by it.' She hesitated. 'I am pleased, my dear, that you honored me with your confidence.'

'I am, too.' Alison laughed shakily. 'I could not begin our relationship with a lie, and I felt at ease with you. I am glad now that there are no falsehoods between us, for your friendship has grown to mean a great deal to me, Lady Edith.'

The older woman brushed Alison's fingers in a gesture of affection. 'Thank you, my dear. However,' she continued gravely, 'I do think you are making a mistake. At any rate, as I said, March has no idea that Alison Fox is the mysterious Lissa Reynard for whom he has been searching all this time. He merely thinks you a plain, garden-variety unprincipled vixen. What is it?' she asked as Alison laughed shortly.

The young woman pressed her fingers to her lips, embarrassed. 'Oh, it's nothing, really – the irony of it, I guess. When I was in school, that's what my particular friends called me – Vixen. Because of my name, you know.'

Lady Edith smiled indulgently. 'Your friends must have had a delightful, if somewhat misplaced, sense of humor. At any rate, getting back to March, we must simply assure him of the purity of your character, and he will be gone back to London and his dismal bride-to-be within a week.'

Alison breathed a troubled sigh.

'I fear the purity of my character is going to escape him when he learns of your plan to provide me with additional funds at the end of the year.'

'Nonsense,' the old lady replied briskly. 'I am pleased to gift you with your heart's desire, though I do not like the idea of your leaving me. When you do so it should be to marry. I shall never understand why someone as young and lovely as you should deny herself the support of a good husband and her own home, merely to open a seminary for young ladies.'

'We've been over that, my dear Lady Edith. I am eight-and-

19

twenty and firmly established on the shelf. Added to that, I have no desire for a husband. As far as I can see, unless a female has her heart set on children, she is much better off without one. As the old joke goes, "I can purchase a parrot that talks, a fish that drinks, and a cat that will stay out all night. Why do I need a husband?" '

Lady Edith did not respond, but waved her hand distressfully. 'I have never wed myself, of course, but I know marriage can be so much more.' She sighed. 'Very well, I shall say no more on that head. If a school is what you want, a school is what you shall have. My dear,' she continued, observing familiar signs of protest in Alison's eyes, 'I have more money than is good for any Christian woman, and I shall never even miss such a paltry sum!'

'I would not consider fifteen hundred pounds a paltry sum!'

'Never mind that. My only regret is that I shall never find someone to live with me who is half as compatible as you have been.'

'I do not think Lord Marchford will regard such a – a munificent gesture on your part in precisely the same light. In fact, it will merely fuel his suspicion that you have been set upon by the lowest form of criminal – one who preys on the innocent and openhearted.'

Lady Edith uttered a sound that was perilously close to a snort.

'I do not think I shall experience much difficulty in persuading my nephew that I am not a gullible old woman to be caught by a clever sycophant.'

Alison smiled faintly. 'I am sure Lord Marchford already knows you better than that.'

Lady Edith returned a demure grin. 'And so I should hope. Now,' she continued briskly, 'the dinner hour approaches. I think the midnight blue lutestring would be a good choice for you this evening. It is becoming, and it sends an unmistakable message of respectability, which is the impression we wish to create – at least for now, *n'est pas?*'

*

An hour or so later, Alison eyed herself narrowly in her looking glass. Adrienne, the highly superior lady's maid provided for her at Lady Edith's insistence, had gathered her dark hair into a becoming sweep atop her head. A few curls were allowed to escape their confines to float about her cheeks in engaging tendrils. Still, she did look – respectable. The blue lutestring boasted a modest décolletage, but so well was it cut that the curves thus concealed were softly delineated beneath the silky fabric cunningly gathered over her breasts and thence falling away in a luxurious sweep to a Vandyked hemline.

She was sure she would look to Lord Marchford precisely what she was, a valued companion to a generous employer. She paused in the act of fastening a necklace of amethysts about her throat. Perhaps Lady Edith was right – and she had no reason to fear the earl. She closed her eyes and a mental image of his lordship took shape behind her closed eyelids. She examined him carefully. He was certainly not frightening to behold. He was tall, with light brown hair cut shorter than the current mode, waving in an unfashionably neat curve over a broad brow. His frame was compact rather than muscular, and his features were regular, if a trifle harsh, with a square, resolute jaw. There was certainly nothing out of the ordinary about him – at least, until one came to his eyes. They were a light golden brown, and from their depths shone a quiet confidence. No, there was nothing out of the ordinary about Lord Marchford, except ... There was something, Alison mused uncomfortably, that gave one the impression that he would be a dangerous man to cross. He exuded an inescapable impression of strength. A shiver passed through her as she pictured those tawny eyes turning on her in rage and contempt.

It was not fair! The cry welled up from deep within her. She had done nothing wrong! Her only crime had been to help a friend. How could she have foreseen the disaster that would result from doing a favor for Bethie.

'Please,' Beth had pleaded, tears sliding down her ashen cheeks. 'I know Jack should not have gambled so heavily – and to steal to cover his losses was very wrong. But, if he can just restore the money. . . .'

'But, Bethie, four thousand pounds. . . !' Alison had simply gasped when Beth had told her the sum required.

'I know, Alison – that's why I came to you. He has only four months in which to return the money, and you are the only person I could think of who could acquire that much in so short a time.'

So Alison had left her home and an ailing father to make her way in the treacherous altitudes of high-stakes gambling in the beau monde. Unwilling to tarnish the good name of her family, she took the name Lissa Reynard and disguised herself with a brown wig and tinted spectacles, content to be considered an eccentric. Another school friend, Molly Selwyn, now the Viscountess Callander, was apprised of the scheme and declared her enthusiastic participation by installing the odd Miss Reynard in her own home, declaring her to be an acquaintance made recently in Brighton.

All went as planned. Alison's success at the tables was phenomenal, and she was able to accrue the needed pounds well before the expiration of Jack's deadline. Shedding wig and spectacles in great relief, she accepted Beth's tearful expressions of gratitude and fled to the sanctuary of her father's vicarage.

It was not until many months later that Alison learned of the tragedy she had left in her wake. A chance mention in a letter from a distant acquaintance led to further inquiry and at last it was Molly who confirmed that young William Brent, the second son of the Earl of Marchford, had expired with his wife, Susannah, in a tragic accident that many were saying was no accident at all.

Young Susannah was known to have gamed frequently with the mysterious Lissa Reynard, in the process losing great sums of money. She had loudly bemoaned her fate, declaring that the Reynard woman was nothing but a card sharp. The *ton* nodded its head wisely, remembering the astonishing dexterity and the phenomenal luck displayed by the Reynard woman, whom no one really knew, did they? Whether Susannah's husband believed his wife had been cheated was never ascertained. It was more than evident that he was severely displeased with his spouse. It was whispered that he had made arrangements to have her banished to Marchford Park, the earl's seat in Hampshire. Lord Marchford, William's father, was believed to be striving for a reconciliation. Unfortunately, Viscount Rivington, William's brother and the one person in the family to whom William might have listened, was out of the country. Of the elusive Lissa Reynard, no trace could be found.

A bare three weeks after Miss Reynard's departure from the glittering landscape of London, Lord Rivington returned to London to be greeted by the news that William had perished in a futile attempt to save the life of his wife as she flung herself one dark night into the swift running waters of the river that ran through the Marchford estate. A year or so after that, the old earl succumbed to an inflammation of the lungs and Lord Rivington became the new earl. Some said the old man's constitution had been weakened by grief.

Alison learned from Molly that the earl's son, Anthony Brent, now Lord Marchford, had mounted a frenzied campaign to find Lissa Reynard and destroy her.

'Honestly, Alison,' she had written, 'when he came to see me, the man was positively livid. I tried to dissuade him of his belief that you virtually robbed his sister-in-law of her sustenance, but he wasn't having any of it. He took everything I said as an effort to excuse my own poor judgment of character in inflicting you on an unsuspecting public. My dearest, whatever you do, stay away from London, and above all, pray that you never run into the Earl of Marchford!'

Alison viewed herself again in the mirror and sighed. Upon the death of her own father, shortly after her return home, her Uncle Matchingham had arranged for a position for her as companion to the reclusive Lady Strangeways in the blessedly remote wilds of Northumberland, and it was while she was there that she received news of Beth's death in childbirth. Alison had grieved unrestrainedly, not only for the passing of her dear friend, but for the meaningless sacrifice made on behalf of her ne'er-do-well husband, Jack Crawford. Alison remained in

Northumberland, safe and guilt-ridden until taken under the capacious wing of Lady Edith.

She had begun to believe that she had created a cocoon of security for herself, one that would be truly impregnable as soon as she had immured herself in the fastness of her school for girls. Then she made the discovery that retribution was indeed at hand, in the form of her employer's nephew, and her world had crashed anew. Even then, when no nephew appeared on the horizon with fiery sword in hand, she had begun to think herself safe again.

Until today.

She swept from her dressing table a shawl of Norwich silk, last year's Christmas gift from Lady Edith, and arranged it absently about her shoulders. Perhaps her ladyship was right. Thank God she had gone about her unsavory business in London under an assumed name and in disguise. There was no reason, after all, that Lord Marchford should discover she was anything but a country vicar's daughter.

With one last worried glance in the mirror, she strode from the room.

CHAPTER 3

His aunt had been right, mused March idly as he allowed the ladies to precede him into the elegant building in Bennet Street that housed the Upper Assembly Rooms. The company was indeed thin tonight. His gaze wandered over the swirling groups of ladies and gentlemen garbed in festive attire. He recognized a few of the persons visible, but saw no one with whom he wished immediately to engage in conversation.

March and Alison had traversed the short distance between Royal Crescent and the Upper Rooms on foot, accompanying Lady Edith as she was borne in her sedan chair. Conversation had been desultory among the three, but March was aware of the tension in the slight figure beside him. Her contribution to their light chatter had been minimal and he had sensed her relief when they arrived at their destination.

'Now, which shall be first?' asked Lady Edith after they had divested their outer garments in the cloak room. 'Dancing or cards – I rather think none of us is ready for refreshments yet. Dancing, I think,' she finished without waiting for an answer. 'Will you join us, March, or are you going to vanish into the card room?'

'Perhaps later, Aunt,' replied her nephew dutifully. 'I should be delighted to accompany you into the ballroom.'

A country dance was just concluding as they entered the spacious chamber, and Lady Edith, spying a favored acquaintance, moved immediately to seat herself beside the lady in one of the chairs placed around the perimeter.

'You two have my permission to dance.' Her eyes sparkled as

she waved an airy hand at the earl, who turned to face the lady by his side.

'It seems we have been deserted, Miss Fox. I see a new set is forming. May I have the honor?'

Alison shrank from him as though he had brandished a hot poker in her face. 'Oh, no, my lord! That is – I do not customarily dance. I feel it is improper—'

'Improper fiddlesticks!' The speaker was Lady Edith, who had overheard. 'Alison, you know you enjoy dancing, and there is nothing the least improper about an attractive young woman enjoying herself in such a fashion.'

Reluctantly, Alison allowed herself to be guided into place by the earl. Fortunately, the dance in which they found themselves was a country dance, which permitted only a minimum of contact, physical or conversational, between partners. Nevertheless, Alison was intensely aware of his proximity, as she had been since he was shown through the front door for dinner that evening. This afternoon, in his moderately taped great-coat and shining top boots, he was all that was proper, and every inch the gentleman. In evening wear, his burnished brown hair reflecting the candlelight, he was disturbingly attractive. In daylight, his eyes had appeared merely light brown. Now, at night they had taken on the lazy, tawny glint of a lion.

She shrugged off her fanciful reflections, realizing that the dance had come to an end. The earl guided her from the dance floor, maintaining an inconsequential flow of chatter. Bereft of speech, she looked around rather dazedly and saw with some relief that Colonel Rayburn was approaching. She was forced to smile inwardly, for this was the first time that she had beheld the retired military man with anything but resignation. The colonel had been most persistent in his attentions of late, making her feel rather like a besieged fortress. Not that George Rayburn wasn't a very nice man, but she was not in the market for a man – very nice or not.

Nonetheless, when the colonel solicited her hand for the next dance, a waltz, she accepted with almost unbecoming alacrity. Though her partner held her perhaps a fraction closer than was strictly permitted, Alison never noticed. Indeed, she admitted later to herself, the man could have quoted salacious poetry to her and she wouldn't have heard a word, for her attention was wholly taken up by the figure of Lord Marchford, who impinged continually on her vision. He was not taking part in the dance, but wandered in amiable conversation with various other nonparticipants seated on the settees that surrounded the dance floor. Occasionally, he glanced in her direction, and her pulse pounded uncomfortably in her throat. She was reminded very unpleasantly of a jungle predator stalking its prey. And, to her annoyance, she seemed unable to keep her gaze from returning to him.

'Indeed, Lady Fortescue,' March said, bending a smile on the elderly beldam with whom he stood in conversation, 'I could not agree with you more. The latitude allowed young people today is most disturbing. Scandalous, no less. Their goings-on in London are simply appalling.'

Bidding a firm adieu to the lady, who obviously wished to hear more on this fascinating subject, he moved to a position near the doorway where he could watch Miss Fox unobserved.

How could he have thought her colorless? he wondered again in bemusement, observing her head thrown back in laughter at a witticism delivered with what the earl could only consider a fatuous guffaw by her partner. Below a graceful sweep of midnight hair, her eyes sparkled like sunlight dancing on a tropic sea. The flush tinting her cheeks put him in mind of roses on snow and the skirt of her silk gown swirled to reveal the lush curves beneath it. March felt his throat tighten.

Steady on, my lad, he told himself grimly. Casual seduction had never appealed to him, and this woman above all was forbidden territory. He watched sourly as the set ended and another gentleman approached to gather her decorously in his arms for a quadrille. Slightly younger than the colonel, this fellow possessed more hair on his head and was also somewhat plumper than the retired warrior. Probably plumper in the pocket, too, surmised the earl with a certain degree of cynicism, judging from the warm smile with which she greeted her new partner.

27

'Haven't seen you out and about much, Miss Fox,' Squire Hadley said, beaming at the glowing face before him.

Alison relaxed momentarily. The squire could also be said to be her admirer, but his attentions were so obviously spread among every other presentable female in Bath that she did not feel threatened by them. Indeed, with his self-deprecating sense of humor and genuine appreciation of her company, she thought more of him as a valued friend than a suitor to her charms.

'I see Marchford is in town,' continued the squire. 'Come to visit his aunt, has he?'

If Thomas Hadley noted the sudden stiffening of the slender back beneath his gloved hand, he said nothing. 'Yes,' said Alison quietly. 'He arrived this afternoon. Lady Edith was most pleased to see him,' she continued in rather a breathless rush. 'I believe he plans to stay a week or so.'

'Ah,' replied the squire. 'I hear he is on the verge of falling into parson's mousetrap.'

'As to that, I could not say.' Her voice was cool and she turned the conversation to a more innocuous subject. She stepped away from Mr Hadley quickly as the music faded into silence, intending to return to Lady Edith's side, but she was halted by a now-familiar voice speaking behind her.

'I understand they are going to play another, Miss Fox. Having observed your skill, I should be honored if you would try me as a partner.'

Wildly, Alison tried to form words of refusal, but without waiting for an answer, Lord Marchford swept her into the rhythm of the music. She almost gasped as he placed his hand on her back, its warmth penetrating the thin silk of her gown. She could only be grateful that the mechanics of the dance would keep them apart for most of its duration. Her temperature seemed to rise in an alarming fashion as he bent to whisper to her. His mouth was terrifyingly close to her ear.

'Since this is the second time we have stood up together,' he whispered, 'I may not have another opportunity to speak with you in such, er, close proximity.' Alison's heart pounded wildly. 'I would very much appreciate,' he continued, 'the opportunity to speak to you in private.'

The words were an icy shower that effectively quelled her temperature if not the beat of her heart, which plummeted into her shoes. Her gaze flew to his and her eyes widened.

'I d-don't understand, my lord,' she quavered.

'Please,' he responded, and it seemed to Alison that he must be overset, for he was somewhat breathless, 'I have no evil designs on your person. There is, merely, a matter that we must discuss.'

'I see.' Alison forced her voice to a semblance of composure.

'May I suggest a stroll through Sydney Gardens tomorrow? That is, if your duties to my aunt will permit,' he added with some irony.

'It would have to be fairly early, my lord.' Dear God, surely he must hear the thundering of her heart beneath its modest covering. Taking a deep breath, she continued. 'Lady Edith rises at eight and breakfasts in her room. She will want to visit the Pump Room afterward. I would have to return to accompany her by eleven or so.'

'Excellent. An early appointment will assure us of some degree of privacy. I shall call for you at eight.'

As the earl predicted, Alison saw little of him for the rest of the evening, for later he left the two ladies at the door to their home with a tip of his hat, promising to be on hand for what would probably be the boisterous arrival of his sister, Meg, on the morrow.

Lady Edith retired promptly and Alison soon followed, only to spend most of the night staring at the ceiling above her bed, conjuring up visions of the imminent conversation with the Earl of Marchford. None of the scenarios she envisioned were pleasant to any degree, and when she finally fell into a fretful sleep an hour or so before dawn, her rest was disturbed by fitful dreams in which his lordship either drove her from his aunt's home in a flaming rage or screamed her perceived iniquity from the rooftops of the Royal Crescent.

'You're being quite absurd, my dear,' Lady Edith had told her on their return from the Upper Rooms. 'But if you are frightened, I will talk to him myself.'

'No – thank you, my lady. He will want to determine my character for himself, and for this I cannot blame him. I shall see him as arranged.'

Thus, when the earl arrived at the appointed time the next morning, Alison was waiting for him in the library. She was icy with apprehension, feeling that she was congealing into a rigid pillar of pure anxiety. When he was announced, she affixed what she hoped was a confident smile to her lips and rose to greet him.

'How charming you look today, Miss Fox,' said the earl. Since she had changed her clothing four times before descending from her bedchamber in a sturdy ensemble of brown wool left over from her days at the vicarage, she was in no danger of interpreting his words as a compliment. Shooting him a sidelong glance, she contented herself with a cool, 'Thank you,' and allowed him to escort her from the house.

The walk from Royal Crescent to Sydney Gardens was long and seemed even longer, but Lord Marchford had little difficulty in filling the time with light conversation. By the time they had reached Bath's version of Vauxhall, Alison had learned more than she really cared to know about the situation in Spain, the likelihood of the Prince Regent divorcing his unattractive wife, and the difficulties posed to England's underclass by the Corn Laws. Once inside the gate, however, he steered her with unnerving speed to a bench that was private without being indecently secluded – though, in truth, there was no one else in sight along the leafy paths at this hour of the morning.

'Now then, Miss Fox,' the earl began pleasantly, 'I am not a man to waste time in unnecessary preliminaries, so let me get right to the point. You have been with my aunt for some two years, have you not? And in that time,' he continued without waiting for an answer, 'you have insinuated yourself most cleverly into her affections.'

Alison resisted an urge to rise abruptly and sweep out of the gardens. She clenched her hands in her lap instead and faced Lord Marchford squarely.

'I find your tone and your words offensive, my lord. It is true that Lady Edith regards me with affection, but it is an affection that is sincerely returned. As far as insinuating myself – I began by being agreeable to her because that is what I was hired for, but before long I found her to be all that is genuinely good and kind. Now, I hold her in very high regard, and I feel honored by the kindness she has shown me. Not that it is any of your business,' she finished tartly.

'Now there you are quite wrong, Miss Fox,' he replied amiably, although Alison sensed the soft threat behind his words. 'Your involvement with my aunt is very much my affair, and, though I fear it will distress you greatly, I am here to put a stop to it.'

'I'm afraid,' said Alison tightly, 'that it is beyond your power, or your wealth, to put a stop to genuine friendship.'

To March it seemed as though the sky-colored eyes were suddenly tinged with thunder, and he smiled despite himself.

'Ah, yes,' he continued, 'but the operative word there is "genuine," is it not? I remain unconvinced that what you feel for Lady Edith Brent is anything beyond the impending gratification of your dreams of easy wealth.'

Alison felt an urgent desire to slap Lord Marchford across his imposing jawline, but once more she schooled herself to calm. Long ago she had discovered in herself a peculiar sensitivity to the emotions of others – even though those emotions might be masked. This ability was partially responsible for her success at the gaming tables. Now, gazing at the earl in frustrated silence, she was suddenly aware that behind the cynical sneer that accompanied his words was a very real concern for his aunt's welfare. His love for her was patent, and, she considered ruefully, she could hardly fault him for feeling Lady Edith needed rescuing from the grasping adventuress her companion appeared to be. She sighed.

'My lord,' she began again, 'I am truly not what you think me.' She ignored his quirked eyebrow. 'I have no desire to rob Lady Edith of her sustenance. She has been generous to me, and she has indicated that she intends to continue her kindness. You must know,' she continued hesitantly, 'that when she first broached the idea of including me so handsomely in her will, I argued against this at some length.'

'This does not surprise me,' murmured the earl. 'The most successful schemers take great pains to persuade their victims of their altruism.'

'That is very true, my lord.' Alison's fingers were by now clenched so tightly in her lap that she thought she must be digging slits into her gloves with her nails. 'But those who are sincerely altruistic behave in the same fashion, so perhaps it might be difficult to make a considered judgment on such short acquaintance.'

Again, March was unable to suppress a smile. No fool Miss Fox, he thought with reluctant admiration.

'Have you tried simply telling my aunt that you will not accept her bequest?' he asked, still in the same quiet tone.

'No. For, as a matter of fact, I have every intention of accepting it.' She sat back in some satisfaction as his brows drew together in surprise. She continued in a voice of calm reason.

'Every time I mentioned my distress at her munificence, she became distressed herself, and it was soon borne to me that the gift she is planning for me brings her a great deal of pleasure. Perhaps you have never known the joy of bringing happiness to one you love,' she concluded, turning an innocent gaze on him.

The earl flushed but said nothing for a moment. When he spoke again, he didn't bother to conceal his anger.

'Are you saying my aunt loves you?'

'Yes,' she replied defiantly. 'And though I hesitate to say it, for you will not believe me, she is family to me and I love her as well.'

'Your protestations are beyond credibility, Miss Fox,' his lordship snapped.

Alison suddenly knew a surge of exasperation. How was she ever to convince this man that her interest in Lady Edith lay not in her wealth but in the woman herself?

'Lord Marchford,' she said quietly, 'I suppose there is nothing I can say to relieve you of your belief that I am a monster of iniquity, so I shall merely take leave, informing you that I have proferred my heartfelt thanks to Lady Edith for her bequest, as well as for the fifteen hundred pounds she intends to bestow upon me at the end of the year.'

'What?' bellowed the earl, an expression of outrage on his face.

'Yes, for she knows I wish to open a school for young ladies. She has said I may leave my position at that time, but I have, of course, refused that particular offer. Oh, can't you see?' cried Alison, her patience deserting her. 'She wishes to do this. It will bring her great pleasure, and she assures me the cost to her is negligible. To me, however, it is like manna from heaven and I intend to accept her benevolence in the spirit with which it is intended. My lord,' she continued in some desperation, 'my mother died when I was a small child. I was raised by my father – a wonderful man, but not a replacement for a mother. I have found in Lady Edith a warmth and an affection I never expected. Please believe me, her own daughter could not love her more than I do. In reciprocation for her generosity, I offer the only commodity at my disposal – my unstinting friendship for all the years she has left. Be assured, my lord, my hope is as genuine as that of everyone else who loves her that the day I receive her bequest will lie many years away.'

'A splendid way you have of showing your friendship, my dear,' he snarled. 'Love her like a daughter, do you? Permit me to tell you the word "love" is an obscenity on your lips, for daughters generally do not make a practice of grasping with despicable avidity at their mothers' purse strings.' Drawing a deep breath, the earl continued in a milder tone. 'Miss Fox, I do not propose to continue this discussion any further. I am an eminently practical man, you see, and I am prepared to offer you a thousand pounds to leave my aunt's employ at the earliest opportunity. You will no doubt reply that this is a great deal less than you will receive from my aunt's bequest, but I warn you that if you refuse my offer, I shall make every effort to assist my aunt in seeing your true colors. Do not,' he concluded with a narrow smile, 'underestimate me, Miss Fox. I can be a formidable opponent, and I have it in my power to destroy your grand plans – and yourself as well.'

Although she had expected just such a declaration, she nonetheless felt as though he had thrown a pitcher of ice water in her face. She shivered in humiliation and rage, and it was some moments before she was able to control her voice.

'My lord, even if you were to offer me twice the sum Lady Edith has promised me, and even if Lady Edith were to unexpectedly change her mind about the bequest and the gift, I would not leave her. I will stay as long as she wants me with her.'

She gazed directly into his eyes for some moments, and when he made no reply, she rose, and with a brisk twitch of her skirts walked away from him.

March stared after her, stunned. The interview had not gone at all as he had envisioned. The woman had turned down a munificent offer, and had had the poor taste to leave before he could forward negotiations by upping the ante.

But worst of all, he thought with a sinking sensation, he had, for a brief instant, believed her to be sincere. He knew this could not be. He was wise in the way of the world and his experience had taught him that penniless young women did not make themselves pleasant to rich old ladies out of the goodness of their hearts. Loved her like a daughter, indeed. What kind of fool did she take him for? He sighed deeply. Just your average, everyday fool, of course, who could be swept into a pair of deep blue eyes an angel would envy. He rose and with lagging steps headed in the direction of Royal Crescent.

Good God, was he about to be bested by a vicar's daughter who seemingly exuded truth and innocence from every pore? It seemed impossible that she could be so skilled an actress.

And he wished he did not want so badly to believe her.

CHAPTER 4

March was met at the front door of his aunt's house by a small whirlwind composed of pink muslin and golden curls.

'March! Why didn't you tell me you were coming?' The young girl's words cascaded from sweetly shaped pink lips and her brown eyes sparkled with the joyful abandon of youth. 'Did you come just to see me installed in Aunt Edith's home? Can you believe I have finally shaken the dust of that horrid school from my shoes? Oh, March! By this time next year I will have had my Season, and I'll be counting the offers for my hand!'

With some difficulty, March unwrapped himself from his little sister's tempestuous embrace and laughed affectionately.

'Hold, you little hoyden! Obviously, you haven't learned any manners at that horrid school, so perhaps we should send you back for a refresher course!'

Since his words were accompanied by a hearty embrace and a noisy kiss on her cheek, Lady Margaret Brent might be forgiven for ignoring this threat. Watching from the doorway, Alison was astonished at the difference a warm smile made on the normally chilly set of his lordship's features. The man who smiled so engagingly at those he loved, she mused a little sadly, was a wholly different person from the one who bent frigid stares on those for whom he felt only contempt.

Lady Edith had by now joined the group on her front steps, and, clucking impatiently, she led them into the house. Over tea in the library, Meg further proclaimed her relief at having at last escaped the confines of the schoolroom, and could not stop talking about her exciting plans for her Season.

'Oh, Alison,' she cried, clapping her hands, 'you will never believe! Sally Pargeter and I found the most ravishing bonnet in Milsom Street yesterday. At least, *I* thought it was ravishing. Sally says it's fussy. Do come with me this afternoon to look at it again so you can give me your opinion.'

March observed this exchange with some astonishment. It had not occurred to him that Meg would have fallen in with the ranks of Miss Fox's well-wishers, yet they seemed to be on extraordinarily good terms. Indeed, an outsider might consider them a charming pair – Meg with her tumbled golden curls bent close to Miss Fox's sleek, dark head. March pursed his lips thoughtfully as he considered the effect Meg's disastrous friendship with a fortune hunter might have upon his negotiations with same.

What negotiations? The crafty witch had turned him off like a spigot, and had left him feeling oddly guilty in the process – which was patently absurd, of course. He had not been born yesterday, after all. He must assume that her earnest, dewy-eyed protestations of sincerity were merely a ploy to wring a higher price from him.

He wrenched himself back to the scene in progress and discovered to his dismay that Miss Fox and Meg were deep in plans for an afternoon shopping excursion that included an inspection of the bonnet, as well as a search for a ribbon of a particular shade of green.

'It is all the crack, you know,' Meg assured her aunt and Miss Fox. 'And that wretchedly insipid white muslin we purchased last week simply cries for some sort of adornment.'

Miss Fox nodded her head in grave agreement with this assessment while Lady Edith looked on with a fond smile.

'It sounds an excellent plan to me,' the older woman pronounced.

'But, since you will not be going to the Pump Room this morning, will you not wish to go this afternoon?' asked Alison.

'Yes, and I would be delighted if you would accompany me, but once there you may leave me to my gossiping and simply collect me when you are ready to come home.'

'Well,' began Alison, 'if you—'

'I am sure,' interjected the earl, 'that you would not wish to leave my aunt unaccompanied for so long just to indulge in an hour or two of frippery shopping.' His expression indicated that such a program would be akin to abandoning her ladyship in a bawdy house.

'What nonsense!' cried Lady Edith before Alison could respond. 'Alison, after all the hours you have endured listening to me hash over the doings of a parcel of idiots you neither know or care about, you have earned a few hours respite on Milsom Street.'

March could find no reasonable response to that and so offered to escort Lady Edith to the Pump Room himself.

'Good,' she replied promptly. 'Perhaps a dose of the waters will improve your disposition.'

March had the grace to flush.

Such was Meg's excitement over the bonnet in Milsom Street, that they all found themselves rushing through an early luncheon. Not an hour later, Alison and Meg were strolling along Milsom Street, having just purchased the desired length of green ribbon from a mercier in Bath Street.

'There, Alison, in that window!' cried Meg, grasping Alison's arm and pulling her toward the milliner's shop. 'That charming villager hat. Is it not precious?'

Alison peered at the astonishing creation displayed with such hopeful prominence. It could, she supposed, be called a villager, for it had a wide brim, but on the whole it looked more like a coal scuttle, featuring a towering crown surmounted by feathers. A profusion of rosebuds decorated the brim, the whole being anchored to the wearer's chin by several yards of wide, very bright pink ribbon.

After a moment's reflection, Alison said hesitantly. 'It's quite, er . . . tall, is it not?'

'Yes,' replied Meg gleefully. 'That is *precisely* what makes it so dashing. Come, let me try it on for your inspection.'

Dragging Alison bodily inside the shop, Meg motioned to a salesclerk, who brought the desired article to her. Tying the ribbon at a rakish angle beneath one ear, she cocked her head.

'Well, what do you think?'

The kindest word to describe it, thought Alison, was bizarre.

'It is indeed most – uh – most unusual.'

Meg turned to the mirror, examining herself critically from every angle.

'Shall I purchase it?'

'You must do what you want, of course, Meg, but – I wonder. . . .'

Meg swung around, wide-eyed.

'You wonder what? Oh, Alison, never tell me you think it's too sophisticated. *Everyone* says that to me all the time, but I was sure you would not.'

'That's just it, my dear. There is something about it – perhaps all those rosebuds, that makes you appear absurdly youthful. One would not take you for more than fifteen in it.'

Meg whirled to the mirror with a gasp.

'Oh! Oh, dear, I believe you are right,' she concluded after a moment's perusal of her appearance. She sighed. 'And I think those ribbons make me look sallow, in addition. How very lowering.'

'But look over there at that rakish little capote,' said Alison diplomatically. 'I fear Lady Edith will think it quite daring, but I do believe it would suit you.'

Meg raced to try on the capote, and as Alison had hoped, she declared it 'bang up to the echo.' The price was so reasonable that Meg felt almost obliged to purchase a silk bandeau embroidered with acorns as well.

Since Meg had airily dispensed with the services of a maid, she carried the bandbox containing her new purchases herself, and swinging it gaily over one arm, proceeded with Alison down Milsom Street. When they reached the ill-named Quiet Street, Meg bethought herself of a shop that carried yet another essential, a supply of reticules and scarves.

'For I still have enough left from my allowance for another Norwich silk, you know,' she advised Alison, who nodded in complete understanding. Inside the shop, as Meg rummaged through a display of luxurious silk accessories, Alison found herself unable to resist a zephyr scarf shot with silver, and when they again emerged onto the street, the ladies found themselves so burdened with their purchases that they elected to return to the Pump Room immediately.

Moving through the narrow passageway of Bridewell Lane, Meg turned again to her friend.

'Tell me what you think of March,' she said. 'Isn't he wonderful? I am *so* lucky to have him for a brother.'

Alison searched her mind for a suitable response. 'He – he seems quite devoted to his family.'

'Oh, yes. He used to be somewhat of a scapegrace. Indeed,' she continued, observing Alison's expression of disbelief, 'before he went to the Continent, he was quite the man about town – always playing least-in-sight when it came to performing his "peerage duties," as he called them. Papa was always at him to mend his ways. When he accepted the diplomatic assignment – March all but admitted at the time that he took it just to escape his responsibilities – Papa was beside himself. He begged March not to go.'

Meg laughed a little self-consciously. 'Goodness, I am making him out to be a regular care-for-nobody. Truly, he has always been there for all of us ever since I can remember. Mama died when I was about twelve, and Papa – well, Papa was a lovely man, but sometimes rather difficult. When Papa died – oh, Alison, what a dreadful time that was for us.'

Before Alison could utter a word, Meg continued in a rush. 'My sister-in-law became involved with a perfectly horrid woman some years ago. The female cheated her of a great deal of money and poor dear Susannah became so despondent—'

'Yes,' gasped Alison. 'I am aware of—'

'I suppose Aunt Edith told you about it,' continued Meg. 'Anyway, poor March did not learn of the deaths of William and Susannah until he returned to England a few weeks later.' Meg's vivid little face crumpled in distress. 'For a while, we thought March would go mad. He was much closer to William than I was, being more of an age. For that matter, he was closer to Papa,

39

too. March changed then. In just a few weeks he lost all his joy in life and became weighed down with duty and responsibility – as he is to this day. I think he felt somehow to blame for all that happened. He vowed to bring – Miss Reynard, her name was – to justice. Well, more than that. He wanted to make her pay for what she did, although I'm not sure how he planned to bring that about. I know he would have thought of something,' she added, and Alison fought the panic rising within her. 'March searched and searched for Miss Reynard, but she had vanished into thin air, just like the witch we all knew her to be. He's still got detectives on her trail, but we have pretty much given up hope of ever finding her.'

Hating herself for uttering the words, Alison spoke in a strained whisper. 'But – destroying this Miss Reynard would not bring Susannah or William or even your father back.'

'That's just what I said to March,' declared Meg. 'I told him that if anyone was being destroyed over this it was him.' Alison glanced at Meg, surprised at this unexpected evidence of maturity in the youthful sprite beside her. 'But,' the girl said with a sigh, 'once my brother sets out on a course there is no dissuading him. He is all duty and practicality now.'

'Perhaps when he marries,' ventured Alison, 'his wife will move his thoughts in another direction.'

Meg snorted. 'Miss Prunes and Prisms? Honestly, Alison, I cannot imagine what March sees in that insipid monument to propriety. I think it's just another manifestation of his absurd dedication to duty. Why did you know—?' But whatever revelation Meg had been about to make was abruptly interrupted as the girl halted suddenly. 'Oh, look! There is Mr Renfrew!' Meg's gaze was focused on a spot in the near distance before them, her expression beatific.

'Mr Renfrew?' echoed Alison.

'Yes,' Meg breathed, not removing her gaze from the object of her adoration. 'Do you not remember? I told you all about him. He's the drawing master at Miss Crumshaw's.'

'Oh yes,' sighed Alison wearily. Meg's conversation for the last month had been distressingly full of Mr Renfrew's manly attributes. Following Meg's worshipful stare, she gazed with some interest at the slender young man moving down the street toward them. Though the possessor of a lovingly curled, golden mane, he was by no means the Adonis described by Meg. Alison rather thought Adonis might have had somewhat better taste in clothes, and would no doubt have declined the intricately embroidered waistcoat, bright yellow coat, and razor sharp collar points favored by Mr Renfrew.

As the drawing master approached, his eyes lit in recognition, and he lifted his modish hat with a flourish. 'Why, it's Lady Margaret,' he said in mellifluous tones. 'I see you have not yet quitted Bath.'

Meg's eyelashes fluttered and she bestowed upon the gentleman a besotted smile. 'Oh, no indeed. I shall be staying with my aunt, Lady Edith Brent, in Royal Crescent for some weeks before leaving for home. Oh,' she added as an afterthought, 'may I present Miss Fox, who lives with my aunt.'

Mr Renfrew expressed his pleasure in meeting Miss Fox, then nodded at Meg. 'Perhaps we will see each other again before you leave.'

'Oh, yes,' breathed Meg. 'I hope so.'

Mr Renfrew made no response, and with another smile and a tip of his hat, he bade both ladies good afternoon and continued on his way. Meg stared after him in a blissful reverie until Alison's gentle tug at her elbow recalled her to her surroundings.

'Oh, Alison,' she cried, craning her neck to look after him, 'isn't he wonderful? And did you see the way he looked at me? I know he feels the attraction between us. I wonder if he will come to call?'

'I think that extremely doubtful, my dear,' replied Alison carefully. 'He has a position to maintain, after all. It would be considered the height of impropriety for him to appear to be making advances.'

'What fustian!' retorted Meg. 'He cares no more for the opinion of others than I, and—'

'In addition, the man is so much older than you. He must be almost thirty.'

'I care nothing for that!' By now, Meg's voice had begun to tremble, and angry tears sparkled in her eyes. 'Alison, I thought you would understand!'

'Oh, believe me I do, my dear. I do admit he is splendid, and I certainly do not blame you for being in alt over him.' She forbore to remark that the foppish Mr Renfrew did not appear to be overcome with feeling for his erstwhile pupil. She wondered bemusedly if there were some unwritten universal law that first love must always be painful.

The two had by now reached the east entrance to the Pump Room, and they hurried inside to find Lady Edith and her nephew.

Almost at once they spied her seated on one of the benches sprinkled along the edges of the room, deep in conversation with a large lady whose feathered bonnet fluttered in such turmoil that it appeared ready to take flight. Alison glanced about and discovered Lord Marchford standing at the far end of the chamber, talking easily with a group of older gentlemen.

Seeing Meg and Alison, Lady Edith waved them to her side and directed her maid to have their parcels carried home.

'Good afternoon, Lady Wilbraham,' Alison said with a smile, trying very hard not to stare at the matron's absurd hat. Meg followed suit, bobbing a careless curtsy to the woman she had known since she was in leading strings.

'Lady Wilbraham and I were just discussing your come-out, Meggie,' said Lady Edith. 'We—'

'Your sister will have the dressing of you in London, I presume,' Lady Wilbraham interrupted with a glance of disapproval at Meg. 'Good. Tell her to try Madame Olivette. She's new in London and prodigiously talented. I have decided to let her do my Clarice.'

Clarice was known to both Meg and Alison, as well as to Lady Edith, and the latter sent a quelling glance toward Meg, whose eyes were already glinting mischievously.

'Why thank you, Horatia,' said Lady Edith mildly. 'I shall certainly forward your recommendation to Eleanor. Clarice always dresses with a great deal of, er, élan.'

Alison admired Lady Edith's diplomacy, particularly since Clarice, who possessed the same shape and general appeal of a bag pudding, had an unfortunate tendency to appear at every occasion in a full complement of ruffles, ribbons, laces, jewelry, and every other form of adornment she could affix to her plump person. Lady Edith's expression, however, indicated nothing beyond a courteous attention. Lady Wilbraham heaved herself to her feet.

'I see Mary Glenham over there, boring the ears off the poor rector, Mr Rayburn. I must be off to rescue him.'

She had barely begun to make her ponderous way across the polished wooden floor of the room when Meg fairly exploded with the giggle she had been stifling for the past several minutes.

'Meg!' rapped Lady Edith. 'That will be quite enough.'

'Oh, but, Aunt,' gasped her niece. 'We must send a card of thanks to Lady W. for telling us which of all the modistes in London is to be avoided at all costs.'

Lady Edith's lips twitched, but her stare was minatory and Meg soon subsided. Alison took pains to hide the smile that curved her own lips.

Across the room, March watched Miss Fox's efforts. He was forced to acknowledge that in her quiet loveliness, she was one of the most provocative females he had ever met. Her austere walking dress of Cheshire brown twilled silk should have obliterated the lush body hidden beneath its stiff folds; instead, it merely created in him an uncomfortable desire to push the folds aside to discover the beauty that lay beneath them.

He excused himself from the group with whom he had been conversing and made his way to where the ladies sat before one of the long windows that overlooked the King's bath.

'March,' cried Meg, 'have you spent all this time here? You must be ready to expire from boredom!'

'On the contrary, infant,' he returned, an amused twinkle in his eye. 'I have spent a pleasant afternoon renewing old acquaintances. Unlike you, my pleasure does not hang on how many fripperies I can purchase in a given amount of time. May I assume,' he continued, 'from the astonishing number of parcels

43

under whose weight you staggered in, that you were successful in the Great Bonnet Quest?'

By unspoken consent the group rose to depart, and on the way home, Meg regaled them with the details of the shopping expedition.

'A zephyr scarf?' asked Lady Edith of Alison. 'It sounds perfect for the cerulean satin we had made up for the Budwell soirée.'

'Yes, so I thought, my lady. Although, I am still not wholly reconciled to attending Mrs Budwell's party.'

'Why not, for heaven's sake? It will be one of the grandest events of the season.'

'That's just it.' Alison glanced surreptitiously at Lord Marchford. 'It will be thought coming of me to attend such a function. There will be dancing, and—'

'Of course there will be,' interjected Lady Edith impatiently. 'And you will not lack for partners. Now see here, Alison, I will not countenance any longer this – this obsession you have with fading into invisibility. One would think you were some jumped-up little mushroom instead of the granddaughter of the Earl of Trawbridge.'

March's eyes widened. He had not known this. How was it that the granddaughter of an earl was reduced to earning her bread in service as companion to a septuagenarian? Was it the oft-told tale of an enraged peer whose daughter married beneath her? Had the earl severed the connection, leaving his impoverished descendant to make her own way in the world? Such was the stuff of high drama, he concluded briskly. If this was the case, the offspring in question had certainly landed on her feet. Good God, his besotted aunt was indeed treating the woman like a beloved daughter. Cerulean satin and fashionable soirées, indeed.

When the party reached Royal Crescent, the earl declined to enter, but bade the ladies farewell on the doorstep, claiming a prior engagement. It was in a thoughtful mood that he strode down George Street en route to his temporary abode in the Royal York Hotel. To his surprise, he was informed on entering that elegant hostelry that a visitor awaited him in a private parlor just off the coffee room.

'Good afternoon, my lord,' said the man who leapt to his feet at the earl's entrance. He was slight of build and dressed in somber garb. His features were small and pointed, but kindly in their way, so that he looked rather like a benevolent rodent.

'Ah, Mr Pilcher,' said the earl, closing the door behind him. 'I presume you have come with news of Miss Reynard.'

CHAPTER 5

'Well, as to that, my lord' – the little man sank nervously into a chair at the earl's gesture of permission – 'I fear my news is no better than before. Lissa Reynard has disappeared from sight as though she'd never been. Which, I should imagine, is very much the case.'

March's brows snapped together. How could one female be so impossible to locate? Upon his return to England and the discovery of the tragic deaths of William and Susannah, he had begun an immediate search for the mysterious Miss Reynard. His first move was to question Lady Callander concerning the viper she had nourished in her bosom. The woman had declared herself unable to help him. She really hadn't known Miss Reynard all that well, she explained with sympathetic regret. They had become chance acquaintances in Brighton and Lady Callander had invited her to visit on a whim, never really dreaming she'd accept. No, she did not know where Miss Reynard had gone upon leaving London, but if she were to hear anything she would assuredly let his lordship know at the earliest opportunity. Apparently, the viscountess had not heard anything, for March received no more information from her.

He growled aloud. 'We had already surmised that the woman was using a pseudonym, Pilcher. Still, she cannot have simply vanished.'

'I recently paid another visit to the Lady Callander, my lord, with no more success than on my previous efforts. She insists she has no knowledge of Miss Reynard's whereabouts, and further contends she really didn't know her very well to begin with.'

'In short, you learned nothing from her that she had not already told me on the occasion when I went to see her. Do you believe her?'

'As to that,' replied Mr Pilcher, chewing on his lip, 'I could not say. She seems sincere in her embarrassment at being so easily taken in by a woman of that sort – she seems precisely the flighty type of woman who could easily be gulled. To a woman like Lissa Reynard, she must have seemed the perfect tool with which to wangle an introduction to the beau monde.'

'At any rate,' continued the earl, 'it sounds as though we will get no more information from her.'

Mr Pilcher smiled mirthlessly. 'Indeed, my lord, she was quite short with me on my last visit, and as much as told me she was tired of seeing my face. I shan't be welcome there again, I think.'

'And nothing new from your sources in Brighton?'

'No, and that's another odd thing. My acquaintances there do not mingle with the *ton*, but they do, er, keep abreast. My sources indicate that Lady Callander was indeed a visitor in Brighton not long before Miss Reynard made her appearance in London, but no one remembers hearing that name in Brighton.'

'Odd.' March drummed his fingers on the table at which he had taken a chair, then poured a glass of wine from the decanter that had been set unobtrusively at his side by the inn's host. He offered it to the little detective and filled one for himself.

Mr Pilcher drew a long breath. 'My lord, I am at the end of my resources. I have meticulously checked out the possibilities, from searching out descriptions of female coach passengers leaving the city to interviews with modistes and shopkeepers who were patronized by Miss Reynard. I shall, of course, continue my efforts if you wish, but it has been four years now. The trail is cold as ashes, and I must tell you in all conscience that I believe I can no longer be of help to you. I am sorry.' Mr Pilcher seemed to truly regret his failure, and his expression resembled that of an unhappy marmoset.

March's fingers tightened around his glass. Had it come to this, then? The rage that had boiled within him for so long would be allowed to trickle away in defeat, and the grief that

47

still consumed him would harden and continue its acid destruction of his soul. Behind it all lay an inescapable sense of guilt that in his desire to avoid responsibility, he had been absent during the whole fiasco. *Dammit*, he should have been able to prevent the tragedy that had befallen his family. The knowledge that such a feeling was irrational did nothing to relieve him.

He rose wearily. 'I am sorry, too, Mr Pilcher. I know you did your best. I shall continue the search on my own, for I cannot bring myself to abandon it.'

'I understand, my lord.' He turned to leave.

'One moment, please, Mr Pitcher.' The little man halted in his exit and swung to face the earl.

'I have another, smaller commission for you. I would like you to look into the background of one Alison Fox. She claims to be the daughter of the deceased vicar of Ridstowe in Hertfordshire. I merely wish to ascertain the truth of this statement.'

'Of course, my lord. It sounds quite straightforward – I should have a report for you within the week.'

The earl nodded, and, bowing once more, Mr Pilcher departed the room, leaving the earl to stare into the flames of the fire that crackled with vexing cheerfulness in the grate.

'Lissa Reynard.' March whispered the words, almost savoring the bitterness they left on his tongue. She must be out there somewhere, and someday, by God, he would find her. When he did, he would ruin her. Destroy her – and make her rue the day she had chosen Susannah for the target of her greed.

He rose to repair to his room. He was promised again to dinner with his aunt, and planned to take the opportunity to draw the redoubtable Miss Fox aside for further conversation.

When he arrived in Royal Crescent, however, he found his aunt, Miss Fox, and Meggie in the library, immersed in a spirited discussion concerning the propriety of attending a masquerade ball in the Upper Rooms before one was officially Out.

'But this is Bath!' Meggie spoke in impassioned tones. 'The only people we'll see are the same ones we invite to our own parties, and you know we have dancing then.'

'That is quite different, Meg,' replied Lady Edith sternly.

'There will be persons of many stations at the masquerade ball, as well as some of the high sticklers who would rend you limb from limb once they returned to town. You would not have a shred of reputation left.'

'Why do you wish to go to an assembly, Meg?' interjected Alison. 'You have frequent opportunities to dance with all the young men of your acquaintance either in your own home or that of your friends. Just last week, the Brintons held an impromptu hop that lasted until well after midnight. You said you had a lovely time.'

'I don't *want* to dance with the young men of my acquaintance, I want to dance with—' Meg caught herself. 'That is, I'm tired of the same old faces all the time. And a masquerade would be such fun!' She pointedly turned her back on the company and flung herself into a damask-covered armchair.

March, moving into the room, felt a stirring of sympathy for the young girl, but spoke calmly. 'Meg, your behavior reveals just how far from ready you are to take your place in adult society.'

Meg whirled about in her chair. 'March!' She leapt to her feet and ran to his side. Lifting her face, she pouted prettily at him. 'I can surely be forgiven for flying into the boughs – or, at least into the lower branches. I am surrounded by people who are forever denying that I am a young woman now, and not a child. There is to be a masked ball at the Upper Rooms the evening after next, and I do so want to go!'

March's eyes lifted. 'You cannot be serious. I did not realize the standards at the Upper Rooms had so deteriorated. Of all the functions you might wish to attend, a masked ball is the least likely for which I would grant permission. They always have a tendency to turn into the worst sort of romp.'

'But, I could leave if it started to get rowdy,' pleaded Meg. 'And no one would know who I was anyway, so—'

'That will do, Meg,' said March, his patience deserting him. 'Your aunt disapproves, as does, I take it, Miss Fox. . . .' He shot a questioning glance across the room, and after a moment's hesitation, Alison nodded. 'That should be enough. Now, let us change the subject. I understand there is to be a gala held in Sydney Gardens next Thursday, with supper and fireworks. Perhaps we—'

'I don't *care* about stupid old Sydney Gardens,' wailed Meg. 'I want—'

'That will be quite enough, young lady,' snapped March. 'If you wish to behave like a spoiled child, you may leave the room.'

Across the room, Alison drew in a sharp breath of dismay. Lord Marchford might think himself awake on every suit, but it was obvious he had not the slightest notion of how to handle a volatile girl in her teens.

Rising again from the chair into which she had once more flung herself, Meg posed for an instant, her hand to her throat. Then, in a throbbing voice, she cried, 'Yes, I shall spend the rest of the evening in my room. Better a crust of bread in solitude than a banquet among – among those who – people who cannot. . . .' Unable to complete the sentence to her satisfaction, she took refuge in a dignified silence and swept from the room.

'I shall, of course, have a tray sent up to her,' said Alison with a questioning lift of her brows to Lady Edith, who laughed aloud.

'Of course. Although it seems a shame to deprive her of the marvelous drama she has created, of immolation on the altar of family repression.'

'I'm sure she'll recover by the morrow,' added March with a wry smile.

Alison wondered if she should make mention of Meg's current passion for Mr Renfrew, the drawing master. It was obviously the hope of seeing him there that had prompted her desire to attend the masquerade. She shrugged. Meg's passions were frequent, but mercifully brief. By this time next week, she would no doubt have shifted her affections to someone else.

Without the stimulation of Meg's presence, dinner was a quieter affair than it would have been otherwise. Nevertheless, conversation was lively.

'You do not mean to tell me, March,' said Lady Edith, 'that

Gertrude Tissdale actually appeared in public dressed as the goddess Diana.'

' 'Pon my honor, Aunt. For the Jerseys' costume ball. She appeared swathed in semitransparent draperies and carried a bow and quiver of arrows. Around her waist hung two very dead pheasants and a hare.'

'But, March, she is almost my age and must weigh well over fourteen stone.' She swung to Alison. 'Don't you remember? She came to take the waters last year, and there are those of us ready to swear that the level of the Cross Bath rose nearly to overflowing when she stepped in.'

'Lady Edith!' By now, Alison was gasping with laughter. 'You are exaggerating. Lady Tissdale is somewhat ... plump,' she said unsteadily, 'but—'

'Somewhat plump!' echoed March. 'My dear Miss Fox, unless you are speaking of another Lady Tissdale altogether, you have a talent for understatement.'

March watched Alison's laughing confusion in some bemusement. The pink of her cheeks enhanced the sparkle in her magical blue eyes, and his fingers itched to know if the dark waves of her hair would feel as silky as they looked. He turned abruptly to his aunt, and he was dismayed at the expression of open affection displayed in the gaze she bent on Alison. If he was successful in dislodging Miss Fox, what would be the effect on Aunt Edith when this darling of her heart suddenly decamped with a flimsy explanation? Would the adventuress, deprived of her prey, spin a tale of having been driven away by a vindictive relative? If so, he would tell his aunt the whole, and surely she would understand that what he had done was for her own good.

Finding his reflections annoyingly uncomfortable, he applied himself with industry to the gâteau mille-feuille just set before him. After dinner, he declined to sit alone at the table with the brandy decanter, and accompanied the ladies to the drawing room on the floor above. He watched Alison, observing the unobtrusive attention with which she performed her duties to Aunt Edith. A pillow placed at the older woman's back, embroidery and books set within easy reach, and a watchfulness for her smallest need were all accomplished with a lightness of spirit that removed them from the realm of imposed tasks. Rather, they seemed accomplished with quiet pleasure. Was Alison Fox merely a skillful actress? She certainly moved with a grace suited to the stage, he mused appreciatively as he watched the silk of her gown mold itself to her lovely, lithe body.

'I hope you two do not mind' – March jumped a little as his aunt's clear tones cut into his reverie – 'but I believe I shall retire early this evening. It has been a tiring day, and tomorrow will be busy as well. We have arranged an outing for Meg and some of her young friends,' she said to March. 'They are planning a walk to Beechen Cliff, with a picnic at the top. I shall not participate in the climb, but will come by carriage and join them at the top for the picnic. Alison and the parson, Mr Rayburn will be there to chaperon, as will Sally Pargeter's mother. Sally, as you will remember, is Meg's particular friend. You do not have to go, of course. I should imagine an afternoon spent with the infantry would bore you into a decline.'

Alison held her breath. She could not look forward to an afternoon spent in the earl's company with any degree of equanimity, and she leaned forward in anticipation of his refusal. She sank back in dismay at his answer.

'I hope I am made of stronger stuff, Aunt,' March said, forcing a chuckle. 'As long as I am in Bath, it behooves me to take my part in overseeing the doings of my little sister. I shall be pleased to join you.' Alison thought his words sounded heavy and pompous, and she watched with some relief as he rose to see his aunt from the room.

Unfortunately, just as she, too, rose to leave, the earl came back into the drawing room.

'Since Lady Edith has—' she began nervously, 'that is, I believe I, too, shall retire, my lord.'

'What, and leave an honored guest of the house sitting abandoned in the drawing room, Miss Fox?' His smile curled ironically on his lips. 'Particularly since my aunt has gone to such pains.'

Her eyes flew to his. 'What do you mean?' she asked anxiously.

'Evidently, Miss Fox, Aunt Edith is trying to throw us together, with what end in mind I scarcely dare to venture a guess.'

Alison flushed. 'That is absurd, my lord. Perhaps she merely wishes us to become better acquainted, since. . . .' Her voice faltered. She straightened her shoulders and looked directly at him. 'Since she loves us both, and since we shall probably be meeting again with the passing of time.'

Taking her hand in his, he drew her down beside him on a convenient settee. She was struck by the warmth of his touch. 'I am so glad you brought that up,' he said silkily. 'Have you reconsidered my offer?'

She glared at him. 'Frankly, my lord, I do not even remember what it was. It was completely irrelevant, after all.'

'Why, I believe you hold me in dislike, Miss Fox,' he murmured, moving closer. Alison stared at him, wishing that were the case. He was smug and arrogant, and his assumptions about her were insulting, but they sprang from a genuine love for his aunt. Try as she might, she could not fault him for his behavior, irritating though it might be. In addition, she was dismayingly aware of the man's disturbing physical attractions. Why should she experience an urge to trace the strong line of his jaw with her fingertips was a mystery as unsettling as it was dangerous. She started, aware that he was speaking again. 'So unnecessary, I assure you. Why don't you tell me what it is you will accept to leave my aunt's employ? If it is not outrageous, I will do my best to see that your demand is met. After that, we can part company – all with an absence of any disagreeable wrangling.'

His words were reasonable enough, but she had no difficulty in sensing the hostility that bubbled beneath them. No, my lord earl had nothing but contempt for the adventuress, Alison Fox. A tremor shook her. God knows what his reaction would be if he knew that he faced Lissa Reynard, as well. She raised her eyes once more to his.

'My lord, you are wasting your time and your energy, and your breath. For all your talk of practicality, you do not possess enough money to entice me away from this house. I like it here, and I love Lady Edith. I suppose it is within your power to poison her ladyship's mind against me, or to remove me by force, but you will be doing your aunt a grave disservice by doing either. She is, by the by, perfectly aware of the reason for your visit and is highly amused. Now, I most earnestly suggest that you pack your bags and your money and your pathetic suspicions and go back to London. Marry your Miss Whatever-her-name-is and leave me in peace. I promise you will not regret it.'

Lord Marchford rarely found himself at a loss for words, but at this moment he could think of nothing to say. Indeed, rational thought of any sort was proving difficult. He had the strangest sensation that he had become lost in this vixen's amethyst eyes. He wanted nothing more than to fold her in his arms and kiss her until she melted against him in an acquiescent pool of violet-scented desire.

Horrified at the direction his thoughts had taken, he tried to focus on the words she had just spoken. For a long moment, he simply looked at her, surprised that she endured his scrutiny without any outward sign of discomfort. She returned his regard with an expression of steady calm.

'I am not ready to return to London yet, Miss Fox,' he stated, trying a different tactic. 'However, may I suggest that we call a truce?' She lifted one hand as if to interrupt, but he pressed onward. 'I shall cease in my efforts to, er, pry you from my aunt's vicinity, at least for the time being. I do not wish to ruin the pleasant occasion of a visit to my aunt with this continued bran-gling.'

'I commend your good sense, my lord,' she said with an air of surprise. Extending her hand, she rose and faced him. 'I look forward, then, to seeing you tomorrow.'

March thought he detected a spark of amusement in her face.

'Ah, yes, the picnic,' he replied. 'I have the melancholy suspi-cion that I am going to feel like the veriest graybeard, forced to endure the chirpings of a group of dewey-eyed young misses and their adolescent swains.'

'The company of Meg's friends can be somewhat wearing,' she replied with a smile. 'However, there will be plenty of gingersnaps with which to fortify yourself. Your aunt tells me they have always been a great favorite of yours. Indeed, I am told you were not above theft from the biscuit jar in your misspent youth.'

'Ah, the curse of a relative with an inconvenient memory,' he groaned. He paused, unable to control his interest. 'By the way, speaking of Meg, you and she appear to get on uncommonly well.'

The smile dropped from Alison's lips, and she stiffened. 'Yes,' she replied defiantly. 'Am I now to be accused of plotting to steal her fortune, as well?'

March drew back, startled. In the enjoyment of the moment, he had almost forgotten his original suspicions. He smiled rather rigidly. 'You wrong me, Miss Fox. Have you forgotten our truce? Having pledged my courtesy, I shall not go back on it, and I hope the same will be true of you.'

Feeling somewhat ashamed and a little ridiculous, Alison merely nodded her head. She had led the way to the front door as they spoke, and now opened it for him.

'In that case, my lord, I will bid you good night.' Without giving him a chance to respond, she handed him the hat and walking stick that Masters had laid on the hall table and shep-herded him hurriedly from the house. Closing the door, she turned and leaned against it. Her breath came quick and shal-low, like a child running from shadows in the night.

CHAPTER 6

Alison sat smiling among the ruins of a substantial picnic lunch, listening to the merriment around her. Meg's *mal d'esprit* had apparently vanished during the long reaches of the night, for at breakfast this morning she had been her usual sunny self, full of plans for the afternoon's expedition. On the walk to the top of Beechen Cliff she had entranced the male members of the party, although they were still of an age where they liked to pretend that the existence of females on the planet indicated a momentary lapse on the part of the Creator. Nonetheless, her every whim had been catered to by budding gallants, with the result that at present, young Lady Meg was quite flown with lemonade and compliments. A game of catch was in progress.

'I say, Sukey,' cried Mr Peter Davenish to his sister, a shy maid of fifteen summers, 'perhaps if you aim for Grenby over there, you might get the ball over here.'

'Now, Peter,' called Meg from some distance away, 'you leave Susan alone. Just because she doesn't have your natural athletic ability is no reason to poke fun.'

Not surprisingly, Peter did not take exception to this dictum. Instead, he threw the ball down and strode over to where Meg stood in conversation with Sally Pargeter. Sally was tall and slim, forever bemoaning her fate as a maypole. She was graceful and attractive, however, and of such sweetness of disposition that she attracted admirers of both sexes. She laughed unaffectedly as Peter flung himself full length on the ground and lifted his hand in petition for the two damsels to join him there.

'It's too hot for running about,' he complained, assisting the girls in settling themselves near him. In a moment all three heads were bent together in a lively conversation.

'The young sprig is right,' said a familiar voice in Alison's ear and she turned to behold the earl lowering himself into a chair near her. 'It's only April, but today one would think it July.'

'Are you enjoying yourself, my lord?' she queried, wishing that Lady Edith were not some distance away, talking with Mrs Pargeter and Mr Rayburn.

March followed her glance. Why was that Rayburn fellow about, he wondered irritably. He had noticed him as one of Alison's more vocal admirers the other night at the Assembly. This afternoon the man was making a perfect ass of himself, hovering over Alison as though she were an invalid, incapable of procuring her own cold chicken and salad.

'Yes,' he answered shortly. 'I am enjoying myself immensely and will enjoy myself even more when these chattering children have all gone back to their nurseries and I can put my feet up in a quiet room with something large and cold in my hand.'

'Oh, but there is plenty of lemonade,' replied Alison, her eyes wide and ingenuous.

'Ah, you relieve my mind. More lemonade is, of course, precisely what I require right now. Minx.'

Alison laughed engagingly, bringing March to a startled realization that he was indulging in banter with the enemy. But, was she really his enemy? he wondered, as he had been doing with increasing frequency over the last few days. He wished her company weren't so damned enjoyable. This was not surprising, of course. Any adventuress worth her salt would have to be charming, and just as surely, he reminded himself, an engaging laugh must be a stock in trade for her sort. She was probably laboring under the delusion that she could charm him into acceptance of her as a suitable companion for his aunt. He intended to prove her wrong.

Apparently his thoughts were easily read on his face, for after a quick glance at him, Alison rose to her feet and made as though to join Lady Edith. Perversely, he held out a hand to stay her.

'Tell me about this school of yours.'

Alison's eyes widened. 'Well,' she began warily, 'I thought of setting it up just outside London. In Kensington, perhaps. On the other hand, I may join the number of select academies already in Bath – so that I may be near Lady Edith,' she concluded a little self-consciously.

March looked at her in some astonishment. If she was telling the truth, she had chosen an odd occupation for an adventuress.

'Do you plan to teach in the school yourself?' he asked.

'Oh, yes, at least at first. If we are a success, the administrative duties will keep me quite busy, I suppose.'

Alison's eyes had taken on a sparkle of enthusiasm as she spoke, but at the earl's next words, they became shuttered.

'And for this, you are proposing to leave my aunt at the end of the year, after your protestations of devotion to her?'

'Of course not,' she replied in a weary tone. 'I told you – I have informed Lady Edith that, while I appreciate the gift she plans to bestow upon me then, I shall set it aside for the time being. I shall remain here in Bath with her as long as she needs me.'

'Ah, well then,' March retorted, unable to keep the sarcasm from his voice, 'she is, after all, in her seventies. Perhaps you won't have long to wait.'

At this, Alison stood abruptly. 'Her ladyship is in excellent health, which I hope will continue for some years to come. Now, if you will excuse me. . . .' She walked swiftly away in the direction of the other adults.

March cursed his unruly tongue. He had glimpsed the tears that had flashed in her eyes before she turned away, and he could only conclude they were genuine. He sighed, feeling a twinge of guilt. Was he wrong about Miss Alison Fox? Everything in his experience led him to mistrust her, but her sincerity, and the unconscious affection she had shown his aunt during the time he had observed her was beginning to overwhelm him. Could he have been so mistaken in his assessment?

She had turned down a substantial bribe, and displayed no inclination to negotiate further. Perhaps, he thought, it would behoove him to remain in Bath for another week.

He should, of course, be getting back to Frances. But Frances, he was perfectly aware, would wait on his return. She and her doting parents had made it plain that in the Earl of Marchford – or at least in his title and his wealth – they beheld the realization of their dreams for the Honorable Frances Milford.

Abruptly, he pushed this uncomfortable notion from his mind, dimly aware that the careful business-like approach to marriage on which he had prided himself now brought him only a profound sense of depression. He also preferred not to dwell on the anticipation stirring within him at the prospect of spending another week in the company of Alison Fox.

Dinner that night was a lively affair, for Sally Pargeter had returned with Meg from the picnic and had been invited to spend the night. The two young ladies were still very full of the events of the afternoon, and most of the conversation was taken up with the exploits of the various young males in attendance at the picnic. After dinner, they retired early, Meg explaining that they had much to talk over, as though the house were not still ringing from their airy prattle.

'I had no idea,' commented March as he and Alison and Lady Edith took their ease in the drawing room, 'that the doings of a group of the greenest young halflings I've seen in quite some time could provide so much food for conversation.'

'I assure you,' replied Lady Edith, 'their doings are only of interest to very young ladies.'

Alison made no comment, merely wondering to herself over Meg's demeanor this evening. The girl had been almost febrile in her excitement, her eyes fairly blazing. Several times she had started to say something, then caught herself with a meaningful glance at Sally, whose returning look was one of sheer terror, if Alison was not very much mistaken. What was the imp up to now? Alison supposed she need not be overly concerned. Meg was well bred, and if her volatility sometimes led her into actions bordering on impropriety, they were no more than might be expected from a high-spirited young damsel who had been pampered and doted upon since birth. There was no denying she was a rare handful, but she was also well aware of the fine line between what was acceptable in a well-bred young miss and what was most definitely not. At least, she had been up till now. Aware that Lady Edith was speaking to her, Alison pushed her concern to the back of her mind.

'Of course, my lady,' she replied mechanically. 'A drive to Whitestone Abbey tomorrow sounds lovely. And I'm sure Lady Melksham and Mrs Busey will enjoy it, too.' The estate, owned by the Dowager Countess Melksham's son, boasted an impressive ruin, which the ladies visited periodically. 'But you do not wish to tire yourself. You are invited for cards at the Dunsaneys' tomorrow evening.'

'Pooh,' said Lady Edith briskly. 'A ride in the country is not going to tire me out.'

It was late when the earl bade a sedate good night to the ladies in Royal Crescent. At Lady Edith's behest, Alison accompanied him to the door.

'Are you, too, looking forward to a drive to Whitestone Abbey, Miss Alison?' he inquired innocently.

Disconcerted, Alison stared for a moment into his sleepy-lion eyes before replying.

'Of – of course. It promises to be a pleasant outing.'

'Just what I was thinking,' came the placid rejoinder, his amusement plain at Alison's obvious discomfiture upon realizing that he would make up one of the party. Settling his hat on his head, he lifted her fingers to his lips for a casual salute. At the last moment, he turned her hand over in his and pressed a kiss on her palm. She jerked her hand away from him as though she had been burned.

'Good night, my lord,' she whispered harshly, and whirled on her heel. The last thing she heard as she fled up the stairs was the door closing on his soft laughter.

Now what was he up to? she wondered as she made preparations for bed. Did he think to charm her into relinquishing her place in his aunt's home? She sniffed. Charm was certainly not the man's forte. He could lay no claim to being a lady's man, for he was arrogant to a fault and not particularly handsome. His clothing was of excellent quality and he wore it with great style, but he could hardly be called a top of the trees. His features were nothing out of the ordinary – if one discounted the way his eyes looked in candlelight. And, if truth be told, she assured herself, his jaw made him look pugnacious rather than handsome. In short, she concluded with some satisfaction, she was in no danger of succumbing to Lord Marchford's feeble attempts at seduction. But as she curled her body into sleep that night, her fingers closed tightly over the place where he had dropped a kiss, and she drew her hand to her breast with an unconscious sigh.

She found herself continuing the earl's catalog of flaws the next afternoon during the journey to Whitestone Abbey. She was sharing the coach with Lady Edith and her particular cronies, Gertrude, Lady Melksham, and Elizabeth Busey, known as Bessie to her friends. All three ladies were of the same generation and spent many happy hours gossiping about events that belonged to the distant past; there was great delight to be had in shredding the reputations of persons who had long since passed to their rewards.

Alison smiled at the scurrilous tales, told with such relish, and returned her gaze to the straight figure who rode on horseback just beyond the window. He sat a horse well, but then so did most men of his class. Whether any of them could have managed the mettlesome bay he guided with such ease was debatable, but he could not really be called dashing, could he? No, certainly not. Practiced, perhaps, but nothing more.

Once the party arrived at the abbey, Alison was kept blessedly occupied, with little time to mull over the earl's appearance and character. The ladies, of course, were unable to walk up to the abbey ruins, but the coachman manipulated the vehicle close enough so that the beauty of the ancient monastery could be admired. A small luncheon was spread for their delectation, after which Lady Edith and Mrs Busey dozed. Lady Melksham, however, was made of sterner stuff, and declared her intention of sketching the main arch, which, happily was just a few feet from the roadway. She accepted with many thanks Alison's arrangement of cushions and scarves, declaring herself perfectly comfortable – but would dear Alison mind fetching the small pillow she always used when she sketched? She was quite sure her maid had packed it in a box that had been placed near her sketching supplies. When fifteen minutes' worth of rummaging produced the desired article, Lady Melksham again offered her profuse thanks and remarked that if dear Alison would just procure the shawl she had a mere few moments ago tucked behind the squabs of the coach, she would be quite settled. March found himself forced to admire Alison's undiminished good humor as she found the shawl – eventually – and the lady's spectacles, and poured her a glass of wine to sustain her through her labors, and adjusted her stool a number of times before she was at last able to take pencil in hand. By this time, the other two ladies had awakened from their slumber, and with a languid gesture Lady Melksham stated that she was quite tired of sketching and perfectly willing to return home as the ladies requested.

March parted from the ladies in Royal Crescent immediately on their return home and made his way back to York House, where he was presented with a missive from Jonas Pilcher. With an unexpected tension, he tore open the letter and scanned its contents hurriedly.

'Miss Alison Fox,' wrote Mr Pilcher in a precise hand, 'is the only offspring of the Reverend Martin Fox, who died some four years ago. Miss Fox is described as being in her late twenties – tall and slender with dark hair and blue eyes. All the persons I contacted spoke of her with respect and affection. She has lived in Ridstowe all her life, except for a period not long before her father's death, when she visited a cousin in Yorkshire for an extended length of time. After her father's death. . . .'

The neat writing went on to detail her departure from Ridstowe to become companion to Lady Strangeways. Here, Pilcher said, his investigation had stopped. Did his lordship wish to proceed?

No, sighed March to himself, his lordship did not wish to proceed. Miss Fox's life was, apparently, an open book, clean and pure as the first snowfall of winter. He felt an odd sense of relief at the news, as though a burden had been lifted from him – which was quite ridiculous. He was pleased, of course, that he would not be put to the trouble and expense of ridding his aunt of a disastrous encumbrance. In fact, it was beginning to sound as though Alison Fox was the best thing that had ever happened to the old lady. This, however, hardly accounted for the sense of lightness – almost of exhilaration – that swept over him at the thought of Alison's blameless existence. Nor was there any particular reason why he was looking forward to a tame evening of cards with some of the most hideous bores of his acquaintance, none of them under seventy years of age, solely because the company would include a certain woman 'in her late twenties – tall and slender with dark hair and blue eyes.' Blue eyes, he mused. What an inadequate description – like calling the Sistine Chapel an old church with a few pictures painted on the ceiling.

An image suddenly thrust itself upon him of his soon-to-be betrothed. Good God! he exclaimed silently. He could not bring to mind the color of Frances's eyes. Some shade of gray, he rather thought. Steel gray. Like a pistol barrel. He shook himself. Lord, where had that thought come from? Frances, of course, was not to be compared to a mere lady's companion – as she would be the first to remind him if she were here, he added, smiling sourly to himself. He rose suddenly. What the devil was the matter with him? Shrugging himself out of his riding coat, he rang for his valet. Time to ready himself for the evening, he told himself firmly, ignoring the traitorous stab of anticipation that left him a little breathless.

Several hours later, Alison stood poised in the doorway of the drawing room in the home of Sir Arthur Dunsaney and his wife, Millicent. Lady Edith had preceded her into the room, and Lord Marchford stood directly behind her. She did not wish to delve into the reason she had elected to dress with particular care this evening. She knew that her gown of turquoise gros de Naples was vastly becoming, having been told on a number of occasions that it made her eyes glow like jewels. It also possessed a lower décolletage than any of the gowns she had worn so far in Lord Marchford's presence. It boasted a lavish sweep of embroidery across the bodice and the hemline, and, after adding her

mother's pearls, she felt complete to a shade wearing it. In justi-
fication, she felt she needed the added confidence the ensemble
brought her, for she believed she was taking an extraordinary
risk in attending a card party in the earl's presence. She knew
her fear to be irrational, but she imagined that she would only
have to pick up a hand of cards to be immediately recognized by
his lordship as the hussy who had supposedly cheated his sister-
in-law of thousands of pounds.

There was, she admitted to herself reluctantly, another consideration. The anger and contempt with which the earl had treated
her before was nothing to the rage he would feel toward her if
he suspected the truth. She had noted what seemed to be a soft-
ening in his attitude toward her. This afternoon they had
conversed quite amiably and she had found much enjoyment in
his company. She laughed a little at her surprise when she
discovered that the Earl of Marchford actually possessed a sense
of humor. She knew he had threatened to ruin Lissa Reynard,
and she knew he was a man to be feared, but even more she
feared the idea of seeing those tawny eyes cloud over with
hatred for her.

'Good Lord, Alison,' Lady Edith had exclaimed impatiently at
her request to be left at home that evening, 'you are becoming a
positive ninnyhammer over this business. You have played
cards on any number of occasions since you have been with me,
and never have you displayed so much as a hint of – of an
unwarranted expertise.'

Which was perfectly true. It was difficult to escape the occasional game of piquet or whist when one lived in Bath, but
Alison had taken great care to display nothing but the most
mediocre skill. She generally managed to lose more than she
won.

'At any rate,' continued Lady Edith, 'with the masquerade
being held at the Upper Rooms tonight, we must rely on a
private party for entertainment, which is why I accepted the
Dunsaneys' invitation. Now, let us hear no more about it.'

So, here she was, and as luck would have it, she found herself
partnered almost immediately with the earl for a game of whist.

The other players were Lady Edith and Mr Rayburn.

'Do you play often, Miss Fox?' asked the earl.

Alison's heart leapt into her throat, where she thought it would choke her, but she answered calmly enough, 'Oh, no, my lord. I – I do not enjoy it much.'

'Ah, you are not a gamester, then?' The words were innocently spoken, and she could read nothing but the most casual interest in his eyes. She forced her hammering pulse to still and drew a deep breath.

'Not at all,' she said quietly.

'As I can confirm,' interjected Lady Edith, smiling. 'Alison is a dear child, but I wish you well of her as a partner. You will be lucky not to lose your shirt.'

When play commenced, Lady Edith's dictum was borne out. Alison made one blunder after another, so that at the end of the evening, the Earl of Marchford declared his pockets wholly to let.

When the three arrived back in Royal Crescent, Lady Edith said good night at once and climbed the stairs toward her bedchamber, again leaving Alison to bid the earl good night.

'You did not appear to enjoy yourself tonight, Alison,' he said slowly. She was intensely aware of his nearness and of their isolation in the candlelit shadows of the hallway. The use of her first name did nothing to quiet the racing of her pulse. 'A skill at cards is not considered a social necessity, after all,' he concluded, and, while she did not doubt that the statement was intended to comfort her, her heart lodged once more in her throat, and she swallowed convulsively.

'No! That is' – she knew her smile must be a grimace – 'I would not mind for myself, but I fear I must be a sad aggravation to anyone unfortunate enough to partner me.'

'Believe me, Alison, the loss of a few pounds did not outweigh the pleasure of your company this evening.'

The earl leaned closer as he spoke, and Alison fancied she could see her consternation reflected in his eyes. The pounding of her heart threatened to suffocate her, and she was sure he must hear it. 'It – it is getting late, my lord. I must. . . .'

'Do you think we could dispense with "my lord"? ' His smile was decidedly leonine, she thought desperately. 'Please call me March, as do the others in this house.'

'Oh! Oh no, I don't think I could—' She was interrupted by an odd sound that seemed to come from the back of the house. It progressed in a series of muffled thumps, culminating in a crash. The earl stepped back abruptly. His eyes were still on her, however, and they contained an expression she could not fathom. He looked away, finally, toward the direction of the sound.

'What the devil. . . ?'

The two hurried toward the door that led to the service area belowstairs. March wrenched it open and immediately found himself clutching a small figure, swathed in a hooded cloak.

'Who—?' growled March. 'What. . . ?'

A sob escaped the figure and the hood slipped to reveal a tumble of golden curls.

'Meg!' gasped Alison and March in unison.

CHAPTER 7

'Meg!' repeated March, this time in a voice of thunder. 'What the devil are you about? Have you just come into the house?' Observing the satin mask that hung about the girl's neck, his eyes narrowed. 'The masquerade! My God, Meg, did you attend that infernal ball?'

For the first time, Meg lifted her head, and Alison observed that her cheeks were tear-stained and her eyes swollen from crying. Her bodice was torn and an expression of lingering terror lay on her delicate features.

'Answer me, Meg,' continued March, the fiery thunder now hardened to ice. 'What have you done?'

At this, Meg broke into sobs so loud and violent that she couldn't speak. The earl observed her in silence for perhaps ten seconds before reaching to shake her by the shoulders.

'By God, Meg, we'll have none of your histrionics. Tell me what happened. Did you actually go to the Upper Rooms unattended? Have you been out alone on the streets at this time of night, like the veriest drab?'

Observing the very real signs of imminent collapse displayed on Meg's face, Alison intervened hurriedly.

'My lord, she is genuinely distraught. As you can see, she is unable to speak right now. Let me take her to her room and you can talk to her tomorrow.'

March opened his mouth, but the denial he had been about to utter died on his lips. He very much wished to inform Miss Fox that her interference in a family matter was quite unnecessary. On the other hand, it was obvious that she was eminently correct in her assessment of Meg's mental state, and he experienced a craven desire to remove himself with all possible speed from the vicinity of a young woman who gave every sign of bursting into strong hysterics.

With a dignified nod, he drew his coat about him. 'Very well, I shall return in the morning.' He shot a minatory stare at Meg. 'At which time I shall want a full explanation of what transpired tonight.' So saying, he made a hasty exist from the house, closing the door behind him with unnecessary force.

Alison turned to minister to Meg, who was leaning heavily against her. The girl's sobs increased on the way up the stairs as she began an incoherent explanation. Alison forbore to say anything until they had reached her room, where Finster, Meg's maid, was awaiting the return of her mistress. Her eyes widened on observing that Lady Margaret was accompanied by Miss Fox, and on being told rather sternly by that lady that her services were not required any further that evening, she flew from the room in obvious relief.

Alison guided her tearful charge to the bed and, lowering her gently, sat beside her and began unfastening the ties of the crumpled domino.

'You're all right now, Meg,' she said soothingly. 'Safe and sound at home. Now, tell me what happened.'

'Oh, Alison!' cried Meg. 'It was so awful! Yes, I did go to the masquerade – with Sally. It seemed like such a lark, and I truly did not think there was anything so wrong in it. I only wanted to dance with Mr Renfrew,' she concluded in a wail.

'And did you?'

'No-oo!' she hiccupped on a sob. 'He was there – and as soon as I saw him I went up to him.'

'Oh, Meg, how could you? What must he think? And what will he tell everyone?'

'Oh, no, Alison. That part is all right. He didn't know it was me. We – we only spoke for a few seconds.' Once more, Meg's eyes filled and tears cascaded down her cheeks. 'I saw him as soon as we entered the ballroom. He was just coming in – carrying two glasses of punch, and we almost collided. I said good evening, and so did he and he said something about what a crush it was and – well, I was just about to tell him who I was when – oh, Alison!' she wailed. 'He was joined by a young woman! He excused himself and turned to her and . . . and gave her a glass of punch and kissed her on the cheek!'

'No!' cried Alison. 'I cannot believe the drawing master at Miss Crumshaw's School would behave so in public.'

'Well, he did – and then he turned back to me and laughed rather sheepishly and said to please beg pardon, but he and the young woman had just become engaged!'

'Meg! Oh, I am so sorry my dear. How awful for you. What did you do then?'

'Sally was standing right beside me, and – she is such a good friend, Alison. She did not say anything, but led me to a nearby bench – otherwise I really believe I would have fallen to the floor in a swoon. There were a great many people there, all in masks, of course, and some of them – particularly the women – were . . . were behaving in a manner that was not at all proper. After a moment, when I had recovered myself, I told Sally I just wanted to go home, and she was more than willing. She really had not wanted to come, after all, and we were receiving some very unwelcome attention from a group of – well, I could scarcely call them gentlemen – who were standing nearby. I think they were somewhat the worse for drink. We had a little difficulty then, because they followed us as we made our way out of the ball-room, but we were finally able to elude them.'

'Did you have any difficulty on the way home?' asked Alison with concern, noting the condition of Meg's gown.

Meg did not answer for a moment, but looked down at her hands. 'Everything was fine until we reached Sally's house. She lives in the Circus, you know, so we had not far to go. And, since it's only a little farther to Royal Crescent, I anticipated no trouble, but' – her eyes widened in remembered terror – 'as I hurried along Brock Street, I was accosted by a *terrible* man. I believe he thought I was a – a woman of the streets. Oh, Alison, I am so ashamed. He said dreadful things to me, and grabbed at my – that is, he tried to – but I managed to tear away from him and I ran and ran and ran. I came into the house through the stables, for Finster left the back door open for me. Oh, dear heaven, I am so glad to be home!'

With this she flung herself into Alison's arms, sobbing once-more in rising hysteria. Alison gathered the young girl to her, murmuring softly and inconsequentially.

'There, there. It's all right now, Meg. It's all over and you are none the worse for your adventure.'

'But I am so very sorry, Alison. It was such a stupid thing to do – especially after you and Aunt Edith warned me, and March – oh, good heavens – March! What am I going to tell him? He will be furious. You don't suppose he will forbid me to come to London, do you? Oh, Alison, I am the most wretched creature alive!'

These words, uttered from the increasingly soggy depths of her bosom, convinced Alison that Meg's most immediate concerns did not include Mr Renfrew's defection.

'There, there,' she said again. 'If you wish, I will speak to your brother when he arrives tomorrow.'

Meg lifted a tear-stained face. 'Oh would you, Alison? I should be everlastingly grateful! He is greatly taken with you, I can tell, and he will listen to what you say.'

Alison flushed uncomfortably and lifted Meg to her feet, ac-complishing in a few moments the removal of the torn gown and the rest of her garments. By then, Meg was more in command of herself and accomplished her nightly ablutions at the pitcher and bowl on her commode without help. Shrugging into her night rail, she settled into bed with a long, shuddering sigh.

'Thank you, Alison, for being so understanding. I truly have learned a lesson.' She assayed a watery chuckle. 'I wish I could say that I shall never do anything so stupid again, but knowing me, I'm afraid I can't make that promise. I will *try* to be good from now on, though,' she added. 'Particularly while I am still staying with you and Aunt Edith. It's not really fair of me, I suppose, to make you suffer for my buffle-headedness.'

With this, she blew a repentant kiss to Alison and snuggled down amid her covers. Smiling, Alison returned the salute and, blowing out Meg's bedside candle, she tiptoed from the room.

On arriving in her own chamber, she retired immediately, feeling quite exhausted by the events of the day. Sleep, however, was a long time in coming. Her thoughts, as they tended to do too often these days, flew to the Earl of Marchford. His presence, she was forced to admit, was having a disastrous effect on her peace of mind. Why just a simple touch from this man, whom she had already decided was a perfectly ordinary example of the species, should make her tremble, she could not fathom. She had been intensely aware of his nearness all afternoon at Prior Park, conscious of his brandy-colored eyes on her and his assessment of her every action. This evening, she had watched with a most unbecoming fascination his strong, slender fingers dealing cards. For once, she had experienced no difficulty in losing hand after hand. His touch at her waist as he guided her through doorways and into sedan chairs produced a spreading warmth that penetrated all the layers of her clothing.

Worst of all, she was beginning to like him as a person. He was certainly a product of his environment, arrogantly conscious of his rank and the dignity due his position. How could he be otherwise when it had no doubt been drilled into him since childhood? Yet, it was obvious that he loved his family with wholehearted devotion – particularly since the tragedy that had befallen them, and with them he was relaxed and unassuming. His laughter and warmth were genuine as he teased Meg and made his aunt giggle with his outrageous flattery. He was well educated without being pompous and displayed a genuine love of learning. For heaven's sake, she thought despairingly, how could one *not* like such a man?

Then again, she reflected with unhappy irony, what difference did it make whether she liked him or not? She was still his avowed enemy and she must fear him. For an instant her thoughts flickered to the words Meg had spoken in Milsom Street. Was his hatred of her partly a product of a guilt he experienced because he felt he had abandoned his family? Not that *that* made any difference, either. She should be taking comfort in the thought that she had apparently convinced him of the sincerity of her affection for Lady Edith and that he would soon take himself off for his town house in London and the company of Lady Frances. If she took great care, she would probably never have to see him again. She was surprised by the profound sense of depression this thought provoked, and although she turned into her pillow with a determined sigh, it was many hours before she at last fell into an uneasy sleep.

Despite Alison's restless night, she woke at a relatively early hour, and, slipping from her bed, went down to take breakfast alone. To her surprise, the earl joined her there before she had finished her first cup of coffee.

'My lord,' she exclaimed, splashing the contents of her cup onto the tablecloth, 'when did you arrive? That is, I did not hear—'

'One of the housemaids was polishing the brasswork on the front door, so I just walked in unannounced,' he explained curtly. He gestured an acceptance of ham and eggs proffered by a footman and held out his cup to Alison, who poured coffee from the silver urn resting on the table. 'Has my sister come down yet?'

'Good heavens, no,' she replied, startled. 'I should be surprised if she were to appear in another two hours.'

'Two hours! But she knows I particularly wish to speak to her.'

'My lord,' said Alison hesitantly, 'she did not retire until very late, as . . . as you know. She was exhausted, and—'

'Yes, I know all about her late night and her exhaustion, but I would have you send for her immediately. I do not have all day to waste.'

So imperious was his tone that Alison's hackles rose unconsciously. Striving for calm, she spoke quietly. 'I know you are . . . unhappy with Meg at the moment, and for good reason,' she added, observing the signs of rising temper in his eye, 'but she is truly repentant of her actions last night.'

The earl snorted, and Alison continued hastily. 'I do not think I am betraying her confidence when I tell you that her wish to attend the masquerade was not mere willfulness, but the result of a childish, albeit very painful infatuation.'

March raised his brows disdainfully. 'Are you telling me, Miss Fox, that my sister divulged her plans to you and you said nothing to Lady Edith or me?'

Alison stiffened. 'Of course not. I was aware of her interest in this person, but I knew it for a schoolgirl crush and never dreamed she would carry it so far.'

'Go on.' His words carried the merest hint of an apology, and Alison, still bristling, told him of Meg's harrowing adventures of the night before.

'She is truly sorry for what she has done, my lord, and I believe she has already been punished for her misdeeds.'

March, watching her as she spoke, found it difficult to concentrate on what she was saying. He was, instead, trying to determine the precise shade of her eyes. Their color changed, he decided, depending on her mood. Right now, they had turned from their usual boundless Mediterranean blue to what he rather fancied was the tint of a Renaissance Madonna's robe. She was gazing at him, directly and earnestly, as she spoke, and he felt somehow suspended, as if flung from a precipice out into a dizzying, amethyst void.

'What?' He came to himself with a start. Alison had finished her monologue some moments before and sat staring at him in puzzlement.

'I said, I think your sister has been punished enough. Do you not agree?'

'Oh . . . ah, yes, of course. That is, no, I don't,' he said in some confusion. 'I agree that Meg has apparently learned her lesson, but I cannot let her think I am prepared to simply overlook these adolescent starts of hers.'

Alison frowned. 'Of course, I would not dream of advising you on how to deal with a member of your family, but—'

March grinned. 'No more than you would dream of maneuvering my aunt into getting out of the house regularly and eating proper meals, which I know she did not before you came to her.'

Alison flushed. 'Oh! As to that. . . .'

'As to that,' returned March, a smile still curving his lips as he reached to cover her hand with his, 'I feel that I am about to benefit from your advice whether I wish it or not. I have discovered by this time that you are a rather determined sort.' Alison felt ready to sink. She had apparently won him over. Why, when this ought to put her in transports did she feel like the worst sort of humbug? And why was she so conscious of a running fire in her veins simply because his fingers were gently massaging the back of her hand?

As though he had read her thoughts, March hastily removed his hand to pick up his fork, and for some moments addressed his breakfast with great concentration. He lifted his eyes once more when Alison cleared her throat and began speaking.

'I certainly think you ought to speak to her, but she is already aware of the folly of her behavior last night, and anything more you have to add on the subject would only make her resentful. I think rather than punishing her, it would be more to the point if you were to express to her – briefly – your disappointment in her betrayal of your trust and your hope that she will never do so again. She loves you, you know, and the knowledge that she has caused you hurt will be more punishment than anything else you could inflict on her.'

March sat for a moment in bemused silence, and the ticking of the mantel clock sounded loud in Alison's ears.

'You are very wise, my dear,' he said at last, in a voice so low that she could scarcely hear him. 'And you are right. Betrayal is the worst crime one human can commit against another – and the most hurtful.' Alison sensed that he was no longer speaking of Meg's transgressions, and she held her breath.

To her surprise, March rose abruptly from his chair and said in a brisk tone, 'Very well, Madame *Consigliori*, I will leave you now, and return a few hours hence. I shall speak to Meg then, and you may trust me not to bruise her fragile young sensibilities.'

The smile he bent on her was warm and carried such an intimacy that Alison felt a tide of color rush into her cheeks. She stammered an incoherent farewell, and sank back in her chair, trembling, when he had left the room.

Dear Lord, who was she to speak of betrayal? She had won the earl's trust, but at what cost? She would spend the rest of her life praying that he would never discover her part in the family tragedy from which he had still not recovered. She was forced to admit that the Earl of Marchford had come to mean a great deal to her, although she knew only too well the barriers that separated them. She was the granddaughter of an earl, but his social position, if not his rank, effectively removed him from her, as did his impending betrothal. Not, she was sure, that he looked upon her with anything beyond a friendly acceptance. In other circumstances she would value his friendship as a precious jewel, but she knew she must deny herself even that consolation. He had already invaded her dreams; she must under no circumstances let him creep into her heart, for that way lay sure disaster.

Sighing, she abandoned the cooling remains of her breakfast and made her way to the service area of the house, where she collected the little spaniel Honey for an invigorating walk in the park across from the Crescent. Honey was her usual enthusiastic self and, after clearing the area of any birds who might be threatening the peace and security of the neighborhood, she brought sticks for Alison to throw. An hour spent in this fashion was sufficient to restore Alison's natural cheerfulness, and by the time she bundled the little dog back across the street, much of her equanimity had been restored.

As she approached the house, she was surprised, given the earliness of the hour, to observe a fashionable traveling carriage pull up to Lady Edith's door. When a young woman, casting furtive glances in all directions, was handed down from the vehicle, Alison's eyes widened in astonishment, and she hurried to intercept the visitor.

'Molly!' she cried breathlessly. 'Molly! Molly Callander! Whatever are you doing here?'

CHAPTER 8

'I really should not be here,' gasped Molly breathlessly, her dark curls fairly vibrating in distress. She accepted a cup of tea from Alison and sank back in her chair in the library. Her black eyes darted about apprehensively, as though she feared retribution might be immediately at hand. Alison observed her affectionately, her eyes soft with remembrance.

She and Molly and Beth had been inseparable at school. Alison, the sensible one, was not always successful in restraining Molly, whose snapping black eyes viewed the world as one vast, amusing playground. Beth, golden-haired, pretty, and sweet as the smile that fell from her rosy lips, was the compliant one, always the first to acquiesce to Molly's hare-brained escapades, and always the first to stand side by side with her friends when those schemes inevitably crashed in ruins.

Alison sighed. In the end, it had been her own escapade that had brought ruin – to so many people. She shook herself, attending Molly's next words. 'I am supposed to be on my way to Bristol, where I am to join Callander at his mother's house. The family is gathering, you know, for the christening of his sister's latest. I set out from London yesterday and spent the night in Marlborough. I just had to stop and see you. I know we must not be seen together, but oh, Alison, I have dreadful news!'

'Molly, calm down. Lady Edith is still abed, so we can be private. Tell me what has you in such a pother. Nothing can be all that terrible.'

'Oh, but it is! Marchford is in Bath!'

'Yes, I know,' answered Alison calmly. 'He arrived several

days ago and has spent most of his time here at his aunt's house.'

'But—'

'Really, Molly,' Alison continued with an assurance she did not quite feel, 'the earl and I have met on several occasions, and he has been all that is cordial.'

Molly expelled a gulping sigh. 'Oh, my love, I am so relieved to hear you say that. When I heard he had departed for Bath, I made sure he had discovered all! But,' she continued apprehensively, 'if he has not come to ruin you, why is he here?'

Alison chuckled. 'To deliver his aunt from the clutches of a certified adventuress, of course. Me.'

'What?' Molly gasped once more. 'But I thought you said—'

Alison launched into a somewhat expurgated version of her acquaintance with Lord Marchford, at the end of which Molly broke into a gurgle of laughter. 'Oh, Alison, I might have known you would land on your feet. Certified adventuress, indeed. You, my little Vixen, are one of the most honorable persons I know, and I am glad the earl has the sense to see it.'

Alison smiled at the sound of her girlhood nickname, but immediately, she flushed. 'I hardly think I can call myself honorable, Molly. When I think of how I have been deceiving him—'

'Nonsense,' retorted her friend stoutly. 'It is not as though you are perpetrating a fraud just because you are keeping information from him that would lead to a completely erroneous conclusion on his part.'

'What do you mean? I am indeed the notorious Lissa Reynard whom he has been seeking under every bush in England for the past four years.'

'But you are not the perpetrator of the tragedy for which he has blamed you.' Molly paused and continued hesitantly. 'Have . . . have you ever considered simply going to Lord Marchford and explaining what really transpired between you and Susannah Brent?'

'Yes,' replied Alison sharply, 'and I have come to the conclusion that it would be a great piece of folly to do so. Despite your kind words, Molly, I cannot help but feel responsible for all that happened.'

77

Molly set her cup down so hard on the little table before her that it rattled. 'Alison, I never knew someone with such a – a Methodist sort of conscience. You did not cheat Susannah Brent. You were not even responsible for her horrendous gambling losses. I tell you, Alison, it was all I could do not to repudiate all the lies she told about you.'

'Well, it was a very good thing you did not,' said Alison, smiling ruefully. 'You would have been hard put to convince Lord Marchford after that that you knew nothing about me.'

'Or that dreadful little man he set on to me as well,' added Molly. She smiled, and her black eyes danced wickedly. 'Oh, Alison, I was truly marvelous. I had both the earl and his persistent detective convinced that I was a totty-headed widgeon who had been victimized by a clever female.'

'You should have gone on the stage,' said Alison with a laugh. 'Beth and I always used to marvel at your abilities.' A shadow crossed both their faces at the mention of their friend.

'Poor Bethie,' Molly sighed. 'I knew that her marriage to Jack Crawford would end in tragedy.'

'Yet, she loved him,' Alison's mouth twisted. 'And he loved her, too, in his way. He mourned her death sincerely, I believe.'

Molly nodded her head in agreement. 'Yes, that's true. He came to see me some months after she passed away, and I was quite appalled at the change in him. He had lost a great deal of weight, and become careless in his dress. I'll have to admit, he was one of the handsomest men of my acquaintance, and always rather of the dandy persuasion, you know. Oh!' She sat up abruptly. 'I must be losing my mind! I almost forgot the other thing I have to tell you. Jack Crawford is also in Bath!'

'What?' Alison could only stare in disbelief. 'Here? I have not seen him. What is he doing in Bath?'

'I don't know. Of course, he probably does not move in the same circles as Lady Edith Brent, so it is no wonder your paths have not crossed. However, I'd be on my guard if I were you. I don't see how it would be possible for anyone to make the connection between Lissa Reynard and Jack Crawford, but it seems prudent to keep your distance from him while Lord

Marchford is in town.'

'Yes,' replied Alison faintly, awful visions of imminent retribution rising before her eyes. 'Thank you, Molly, I shall take great care.'

Molly drained the last of her tea and stood up. 'And now, I must leave, my love. I left my abigail cooling her toes in the carriage and must make haste now to reach Bristol at my appointed hour. Do write to me, Alison, and tell me how you go on.' She swept her friend into a scented embrace. 'And it goes without saying that if you get into any trouble, and you find yourself driven from Lady Edith's door with a fiery sword, you are welcome – no, *more* than welcome – to take up residence with me.' She grinned crookedly. 'After all, every good little vixen deserves a safe earth.'

Alison returned the embrace wholeheartedly. 'I am blessed in my friends, Molly,' she said mistily.

'Pooh,' was that lady's response. Bestowing an airy kiss on Alison's cheek, she hurried from the room. As she made her exit from the house, she paused for an instant and looked up and down the street, as though fearful of being observed, before plunging into her waiting carriage.

March, just turning into Royal Crescent observed the woman's careless wave to Alison, and her descent to the street with casual interest. It was not until Molly glanced furtively in his direction that his gaze sharpened. He stopped, rooted to the pavement as he recognized the visitor as the woman with whom Lissa Reynard had resided during her sojourn in the metropolis.

My God, what was the Viscountess Callander doing in Bath? What was she doing in Royal Crescent, apparently on the best of terms with Alison Fox? And why was she creeping away as though the tipstaffs were after her? Whirling, he reversed course into Brock Street and stood for a moment, his stomach churning unpleasantly. Without realizing that he did so, he began walking in the opposite direction and did not come to himself again until he had reached the balustrade that marked the entrance to the Pultney Bridge. Here, he stopped and stared unseeingly at the River Avon rushing below him. A number of things had fallen into place during his peregrination, and he felt as though a bomb had exploded in the pit of his stomach.

He had been extraordinarily stupid, he thought dully. He had, in fact, been duped like the merest greenling by a pair of fathomless blue eyes. How could he have been convinced so easily of Alison Fox's innocence, when it was by now clear as tears that she was the harpy he had originally assumed her to be, and the woman for whom he had searched so long and fruitlessly?

He should have made the connection instantly between the name Fox and its French translation. To be sure, Alison did not match the description given of the elusive Lissa; she had hidden those fascinating eyes behind tinted glasses and covered the glossy black depths of her hair with a brown wig. He swore aloud. There had even been a clue in the report Pilcher had given him a few days ago – 'an extensive visit to her cousin shortly before the death of her father' – which coincided so precisely with the interval Lissa Reynard had spent in London. Fox. Reynard. She was indeed a vixen, more vicious than any female of the species. My God, he would like to return to Royal Crescent right now and strangle her with his bare hands. His fists clenched until his knuckles showed white against the balustrade.

No. He forced his breathing to slow. He would not confront her yet – would not yet take the revenge he had promised himself for so long. He must plan this well, for he intended Lissa Reynard's suffering to equal his own. He had all the time in the world to craft a fitting punishment for her. She had, after all, avowed her intention of remaining in Royal Crescent for the foreseeable future.

And how sweet the punishment would be. At last, he would be free of the corrosive bitterness that had filled him since the deaths of William and Susannah and his father. The rage that even now consumed him would be cleansed from his soul and he could live again, freed from its burden. He reveled in the knowledge that with her ruin he would be accomplishing a double payment. Oh yes, the vixen Fox/Reynard would live to curse the day she had set out to rob the Brent family.

In the meantime, he would go on with her as before, savoring the retribution that was to come. With a smile that caused a young street urchin in his path to cross his fingers in the air, the earl made his way briskly back to his original destination.

He arrived to find both his aunt and his little sister at the breakfast table. Of Alison there was no sign.

'No, don't get up, poppet,' he said to Meg, who had scrambled to her feet at his entrance. An expression of wary relief crossed her features at the sound of his pet name for her. She straightened her shoulders.

'Did . . . did you wish to speak to me, March?'

March gazed blankly at her. Speak to her? Good God – he had forgotten the contretemps of the evening before. Before he could respond, Lady Edith turned to her nephew and spoke without offering a greeting.

'Now, March, Meggie has told me all about what happened last night, and I have already read her a scold. We have agreed that what she did was very wrong, and she is very sorry about the whole thing.'

March's interest in his little sister's escapade was, at this point, nonexistent, but he supposed he'd better see the matter through. 'Is that so, Meggie?' he asked mildly. Meg, for the second time that morning, burst into tears.

'Oh, yes, March. I feel positively wretched about going to the stupid ball against your wishes, and those of Aunt Edith and Alison. I nearly got into terrible trouble, and I will never, ever do anything like that again.' She gazed at her brother through swimming eyes. 'I know I deserve some sort of punishment, and I will accept whatever you choose to dispense,' she concluded with an air of a Christian martyr begging to be thrown to the lions. Despite his agony of soul, March was forced to swallow a smile.

'Sit down, my dear. I must admit that I am terribly disappointed in you.' He noted with a pang that apparently Alison was right, for his words sent a flicker of pain across Meg's pale features. 'However, from what Miss Fox has told me, you have already been punished for your misdeeds. Tell me, Meg, do you truly feel you have learned something from your experience?'

'Oh, yes, March,' the girl breathed. 'I never realized before that when you or Aunt or Eleanor or – or anyone else forbids me to do something I particularly wish to do, I have formed the awful habit of getting my back up and simply doing as I please.' Conscious that she had perhaps not phrased this well, she added hastily, 'That is, my elders have more experience of life than I, and they are probably right in their strictures – besides having only my happiness in mind.'

'What a laudable sentiment, my dear. I could almost fear that you will soon be making arrangements to give away your possessions to the poor and will send to your modiste for a hair shirt. No, no,' he continued, observing the anguished protest forming on Meg's lips, 'I know you are sincere in your desire to mend your ways, and I appreciate it. And, since Aunt has no doubt toasted your ears with her scold, I see no point in delivering one of my own.'

He sat down in the vacant chair next to Meg. 'Will you pour me some coffee, then?' he asked plaintively, 'or must I sit here and starve before your eyes?'

Meg jumped from her chair to fill his request, but before she did so, she flung her arms around him in a violent hug. 'Oh, March! You are the best of brothers, and I do truly promise to become the best of sisters.'

March felt himself sinking into the emptiness within him. If only all his burdens could be lightened so easily. He returned Meg's embrace distractedly, and forced himself to sip his coffee as he listened to a resumption of the discussion that had been underway before his arrival.

'I do love fireworks!' cried Meg, referring to the upcoming gala in Sydney Gardens. 'I won't even mind sitting through a concert first.'

'It is to be composed of Mozart pieces primarily,' interjected Lady Edith. 'To my mind no one has written a decent piece of music since he died.'

'You do not enjoy Handel?' asked March amusedly. 'Or Beethoven?'

'My favorite composer,' said a voice from the door, and March stiffened. 'Ah, Miss Fox,' he said, managing to affix a welcoming smile to his lips with only the greatest effort. 'We were discussing this evening's concert.'

Alison, moving lightly into the room, sent March a brief, intent glance. Something was wrong. She felt it instinctively, as though a chill wind had blown through her. She could discern nothing in his face, which was composed in an affable grin. But his eyes. . . . It was as though a film of ice had formed over his tawny gaze. What had happened? she wondered, and a sick feeling began to tremble within her. In the next moment, she shook off her foolish fancy as he rose to pull out a chair for her at the table.

The next half hour or so was spent in making plans for the evening's excursion. March rose finally, saying that he had an appointment to meet an old friend of his father's at the Saracen's Head Inn for an early luncheon. Aunt Edith declared her intention of repairing to her room to finish the book she had started last night, and Alison and Meg climbed the stairs to Meg's rooms to choose what each would wear to the fête that evening.

Throughout the remainder of the day, March felt as though he were two people, one of whom carried on the normal business of his life, mouthing pleasantries and exchanging gossip. The other seethed with the turmoil that raged within him. He found himself dwelling on the conversation he had held with Alison that morning. Damn the woman and her talk of trust. What was it they had spoken of? Something about betrayal being the worst crime one human could commit against another – and the most hurtful.

He was dimly aware in one corner of his mind – one that he did not at all wish to examine – that the operative word here was 'hurt.' He had come to trust Alison Fox. Worse than that, he had come to like her. Odd that, he mused dispassionately. There were so few people he really liked – including, a small voice whispered, the woman he expected to make his wife. He respected Frances, surely, and admired her, but he did not, he was forced to admit, truly like her, any more than he truly liked, say, Mr

Bratchett, the bespectacled tutor who had dragged him with unrelenting sternness through Greek and Latin as a boy.

He shook himself irritably. All this was beside the point. His betrothal to Frances would be a matter of practicality, and his like or dislike of her had nothing to do with his feelings for Alison Fox, which were a seething cauldron of hatred, humiliation, and betrayal.

His lordship's valet took one look at him when he was summoned to help him dress for the evening, and proffered shirt, cravat, and waistcoat in unnerved silence. When at last he saw his master from his rooms in the Royal York, he fell into the nearest chair with a trembling sigh of relief.

Somehow, March managed to get through dinner. No one, he was sure, even those who fancied they knew him well, could have been aware of the fury contained behind the urbane face he showed to the ladies at the table. He was able to relax a little during the concert, for in the darkness, he felt no need to mask his emotions. Mozart, on this evening, did little to soothe him, but it did help him to think, and by the time the audience had applauded for the last selection, a plan had begun to develop in his mind for the annihilation of the beautiful Miss Fox.

Alison discovered to her dismay that Mozart was failing her tonight. She had looked forward to the concert with delight, particularly since the orchestra was composed this evening of members of the newly formed Philharmonia in London. Their proficiency had been obvious from the start, yet she was unable to lose herself in the music as she usually did. She glanced down the row of seats to where March was seated on the other side of Meg and Lady Edith, but despite the lanterns hanging overhead, she was unable to discern his features. She shifted uneasily in her chair.

She wondered for the hundredth time what had happened to him today. Or was it her imagination that he was indefinably changed? He had laughed and teased at dinner but had eaten practically nothing. He had complimented her on her gown and smiled at her with rigidly curved lips, but his eyes had glittered like ice shards struck from a frozen pond.

She shrugged and consciously unclenched the fingers curled in her lap. Lord Marchford's good spirits, or lack thereof, meant nothing to her. He would be gone soon, and life would return to normal. She had found great solace in her placid existence with Lady Edith, and when her ladyship's nephew returned to his own milieu in London, Alison would continue to enjoy visits to the Pump Room and Duffield's Library. Meg's visit would provide a little needed excitement for a few months, and of course, her quiet moments were always enlivened with plans for her school.

She sank back in her chair. Two weeks ago, this program would have provided her with a great deal of satisfaction. Why it did no longer, she preferred not to consider. She noticed with a start that the orchestra had ceased playing and the sound of applause rose about her. Lord Marchford rose and announced his intention of procuring refreshments to fortify them until the start of the fireworks. Alison watched his departure, admiring despite herself the grace and power in his stride.

Idly, her gaze moved over the throng just leaving their seats. Suddenly she stiffened. Over there, across the little amphitheater, seated with two men and a woman, his head thrown back in laughter – was that. . . ? The man turned toward her as he spoke to one of his companions. Yes! Oh, dear God yes, it was Jack Crawford! She was quite sure he had not seen her and she leapt to her feet in a blind panic. Turning, she ignored Meg's puzzled query and hurtled away from the crowd toward one of the dark walkways that led from the main path. Breathless, she plunged into its leafy shelter, only to be brought up short a few seconds later as she collided with a large, muscular form.

Unfortunately, the large form was juggling four glasses of punch, which flew from his grasp upon impact and shattered on the stone paving at their feet.

'Oh!' gasped Alison. 'I am so— Oh! It's you! I did not see . . . that is—'

'It seems, Miss Fox,' said Lord March imperturbably, 'that you have not curbed your rather unfortunate propensity for dashing into harm's way.' He fished a handkerchief from his waistcoat pocket and began dabbing at the lapels of his coat.

'Oh, dear,' said Alison anxiously. 'I hope you have not ruined it.' She produced her own handkerchief from her reticule and dabbed at the stain nearest her.

'What about your gown?'

'My...? Oh. No, I'm all right,' she replied after a hasty perusal of her bodice. 'But I'm afraid you are rather drenched.' She continued her repairs.

'What were you doing, speeding along a dark path by yourself?' His tone was light, but Alison fancied she detected a note of censure. Good heavens, did he think she was on her way to an assignation? She wished she could explain that it was quite the contrary.

'I did not realize I was speeding,' she replied with some dignity. 'I merely wished to stretch my legs after sitting so long.'

A silence hung between them for a moment, and Alison suddenly realized that her attempts to dry the earl's coat had brought her into disturbingly close proximity to the earl's chin. She looked up and found herself gazing directly into his eyes. Startled, she began to step away, but March placed his hands gently on her shoulders and pulled her toward him. She could feel the warmth of his breath stirring the curls on her cheeks, and discovered that she was having a great deal of difficulty with her breathing. She should push him away. Right now. But lost in the wonder of his nearness, she stayed motionless, aching for him to draw her even closer. When he did, it seemed the most natural thing in the world to lift her face, so that his lips brushed her cheek with a soft caress. He bent over her, and with a sigh, she lifted her mouth to meet his.

His kiss was soft and undemanding at first. He embraced her fully and as his arms pressed her against his length, she arched against him involuntarily. His lips immediately grew hot and urgent and searching, and unknowingly, she raised her own arms to stroke the thick, soft hair at the back of his neck. She felt herself opening to him as a flower might bloom in the heat of a summer afternoon, and she cried aloud against his mouth. The feel of his hands on her back created a fire in her blood, and she moved against him as though she would crawl inside him.

A burst of feminine laughter nearby brought her to her senses, and with a horrified gasp, she stepped abruptly away from him. He made no move to restrain her, and for a shocked moment, she simply stared at him, unable to read his expression in the darkness.

'I should not have done that,' he said harshly.

'No,' she whispered numbly.

'On the other hand, I cannot say I am sorry it happened.'

'No,' she repeated, unable to gather her thoughts into a coherent pattern.

'We had better get back to the others,' he whispered, and putting his hand under her elbow, he guided her back to the crowd that still milled about the little amphitheater. They soon reached the place where Lady Edith and Meg waited.

'I'm glad you two are back,' caroled Lady Edith. 'I was afraid you'd miss the fireworks.'

CHAPTER 9

'Oh, March, thank you so very much.' Meg skipped beside her brother as they emerged from Mrs Vivier's Confectionery Shop in Brock Street. She spoke thickly through a mouthful of pastry. 'I know you must think me the veriest infant, but I am absolutely addicted to Mrs Vivier's meringues.'

'I believe you are not alone,' replied March, indicating a pair of fashionable young ladies who had left the shop ahead of them, each carrying a parcel of sticky treats. 'Where to now?'

'I think,' Meg replied virtuously, 'that we should execute our commissions first – Aunt's writing paper and the new book at Duffield's Library that she requested. Then we may consider our own enjoyment. A stroll along the river, perhaps, and tea at that new little place near Parade Gardens.'

'By which time you will no doubt be suffering from hunger pangs again. I shouldn't be surprised if you will be fat as a flawn by the time you are twenty.'

'March! What a dreadful thing to say.' Meg glanced with satisfaction at her trim form, reflected in a shop window. 'Aunt always says the Brent women hold their figures no matter what. And it is not,' she concluded loftily, 'as though I gorge myself, like Jennifer Wilmont. If you wish to talk about flawns—'

'Never mind, you little cat. Here. Here is Duffield's. You go and inquire about the book, and I shall find the notepaper.'

Casting him a mischievous look, Meg hurried to the counter where a clerk stood in readiness to assist the shop's patrons. March turned away to the other side of the room. Giving a second clerk the order written down by his aunt, he strolled aimlessly among the books on display. The latest edition of the *Bath Chronicle* failed to hold his attention, as did an advertisement for a horse auction to be held three days hence in Lansdown. His vision, it seemed, was clouded this morning by a pair of magical blue eyes that constantly hovered before him, and his thoughts were wholly consumed by the events of last night.

When the propitious, if somewhat messy accident with the punch cups had brought Miss Fox in such close proximity, his first thought was that the gods were indeed with him. His second was an earnest desire to place his hands about that lovely, slender throat and squeeze the breath from her. He knew what he was going to do the moment she stepped close to him, but it was all he could do not to crush her body against him and grind her lips beneath his in a savage kiss. He was almost overwhelmed by a compulsion to violate her in as brutal a fashion as he could manage in such a public place. At the last moment, he found himself oddly reluctant to hurt her and, summoning all the considerable restraint at his command, he had instead brushed her lips with his own in a shy, lover's salute. At the first touch of her mouth against his, he had almost lost control. God, how could evil be disguised in such sweetness? Her lips had been warm and soft, and the body pressed against his in such innocent compliance had been all womanly curves and enticing hollows. If he had not known better, he would have sworn her response was genuine and freely given.

He smiled. Oh yes, she had responded. She had returned his kiss with an unaffected ardor that surprised him. She had opened herself to him freely, and he had been stirred by a desire as urgent as it was unwelcome. If that peel of laughter had not interrupted them, God knows where that moment of passion might have led.

He must be more watchful of his emotions in the future, he mused. His plan had begun well, and with a little careful nudging, Miss Fox would be ready to fall into his arms within a week or two. Time then to savor the fulfillment of his little project. Time then to. . . .

'What?' March stared blankly down at Meg, who stood before him with two books in her hand.

'I said, Mr Wooly Wits, that the nice gentleman over there' – she tossed her head to indicate the young clerk who stood at the counter in blushful reverence – 'told me that *Pride and Prejudice* has just arrived. It is a newly published novel by the lady who wrote *Sense and Sensibility*, and Alison has been waiting and waiting for it. Shall we get it for her?'

'Of course,' agreed March casually. When they were once again out on the street, he asked, 'Is Miss Fox a reader of novels then?'

'Well,' replied Meg thoughtfully, 'I know she loves to read, and I think she amuses herself with novels – though not of the Minerva Press variety.' Meg flushed, for her own purchase had consisted of two Gothic romances, guaranteed, so her friends had told her, to keep her entranced from start to finish.

'What are her preferences, then?' the earl prodded. It would be prudent, he told himself, to know his enemy as well as possible.

'Oh, I don't know. . . . She likes poetry. Coleridge, I think, and someone named Blake. She was quite beside herself when Aunt Edith gave her the complete works of Maria Edgeworth for Christmas. And I think I have even seen her with some of Mrs More's stuff, although why she would choose to immerse herself in a puddle of eternal moralizing, I can't imagine. Lately, she's been perusing a book by someone named Mary Woolen-something.'

'Mary Wollstonecraft?' March lifted his brows in surprise. 'Good Lord!' Was she a disciple of that vigorous advocate of female rights? How odd – particularly if she was also partial to the works of the pious Hannah More.

'A woman of eclectic tastes, one must assume,' he murmured with an air of profound uninterest before turning the subject. Miss Fox's name, however, surfaced again before the conclusion of March's outing with his young sister.

'Oh, that was lovely,' Meg sighed later at the charming tea shop in Parade Gardens. She pushed aside the remains of a plateful of cream cakes and sipped her tea, gazing with satisfaction at the strollers who dotted the park's green sweep. 'I'm so sorry Alison could not have joined us.'

'Mm,' replied March in a carefully noncommittal voice. 'Aunt Edith said something about her being indisposed this morning?'

'Just a headache. Aunt Edith rather thought it must have been all the excitement last night. Goodness, I hope my life doesn't ever become so placid that a wild evening of music and fireworks will put me in bed.'

'I suppose,' said March, speaking almost to himself, 'it depends on the nature of the fireworks.'

Indeed, unknown to March, such had been Alison's reaction to the events of last evening that she had not fallen asleep until dawn. She had awaked a few hours later feeling as though a team of dray horses had taken up residence between her ears.

It was not as though she had never been kissed before. Even before she had left Ridstowe, she had been the recipient of attentions from some of the local sprigs. Mostly reverential, usually shy, their advances had consisted mainly of chaste salutes on cheek or lips. Only occasionally were they followed by a more demanding embrace. She had found some more pleasurable than others, but had never allowed any of them to go beyond what was proper. Nor had she ever wished to encourage her swains to more passionate encounters. But nothing in her previous experience had prepared her for the shattering effect of Lord Marchford's kiss. She had known what he was about as soon as she had looked up into his eyes, even though all she could see in the lantern light was a faint, golden glitter. She should have stepped away right then. She should have let him mop his own shirtfront. She should have. . . . But no, she had allowed herself to sink into his embrace like the veriest lightskirt. At the first touch of his lips on hers she had melted. His hands, moving along her back, had created a trail of molten sensation, and if he had begun disrobing her right there, she would probably have helped him.

Dear Lord, what was she to do now? How could she face him again? When he had pulled away from her at the sound of laughter close at hand, she hadn't even been able to voice a protest at his actions. He had led the way back to the amphitheater, and she had followed like an automaton, unable to speak, or even to think clearly. It was not until she had taken her seat again that she remembered the reason for her flight. Luckily, when she'd sneaked a glance at where she had seen Jack Crawford, that gentleman and his party had left.

The fireworks, she admitted ruefully, had definitely been an anticlimax to the evening.

The house was quiet when she rose at last, and she remembered with some relief that Marchford had made an appointment with Meg for luncheon someplace in the city. She spent a quiet morning helping Lady Edith write invitations to a dinner party she was planning for a week hence, and after their rather Spartan midday meal, the two ladies set forth for their daily sojourn to the Pump Room.

For the first time, Alison felt oddly restless as she followed Lady Edith in her travels about the chamber. She found herself unable to take part in the light conversations of scandal and fashionable gossip. When Lady Edith settled herself in a comfortable chair, her coterie about her, Alison drifted across the room to the pump fountain and dropped a few pennies into the attendant's hand. Sipping absently at the small cup of the famed mineral waters, she moved to the window overlooking the King's Bath and tried to amuse herself with the sight of plump ladies paddling decorously across the surface, garbed in heavy canvas gowns, and dyspeptic gentlemen manfully bobbing up and down in the steaming waters. When a voice spoke suddenly at her elbow, she started so violently that most of the healing liquid splashed from her cup to the floor.

'Alison! Alison Fox, it *is* you!'

With great difficulty, Alison resisted the urge to rush cravenly from the room, and she turned reluctantly to face the speaker.

'Hello, Jack,' she said calmly. 'What brings you to Bath?'

He had not, she thought, changed dramatically in the three years since Beth's death. Molly had described him as distraught and haggard, but he was far from that now. He had regained any weight he might have lost, though his face was naturally thin. He was as she remembered him, dressed in the first stare of fashion, with his glossy black curls artfully arranged in a carefree Brutus. He wore a rather showy waistcoat of Turkish silk but his coat of dark blue superfine was a model of elegance, as were the biscuit-colored pantaloons that lovingly followed the contours of his well-shaped legs.

His black eyes sparkled audaciously as he pressed both of her hands to his lips.

'Why, what should I be doing here? I have come to take the waters.' He laughed engagingly. 'Actually, I am visiting with friends in the area, but I could not tread the streets of this fair city without visiting the pump. Do you live here now, Alison?'

Alison stifled the unreasoning panic that rose within her. 'Yes, I do. I am companion to Lady Edith Brent.' She indicated the older woman, seated with her group of compatriots.

Jack's dark gaze perused Alison thoughtfully. 'I'm surprised to hear that. I would have thought you married to some respectable country squire with a clutch of brats at your skirts. You certainly deserve better than to be at the beck and call of some rich old beldam.'

'I do not believe I wish to discuss Lady Edith with you, Jack,' Alison said with some asperity, 'except to say that she has become my friend as well as my employer.'

Jack whistled softly, his expressive eyes alight. 'No need to comb my hair, m'dear. I'm pleased to see that you've landed on your feet. I wondered what had become of you after—'

'Did you really, Jack? I am, of course, honored by your consideration. Now, if you will excuse me.' She turned to make a dignified exit, but Jack laid his slender hand on her arm.

'Alison, I'm sorry. I did not mean to offend you. Over the years, I have thought of you often and with great affection, particularly since Beth died.' A flicker of pain crossed his regular features, and his voice softened. 'I know I was not a good husband to her, Alison; you and Molly were the only really good things in her life.'

The young man was obviously sincere, and a stab of pity shot through Alison, although it was quickly suppressed. Jack may truly have grieved for Beth, but he had obviously made a full recovery. She said quietly, 'Yes, Beth was a good friend, and is very much missed.' Disengaging her arm from his grasp, she turned away again with a murmured, 'I really must be going,' and moved toward Lady Edith. It was only when that lady ceased her conversation at Alison's approach and glanced questioningly at a spot just over her left shoulder that she realized Jack had followed her across the room.

Alison whirled and intercepted the smiling nod Jack bestowed on the older woman. Lady Edith smiled graciously in return, her sharp old eyes traveling between the two.

Helplessly, Alison performed the introduction.

'John Crawford?' Lady Edith tasted the name on her tongue. 'That rings a bell. Have we met?'

Jack uttered a boyish laugh. 'No, my lady, I'm afraid not. I would surely have remembered.' His eyes crinkled in an expression of youthful admiration, and Lady Edith smiled patiently. 'Alison and I,' he continued, 'are old friends, and I am so pleased to renew our acquaintance. If I present myself on your doorstep to call on her, I hope you won't turn me away.'

Lady Edith glanced quickly at Alison, and observing the tightening of the girl's lips, replied, 'We should both be delighted, I'm sure, although we are often away from home.'

Jack responded with appropriate expressions of delight and bowed himself away from the ladies. It was not until later in the day, when Alison and Lady Edith were at home, removing their bonnets after the day's outing, that the older woman spoke of the encounter.

'What was that young man's name again?' she queried fretfully, stooping to greet Honey, who had bounded up at their entrance to receive the attention that was her due.

'John Crawford. He is usually called Jack, and' – Alison drew a deep breath – 'the reason the name seemed familiar to you is that he was my friend Beth's husband.'

She sat down suddenly, and Lady Edith went to her. 'Oh, my dear, how dreadful to have that rascal show his face here. Why, the impudent blackguard, actually requesting permission to call on you! Well, if he does dare show his face here, I shall know how to go on with him.' She shot a baleful look at the front door as though expecting to find Jack Crawford, armed with sword and battering ram, preparing to make his assault.

'I'm not sure,' said Alison slowly. 'If I should refuse to see him, it will surely be remarked upon. I shall see him alone when he calls, and make it plain that I do not wish to renew our acquaintance.'

Lady Edith shrugged dubiously, but said nothing more on the subject. Thus, when Mr Crawford presented himself in Royal Crescent the next day, a little earlier than the conventional hour for visiting, he found Miss Fox waiting for him, seated sedately in the drawing room.

She offered him sherry, which he accepted, and biscuits, which he did not. 'Now,' he said gaily, 'tell me all you have been doing since you left Ridstowe?'

'You mean since I left for the second time?' Alison responded quietly. A flush rose to Jack's lean cheeks. He stood and took a turn about the room before coming back to sit in a chair beside the settee she had chosen. 'Alison, my dear girl, I can see you still hold a grudge against me for that unfortunate episode, and I cannot say that I blame you. I can only say that I am truly sorry for what happened, and for the unfortunate results of your efforts to help Beth and me.'

'My efforts were solely on Bethie's behalf,' returned Alison sharply.

'Of course,' he said quietly. 'For Beth's sake, then, may we not renew our friendship?'

'I rather do believe friendship is too strong a term for our previous relationship, but, whatever it might be called, I do not wish to continue it. You have no idea of the upheaval my going to London caused in my life, or the tragedy it caused in the lives of others.'

'Ah, you are referring to the Earl of Marchford's family.'

Alison's eyes widened. She had never disclosed to Beth the disastrous results of her foray into the dangerous world of high stakes gambling in London. 'How did you come to know about that?'

'I visited Molly in London not long after Beth died, and she told me all about it. I am truly sorry,' he repeated.

'That's as it may be, but you will perhaps have no difficulty in understanding why I do not wish to see you again.' A trembling had begun in the pit of Alison's stomach and she was forced to grip her hands tightly in her lap lest they reveal her turmoil.

Jack rose from the small gilt chair in which he had been seated and moved unhurriedly to stand before her.

'As you wish, Alison. I have no desire to cause you pain. However, I hope to see you again while I am in Bath, at which time I will take leave to try to change your mind.' The rueful smile that had crossed his features faded. 'I am not a bad man, you know, and I – I am rather in need of a friend right now.'

Once again, Alison experienced a flicker of pity for him, but, saying nothing, she rose abruptly and moved to the door. She inclined her head in an imitation of the regal gesture she had seen Lady Edith use to good effect, and, as she had hoped, Jack bowed in acquiescence and left the room. He crossed the entrance hall and had just reached the front door when it swung open to admit Lord Marchford and Meg, who had gone out together again, this time to view a promising hacking horse that March thought to purchase.

To Alison's dismay, it was evident that Jack recognized the earl immediately, and his glance swung back to her in surprise. Meg, on observing the presence of an attractive young man on the premises, smiled at him in shy invitation. Hands clenched, Alison introduced Jack to Marchford and to his sister, who promptly invited the guest back into the house for tea.

March acknowledged the introduction pleasantly, but his glance at Alison was speculative. Jack had smilingly declared himself an old friend of Miss Fox. Old friend, he wondered, or old lover? He felt a surprising distaste at the thought. He was aware of the tension fairly radiating from Alison's slender body, and wondered further if Jack was here at her invitation. If so, for what purpose?

Alison led the way back to the drawing room, Meg's artless chatter echoing in the hallway. Lord, here was a fresh disaster in the making, March thought grimly. This Jack Crawford, clearly a rogue, must be kept firmly out of the susceptible damsel's orbit.

'My home is in London,' explained Jack carelessly to Meg's query, 'but I have friends who reside permanently in Bath.'

'Oh!' exclaimed Meg, adroitly seating herself next to the visitor on a brocade settee. 'Who are they? Perhaps we know them.'

Jack's hesitation was barely perceptible as he replied, 'Oh, I doubt it, Lady Margaret. Giles – that is Captain Morganton and his wife – rarely partake of the social pleasures of Bath. He has recently sold out and prefers to live quietly in lodgings in the Paragon Buildings.'

March made a mental note of the name. He rather thought he had heard of Giles Morganton since coming to Bath, but he could not remember in what connection.

'But how is it that you happen to know Alison?' Meg persisted.

Once more, Jack hesitated, and March caught the brief glance he shot at Alison.

'Alison was a good friend of my wife, who passed away a few years ago.'

Meg made an appropriate expression of sympathy, but March, turning to observe Alison's reaction, became instantly aware that she was as taut as an overstretched violin string. Her eyes were wide with dismay. Why, the girl was terrified of Jack Crawford! March fought back a sharp urge to move to her side and place himself between her and the object of her distress. Good God, he berated himself, this was ridiculous! Why the devil should he want to protect her?

It was all Alison could do not to run from the room screaming. A nightmarish sense of doom pressed upon her, and she fervently wished that Lady Edith had not taken herself upstairs for a nap, for she felt in desperate need of reinforcement. She could feel March's eyes upon her, and irrationally, could not help succumbing to the belief that he must sense the dark connection between Jack and herself. After several eternities had passed,

97

Jack finally rose, and with a graceful bow declared he must take himself off.

'For,' he said laughingly, 'my hostess has informed me that if I am late for dinner one more time, I shall go to bed supperless.'

'Oh, but, Mr Crawford,' Meg cried, 'when shall we see you again? You and Alison must have a great deal to catch up on, and you have hardly had time for two words together. I know!' She whirled to Alison. 'We must invite Mr Crawford to dinner tomorrow. Aunt was just complaining that we have no engagements and must look forward to a dreadfully flat evening.'

Once again, Jack shot Alison a glance before answering. She opened her mouth to utter some excuse, but to her horror, the earl interjected, 'Yes, by all means, sir. Do join us.' His voice was utterly bland, but Alison could have sworn she heard a hint of menacing amusement in his words.

'How can I possibly refuse?' cried Jack gaily. 'I look forward to seeing you on the morrow, and please extend my best wishes to Lady Edith.' Donning his hat with a flourish, he bowed once more and left the house.

Alison leaned against the closed door, feeling as though her strength were draining away through her shoes. Looking up, she caught the earl's sardonic gaze and she cursed the heat that rose in her cheeks like a tide.

'Well now, Miss Fox,' he murmured smoothly, ushering her back into the drawing room, 'do tell us all about your friend. He seems such an interesting chap.'

CHAPTER 10

'Alison,' said Lady Edith as she and her companion strolled along Royal Crescent some mornings later, 'no offense, my dear, but you look like a death's head on a mop stick. Are you sickening? Have you been sleeping well? Is it that Jack Crawford? Has he been importuning you?'

Alison smiled at the older woman. 'I thank you for your concern, my lady. No, I am not sick, and no, I have not been sleeping well. And no, again, Jack has been nothing that is not proper and unexceptionable. It's just that knowing he is in close proximity to Lord Marchford makes me apprehensive.'

Lady Edith sighed irritably. 'You see what you have brought yourself to? You're afraid of shadows. You are being unconscionably foolish, Alison. March has come to know you over the last week, and he sees you for what you are – a person of goodness and honesty. He has ceased pouring warnings in my ear that you are an adventuress, and now seems pleased that you are with me. If you tell him what happened with Susannah, he will not hold those circumstances against you.'

Alison answered slowly. 'If the circumstances were any other than those that caused the deaths of two – and perhaps three – members of his family, I would agree with you. I realize, having become acquainted with him, that Lord Marchford is an eminently reasonable man – except on this one subject. You have heard his vows of revenge. Should he discover that I am the woman he seeks, his good opinion of me will vanish like a drunkard's good intentions, and he will hate me.'

They had by now reached Lady Edith's house, and she

paused at the steps to face Alison. 'Just what is it you think he will do to you, child – have you burnt at the stake?'

Alison closed her eyes. A vision flashed before her of March's tawny gaze, filled with laughter and affection. Then, the image changed. His lion's eyes filled with contempt and rage. A chill shivered through her as she realized that his hatred alone would be enough to punish her beyond bearing, but she could not speak this aloud. She opened her eyes and stared out at the park.

'I do not know, my lady, but your nephew . . . I feel he can be a hard man with those he deems his enemy.'

Lady Edith sighed again. 'Yes, you are right. I have never seen that side of him, of course, but I have heard he is a dangerous man to wrong. I still think you are mistaken in not telling him everything. He must be brought to realize that Susannah was to blame for her own destruction, though to my mind, her husband had a great deal to answer for, as well.'

Alison glanced at her questioningly, but Lady Edith turned to ascend the steps to her house. Once inside, she moved toward the stairs, declaring her intention of resting awhile before luncheon.

Alone, Alison remained in the entrance hall for some moments, simply staring into space before turning to make her way to a sunny chamber at the back of the house where she kept a supply of articles to be mended. She had not even exited the hall, however, when the front door opened to admit Lord Marchford. Alison tensed to flee, hoping that he had not noticed her standing at the far end of the hall. But, even as he closed the door behind him, he turned immediately toward her and a smile lightened his rather forbidding features.

The smile vanished almost immediately, to be replaced by a look of cool appraisal that created an unpleasant pang in Alison's heart.

'My lord,' she said quickly, moving forward, 'we did not expect you today.'

'No, I am aware of that. As I understand it, Meg is out with friends, and it is not yet time for Aunt Edith's journey to the Pump Room.'

'That is true,' replied Alison, puzzled and inexplicably alarmed. 'Lady Edith is upstairs resting.'

She allowed her voice to lift a little at the end of this sentence, as though to make it clear that he had no reason to prolong his visit, but he did not take the hint.

'In that case,' he said amiably, 'perhaps we might take the opportunity for some quiet conversation. I would like to come to know you better, and this seems like an ideal time for what Meg describes as a comfortable coze.'

A comfortable coze! Alison could have laughed if she had not been so struck with horror at the earl's suggestion. She searched frantically in her mind for an excuse to evaporate, but was forestalled by the appearance of Masters, hurrying in to see who had arrived without his notice. On observing Lord Marchford, he hastened to relieve him of hat and walking stick and, with a reproachful glance toward Alison, asked if tea were wished.

Alison could only nod, and smiling faintly, she led the way to the drawing room on the next floor. Her heart was thudding unbearably as she gestured the earl to a settee covered in straw satin and took a matching chair nearby for herself.

Alison folded her hands in her lap and tried to assume a semblance of calm propriety as she waited for Lord Marchford to begin his coze. When he remained silent, merely gazing at her with that same assessing expression, her hand fluttered toward her throat in an unconscious gesture.

'What – what is it you wish to know about me, my lord?'

'First of all—' he hesitated, 'it seems I owe you an apology.'

This was the last thing in the world she had expected him to say, and her surprise must have shown on her face.

'I said some rather harsh things to you when we first met,' he continued slowly, 'and I have come to realize I was mistaken in my first judgment of you.' His lips curved in a smile that produced an odd thrumming sensation deep inside her. 'I can see why my aunt has quite lost her heart to you, and I can only say that, as head of our little family, I am pleased that you have come to her.'

Alison could only gaze at him in stricken silence. Something in his demeanor did not ring true, but his words were harder to bear than his recriminations would have been.

'Thank you, my lord,' she mumbled inadequately.

'Now' – he leaned toward her – 'tell me something of yourself. Tell me about Ridstowe. Were you happy there?'

Alison's throat tightened. 'Yes, sir, I was. It is a small village, where everyone knows everyone else, and my father was much loved.'

'And you were his only daughter?'

'Yes, my mother died when I was very small, and Father and I were always close.'

'You lived in Ridstowe with him until— Ah, thank you, Masters.' The butler, followed by a footman laden with a tea tray, entered the room and the next few minutes were spent setting out Lady Edith's beautiful porcelain tea service and small, pretty plates of scones, cakes, and watercress sandwiches. Alison, feeling only slightly reprieved, was pleased that her hands did not shake as she handed a cup of tea to the earl and poured one for herself. At her nod, Masters bowed and removed himself and the footman from the room.

'I lived with my father until his death four years ago,' she said quietly. 'I was forced to earn my own keep then, and found a position with Lady Strangeways.'

'I see. It must have been a difficult time for you.' The earl's tone was sympathetic, but Alison somehow knew that his questions were motivated by more than a simple interest in her well-being. 'How did you come to Lady Strangeways's attention?'

Alison drew a deep breath. Lord Marchford's questions were coming uncomfortably close to the bone. 'Through my uncle, Sir Henry Matchingham. He had been acquainted with Lady Strangeways for some years, and knew she was in need of a companion.' She twisted her hands in her lap before continuing in a rush. 'I could have lived with my aunt and uncle, but I chose to earn my own way.'

This was far from the truth, of course. She had declined Uncle Henry's offer of his home because she wished to escape wholly from the civilized world into the haven of Lady Strangeways's reclusive way of life.

'You are an unusual woman, Miss Fox, to choose a life on your own over one with loving relatives. Or perhaps you did not get on with your aunt and uncle?'

'Oh, no! That is, yes, we got along famously. They are wonderful people, and we still correspond. I visit them from time to time.'

'Yes, I seem to remember that on my previous visits to Aunt Edith, your absence was explained in this fashion.' There was nothing in his voice to indicate anything but a courteous interest, but Alison felt perspiration break out on her forehead.

'I wonder where Meg could be,' she said suddenly, in a frantic effort to change the direction of the earl's thoughts. 'She will be late for luncheon if she does not return soon. Will you be taking lunch here yourself, my lord? Lady Edith will be most pleased to see you. Perhaps I should go up and see if she has risen from her nap.'

In a panicked movement, she made as though to rise, but she was stayed by the earl's hand. 'Surely not,' he said pleasantly. 'We have been conversing for less than fifteen minutes, and luncheon is still an hour away. I hope you do not mind my questions, Miss Fox. You are,' he continued after a moment's hesitation, 'an unusual woman, and I find myself interested in how you came to your present situation.'

Alison flushed at the warmth in his expression, and, though she would not have thought such a thing possible, she felt even more wretched in her deception. She laughed nervously.

'I thank you, my lord, but I am really quite ordinary. If you were to interview every other lady's companion in Bath, you would hear my story repeated a hundred times, I daresay.'

'Perhaps.' His smiled declared his disbelief in her statement, and Alison found that she was unable to meet the intensity of his gaze, which, in the late-morning sunlight streaming through the tall windows of the drawing room, reminded her of a lion in a particularly benevolent mood. At his next words, her fingers clenched spasmodically, so that a little of her tea slopped into her saucer.

'B-Beth?' she echoed. 'What about her?'

'I just wondered if she was a friend from your days in Ridstowe? Did she meet Mr Crawford there?'

'No, my lord.' Her heart was beating so wildly she thought it might just possibly leap from her throat. 'I met Beth at school. She and Jack met in London while we were there for the Season.'

' "We"?'

Alison cursed inwardly. 'Yes, I had a London Season – when I was seventeen. I stayed in Beth's home.' The earl's brow lifted questioningly. 'My mother,' she continued unwillingly, 'left a little money for this purpose.'

The earl digested this without comment. 'And did you know Mr Crawford well, also?'

'No!' The word burst from her lips. She sat back in her chair, embarrassed. 'That is, he was a frequent visitor in Beth's home, so I saw him quite a bit, but I did not become well acquainted with him. After he and Bethie were married, I never saw him again until he turned up here in Bath.'

The earl smiled. 'You make him sound like a bad penny.'

'Oh, no – I meant no such thing. I am, of course, pleased to renew our acquaintance. Because of Beth, that is.'

At that moment, the sound of voices was heard rising from the floor below. Nearly gasping with relief, Alison sprang from her chair. 'Meg is home!' she cried, as though the girl had only that moment safely arrived home from a year in the wilds of Africa.

March followed her at a sedate pace as she raced for the door and fairly scrambled down the stairs. The faint smile on his lips was not pleasant. As he had hoped, his questions had definitely touched a nerve in Miss Fox – several nerves if he were not mistaken. For the last few moments there, she had looked as though she were ready to explode, and not once during the entire conversation had she actually looked at him. Which was just as well, he reflected sourly, given his unfortunate susceptibility to her beautiful eyes. He paused on the stairway, and for some minutes watched Alison as she greeted Meg and listened with gentle laughter to the young girl's bubbling account of her morning's activities, while Honey danced around their ankles in a persistent bid for attention.

Alison Fox was an undeniably lovely woman, he reflected with a satisfying detachment that vanished the next moment as Alison, assisting Meg in removing pelisse and bonnet, turned to hand the girl's outer garment to the maid who stood by. The curve of her lithe body in its sedate covering of gray muslin was sweet and almost unbearably tantalizing. It seemed inconceivable that her warm smile and what he could have sworn was an open expression of affection hid the heart of a grasping harpy.

But he could not have been wrong in his deductions. They all fit too neatly. He forced his mind to review what he had learned in his all-too brief conversation with her. So, she had gone to school with a daughter of the *ton*. He would be willing to wager a sizeable amount that she had encountered the future Viscountess Callander at that same establishment. Was there, he wondered, a connection between Beth and Alison's nefarious activities in London, as there had been with Molly?

And what about Jack? It was unfortunate that Meg's arrival had given Alison an excuse to quit his company just as he had been getting to her relationship with him. His sudden appearance in Bath seemed much too fortuitous to be attributed to coincidence. In addition, March had learned through careful inquiry that Giles Morganton, Crawford's host, had an unsavory reputation in Bath as a Captain Sharp with ties to London's underworld. Was there a chance that Alison had spoken the truth that she was not well acquainted with Jack? The fear in her eyes when she spoke his name belied that fact. No, there undoubtedly had been – and perhaps still was – something between them. He was surprised at the anger that surged through him at this thought.

Alison glanced up suddenly, and catching his heated gaze on her, flushed and turned quickly to speak again to Meg. In response, Meg swung to face him.

'March!' she cried delightedly. 'I did not know you would be coming today. You are just in time for luncheon.' She turned back to Alison. 'Is Aunt risen from her nap?'

'Yes, she is,' replied a voice from above them, as Lady Edith descended the stairs. 'As though anyone could sleep through all this racket.' She smiled as she spoke, erasing any hint of censure her words might have created.

More greetings were exchanged, and the little group withdrew to the library to await the summons to the dining parlor.

'How was your visit with Rosamund Pinchot this morning?' queried Lady Edith. 'Has her mother recovered from her bout with influenza?'

'Oh, yes, she's in prime twig now,' replied Meg breezily. 'In fact, she took us shopping. Did you know that there's a new linen draper in Bath Street? Mrs Pinchot purchased two lengths of the loveliest spider gauze there.'

'Oh, yes,' interjected Lady Edith. 'I believe that's the third shop that has opened up there since Smith's closed.' She turned to Alison. 'You were not here then, but a number of years ago a rather extraordinary event took place there. It involve a Mrs Leigh Perrot. I did not know the lady personally, but I understand she and her husband were of unimpeachable character. She was accused by a clerk at Smith's of stealing a piece of white lace. It was all a dreadful misunderstanding, but the poor woman actually was imprisoned in Ilchester Jail and had to stand trial. She was acquitted, of course, but it was a dreadful time for her. The town buzzed about the case for weeks and an account of the trial was published and sold in the bookstores here.'

'Oh, yes,' exclaimed Meg. 'I heard about that. Wasn't Mrs Perrot an aunt to Miss Austen, the authoress?'

'Yes, I understand that to be the case,' replied Lady Edith. 'The Perrots returned to live in Bath, which is surprising. I should think they would have wished to wipe the dust of this city from their feet forever.'

'Indeed,' murmured Alison, her eyes cast down. 'It is a terrible thing to be unjustly accused of a wrongdoing.'

March drew in a quick breath and shot a glance at her. Her comment could not have been directed at him, surely, for she had no idea that he had found her out. The unhappiness in her face struck him almost physically, and, despite himself, he knew an urge to reach out and smooth away the pain he saw there.

He shook himself in some irritation and returned to the conversation to discover that Meg was on another tack.

'At any rate,' she was saying, 'after Mrs Pinchot purchased her spider gauze, Rosamund and I came across an absolutely exquisite white silk shot with silver. Oh, Aunt, I think it would make up beautifully for a ball gown. Since I shall need several when I go up to London, do you not think it would be wise to purchase the silk now? It is only a guinea a length, which I am sure is not nearly so dear as we would be charged in the city.'

Lady Edith laughed. 'You are very convincing, you little minx. Very well, but take Alison with you. Her taste is excellent, you know.'

Meg wriggled in delight. 'Of course. Oh, Alison, that reminds me – we encountered Mr Crawford in Milsom Street. He inquired about you, and I told him you would probably be at the Pump Room with Aunt later today.'

'Oh,' murmured Alison faintly.

'He seems awfully nice,' continued Meg, her interest in Mr Crawford obviously piqued.

'Mmm,' replied Alison discouragingly, 'I really do not know him all that well, Meg, but, I'm sure he is . . . nice.'

'But he says you are old friends!' exclaimed Meg in surprise.

'Old acquaintances would be more accurate, my dear.'

'But you and his wife—'

'Yes,' said Alison, a hint of desperation creeping into her voice. Why was everyone so suddenly and profoundly interested in her past relationships? 'Beth and I were good friends, but I really did not know Mr Crawford at all well.'

'But he is so handsome, Alison. Don't you think?' Alison's heart sank as she realized that Meg's eyes had taken on an all-too-familiar glow.

'He seems most personable,' interjected a calm, authoritative voice. 'He is a little older than you, is he not, Miss Fox? He must be just over thirty.'

If March thought that his observation would dampen that

107

glow, thought Alison sourly, he had another think coming. She reflected on the attraction Meg had felt for the thirtyish drawing master. Jack's advanced years probably only made him more desirable in her eyes.

Not that Jack had made any apparent effort to secure Meg's admiration. At dinner, a few nights before, his manner toward her had been avuncular, and though he paid the girl several extravagant compliments, and declared that she would be the toast of the next Season in London, his words had carried no hint of flirtation. In fact, his behavior that whole evening had been unexceptionable. His manner toward the earl had been respectful but not obsequious, and with Lady Edith, he had been charming and playful. Toward Alison, his demeanor had been friendly but not presuming. Why then, did the very idea of his incursion into Royal Crescent fill her with panic?

Luncheon was announced then, and afterward, the earl took himself off for an afternoon visit to a friend who had recently arrived from London. Alison watched his departure with some relief, and later, with Lady Edith and Meg in the Pump Room, she made a determined effort to join in the conversation among the ladies and their friends. Beneath the friendly responses, however, and the smiles and innocuous chatter that she somehow dredged from her reservoir of social conditioning, her thoughts dwelled on the interview with Lord Marchford earlier in the day.

She could not shake the uneasy feeling that his unexpected expressions of goodwill were not quite genuine, and that his questions indicated more than a passing interest in her background. Did he suspect something? Had she done or said anything since their first encounter to lead him to the truth she wished so devoutly to hide? He had said that he had come to regret his earlier assessment of her as a scheming adventuress, but there was something in his manner that made her profoundly uneasy. She must not allow herself to be alone with him again, nor would she be drawn into any more dangerously revealing conversations with him. Dear Lord, why had Jack Crawford chosen this particular time to come visiting in Bath?

She frowned. Was it possible that his arrival in the city was not coincidental? But that was absurd. She had heard nothing from him since she had fulfilled her obligation to Beth. Even when Beth had died and she had sent a note of condolence, he had not responded. Why then, after all these years, would he seek her out?

So intent was her concentration on her problem, that when a voice at her elbow called her name, she whirled with a start. She stared at Jack Crawford as though her worst nightmare had suddenly materialized in front of her.

CHAPTER 11

'Alison! Are you all right? I did not mean to startle you.' Jack Crawford's face reflected only a sincere distress as he took Alison's hand and led her away from the group with whom she had been chatting.

Alison had gone rigid at the sound of his voice, and knew the color must have drained from her cheeks. Feeling remarkably foolish she replied, 'No, no, of course not. I – I was a little surprised to find you so close behind me.'

'Again, I apologize. It is such an infernal squeeze here, that I very nearly had to pounce on you to get your attention. May I accompany you on a turn about the room?'

Alison suppressed the flutter of unease that gripped her. 'Why, yes, that would be, um, very nice. Meg tells me that she saw you yesterday in town,' she continued as she took Jack's arm.

When he did not reply, she glanced at him questioningly to find that his gaze was lowered and an air of preoccupation lay on his features. She sensed a certain tension in the young man, which transferred itself immediately to her. Jack looked up then, and laughed ruefully.

'I'm sorry. I – I have had rather a lot on my mind of late.' He stopped suddenly in their perambulation of the room and faced her. 'Alison, I must talk to you.'

Alison forced a smile to her lips. 'Go ahead, Jack. I'm all yours, at least until Lady Edith requires my attention.'

'No, no. Not here. I must speak to you alone.'

Alison stiffened. 'I do not know what you could possibly have to discuss with me, Jack, that would require privacy. At any rate, I do not see how we can be private together. I cannot very well bar Lady Edith from her own drawing room when you call.'

'No. No, of course not. But are you never at liberty? Surely Lady Edith allows you some time for your own?'

'I'm afraid—' began Alison quickly.

'Please.' Jack interrupted, his fingers gripping her arm. 'Meet me tomorrow morning in Sydney Gardens. Surely, if you leave the house early, you can return before you are required. Lady Edith need not even know you have been gone.'

'It is not my practice to deceive her ladyship,' Alison responded sharply, and Jack's features suddenly relaxed in a coaxing smile.

'Of course not, but you have become so terrifyingly proper, I would not like to see you compromised in any way with your employer.' He emphasized the last word as though to affirm the businesslike relationship between Alison Fox and Lady Brent. 'Moreover, I do not think you would like others to be party to what I have to say to you.'

There was not the slightest hint of menace in Jack's tone, but Alison felt herself grow cold. She could not bring herself to consider what Jack might want of her.

'Very well.' Her voice came out in a rasping whisper. 'I shall meet you at nine o'clock tomorrow morning.'

For the rest of the day and into the evening, Alison somehow managed to attend to her routine duties and to take her usual part in the activities of Lady Edith's household. But below this amiable surface, a turmoil of apprehension raged. She heartily wished she had not agreed to meet Jack, but felt she had been given no choice. The knowledge that he would not scruple to use her fear of him in gaining his ends only served to increase her unease. To her relief, Lord Marchford did not join them for dinner, and the evening passed in placid tedium. When, at last, Alison donned her nightdress and sank into bed, she lay sleepless for many hours, staring at the ceiling and wishing for all the world that the morning would never come.

*

A lone street sweeper was the only witness the following morning as Alison slipped through the Great Poultney Street gate into Sydney Gardens. Was she to make this a habit, she wondered – sliding through this gate to clandestine meetings with men whose presence in her life could cause her undoing?

A hint of mist floated at her feet as she settled onto the same bench where she had previously confronted Lord Marchford. Like the mist, her thoughts drifted aimlessly, finally settling, against her will, on the earl. Confound the man! What had possessed him to linger in Bath? The date of his planned departure had come and gone, and his only explanation for continuing his sojourn here had been a brief remark that he had found something of extraordinary fascination in the city. His glance had flickered in her direction as he spoke, and in his eyes Alison had noted a disconcerting message. Her thoughts skittered nervously in another direction.

Jack.

Lord, what could he want with her? The only thing she could bring to mind made her shudder with apprehension. Please God he did not still look on her as an emergency source of income.

She shook herself. She was being absurd. Jack Crawford had made his way alone – with reasonable success, by the looks of it – without relying on her help at the gaming tables. It was to be hoped that he had not again found it necessary to steal to cover his losses. Then, what—?

The crunch of apptoaching footsteps jerked her from her unpleasant reverie and she looked up to behold Jack Crawford doffing his hat in an exaggerated gesture and smiling his charming, practiced smile. He inspected the bench carefully before seating himself next to her, whisking the tails of his morning coat behind him.

' 'Morning, Alison – beautiful day.'

Was it her imagination, or was his manner a trifle less respectful than it had been?

'Bath is a restful place, is it not?' he continued. 'Particularly before the hustle and bustle of the city cranks up.'

He studied his legs stretched before him and looked about

with satisfaction.

'Please get to the point, Jack,' said Alison sharply. 'What is it you want?'

He turned to look at her, and in that instant she knew she had not been mistaken. His manner was almost insolent, and bordered on the familiar.

'You're not being very friendly,' he said plaintively.

'No, I am not. I do not consider myself your friend.'

He sighed in mock disappointment, but almost immediately his determinedly pleasant expression slipped, like new paint on a badly primed surface. 'As you have apparently surmised,' he said brusquely, 'I have come to ask a favor.'

She rose swiftly, as though stung by an importunate insect, but Jack was there to lay his hand on her arm. He did not relinquish it when she sank slowly back onto the bench.

'Please, Alison.' He had reverted to his former cajolery, trying out another charming smile. 'I wish I could say that I reformed after your . . . great sacrifice on my – on Beth's behalf, but I can't. I'm afraid I'm simply your basic, nonreformable wastrel.' He assayed a rueful chuckle, which dissipated quickly in the face of her chill response. 'The fact is,' he continued, all business now, 'I need money. Not very much,' he added hastily. 'Five hundred pounds would do it. But, I need it rather badly, and I need it now.'

As he spoke, all trace of his former bonhomie had vanished, to be replaced by a frown of what looked very much like desperation.

'You see, I made a rather serious blunder recently. I lost money to the wrong man. I did not know until I was down nearly a thousand quid to him that the fellow has some powerful connections with some very nasty people in London. I was able to scrape together part of what I owe him, but now I'm tapped out. And if I do not pay up by the end of the month, I shall be properly in the suds.'

As he finished, his voice rose in a painful effort at lightness, but the fear that lurked in the back of his gaze was unmistakable. Alison almost regretted that she could feel no pity for him.

113

She drew a deep breath. 'I am sorry for your predicament, Jack, but I do not see what it has to do with me.'

'Do you not, indeed?' he asked querulously. 'Then you are being peculiarly obtuse.' With an obvious effort, he continued in a more conciliatory vein. 'Please do not make this any more difficult than necessary, Alison. For either of us. I am asking you, of course, to help me recoup my losses.'

'No.' The word burst from her lips without thought. She had known, though. She had known all along what he must want. 'No,' she repeated in a tone that was quieter but no less firm.

'You cannot say no without giving the matter any thought, Alison.'

'Yes, I can, Jack, and please accept it as final. I do sympathize with your plight – though not very much, if truth were told – but I refuse—'

'You refuse!' Jack rose to his feet and faced her, his dark eyes filled with anger. 'Did you not understand me? If I do not hand over four hundred pounds to Gi – to a certain person in three weeks, I'll be ruined! And very possibly dead!'

Alison's hand went to her mouth. 'Oh, Jack! Surely not! What kind of people are you involved with, for heaven's sake? Surely, if you ask for more time—'

Jack seated himself again, and took both Alison's hands in his. His voice grated with the effort to speak calmly. 'No, my poor, simple dear, I cannot ask for more time. I have used up my grace period. As for what kind of people they are, let me assure you they are not proper English gentlemen. They are brutes and murderers who would just as soon cut one's throat as pass the time of day.'

His terror was palpable, but Alison steeled herself. Jack had apparently ruined his life, but she was not going to allow him to complete the ruination of hers. She would help him if she could, but not if it meant sitting down to the gaming table again.

'Do you have any money at all?' she asked suddenly.

'What?' he asked blankly, then recovered himself as he absorbed what she had said.

'A few pounds only. Just enough to live on for a while. You

see,' he continued eagerly, misreading her words, 'it is not just the debt. I am totally at point-non-plus and must have something to sustain me until I can bring things round again.'

'Bring things round?' asked Alison blankly.

'Of course! All I need is a little of the ready. Enough for a small stake. I shall come about eventually. I always do.'

Dear God, thought Alison, the man was completely at the mercy of an addiction, and he was not even aware of the depths of his disease.

She gripped the hands that were holding hers. 'Jack. Listen to me. It seems to me you have another option here. You can leave the country. I will lend you a hundred pounds.' She suffered a pang as she thought of the money so carefully saved. 'You can go to France – or even America – make a new start.'

'Good God, Alison. I don't want to go to France, and I'd turn up my toes for sure in America. Besides, there's no need. I told you. Once I pay my debt, I'll be free to start fresh. Why, within a month or two I'll be able to pay you back – with interest.' He sat back, smiling in anticipation of her capitulation to this final inducement.

Alison wrenched her hands from his grasp in disgust. 'Jack, I am sorry, but I cannot help you.' She attempted to rise, but he grasped her shoulders and pressed her back against the bench. So menacing was his expression that Alison shrank away from him.

'Who the hell do think you are to speak to me so?' he growled. 'You've landed on your feet right enough, haven't you? That rich old crone is besotted with you, and so is her nephew, his high-and-mighty lordship. Oh, yes,' he sneered, in response to Alison's outraged gasp. 'I've seen how he looks at you. Have a fancy to become a rich man's mistress, do you?'

'Jack!' She stared at him in outrage. Dear Lord, was this the man who had earned Bethie's unstinting devotion? Had Alison realized his true nature all those years ago, she would have allowed him to rot in jail, convicted of theft, and thought her friend well out of a bad situation.

Seeing the condemnation in her eyes, Jack flushed and he

shifted uncomfortably.

'Sorry,' he mumbled. 'I shouldn't have let my worries carry me away. You just don't realize what it is to live in a constant state of panic.'

'Oh, but I do, Jack. It is a state I've become very familiar with since I won that four thousand pounds for you, and I have no intention of compounding my error.'

Jack sighed. 'I see what you mean, I suppose.' He laughed shortly. 'I don't know why I expected any other reaction from you.' He sighed again and, straightening his shoulders, gave her a level look. 'It appears it is time to play my ace. It truly pains me to have to do this, but I must. Alison, if you do not do as I ask, I shall tell Lord Marchford that you are the mysterious Lissa Reynard for whom he has been searching and that it was you who caused the deaths of his brother and sister-in-law – and, from what I hear, his father.'

Alison felt as if she were slowly turning to stone. Her heart, surely, had stopped beating and she felt cold as death inside. Her nightmare had become reality.

'But, I didn't—' she whispered through lips numb with shock.

'Didn't cheat Susannah Brent of her pin money?' Jack chuckled mirthlessly. 'No, I don't suppose you did, but that's not important. What's important is that Lord Marchford thinks you did. Fat chance you'll have of hooking him for a protector if he finds out who you really are.'

'Good God, Jack,' she choked. 'Surely, you can't think. . . .' She realized the futility of her denial even as she spoke. To men of Jack's ilk, the fact that Lord Marchford might be attracted to her could only lead to one result for one of her inferior status.

'Aside from that,' Jack continued, oblivious, 'I've heard that he's promised himself a royal revenge on Lissa Reynard. They don't strip women naked and tie them to a pillory anymore, but I shouldn't be surprised if my lord Marchford doesn't have something equally unpleasant for you in mind. You'd be lucky if you don't find yourself in prison – or transported.'

Alison choked, her eyes wide and terrified. 'But I have broken no law!' she cried.

Jack snorted. 'You don't think that makes any difference, do you? Marchford is a wealthy and powerful man. He could get charges trumped up against you with a snap of his fingers.'

'He would not do that,' she said, her voice low and anguished.

'Oh, wouldn't he just? His entire life has been one of privilege, Alison. When he speaks, somebody by God jumps, and those who don't, pay dearly. He believes you to have done him a grievous wrong, Alison, and among his kind, that is grounds for the most brutal retribution.'

Alison sat silently. She did not agree with Jack's reading of Lord Marchford's character, but he was right in one thing. The earl would punish her for her supposed treachery if he were given the chance, and his retribution might well consist of prison or transportation.

She studied her fingertips, panic rising in her like a frozen tide. Her thoughts raced, but she could see no solution to her problem. For the time being, at least, she was in Jack's thrall.

'Very well,' she whispered. 'I will get your damned five hundred pounds, Jack.'

Jack expelled a long, deep sigh. 'That's a good girl, Alison. I knew you'd see it my way. As I said, you have three weeks – although that's cutting it pretty close. The sooner I can pay my tab, the better.' He rubbed his hands with the air of a man who has put in a good morning's work. 'I shall stop by in Royal Crescent in a day or two to see how you're doing.'

'No,' Alison replied sharply, thinking of Meg and the glow in her eyes when she spoke of Jack. 'Don't do that. You seem to have difficulty in understanding this concept, Jack, but I do not like you, and I do not wish to have any more to do with you than necessary. When I have the required funds at hand, I will send for you.'

Anger flashed across Jack's features to be replaced almost immediately by a look of complacency. 'And how do you propose to stop me, my dear? Lady Edith obviously thinks me charming, and as for her delicious little niece, why, I believe she's rather smitten with me.'

Alison gasped. She stood to face him, clenching her fists, and when she spoke, her voice took on the timbre of tempered metal. 'Jack, if I see you cast so much as a single lure at Meg, our arrangement is off.'

Jack's lips curved in a benign smile. 'Now, now, my dear, no need to fly up into the boughs. I was just funning.'

'Well, I wasn't. I mean what I say, Jack.'

The smile dropped from Jack's lips and his eyes narrowed. 'It seems to me you're not in much position to be issuing ultimatums – Lissa.' He rose leisurely and, reaching for her hand, pressed her fingertips against his lips. 'You may go now. Just remember, the quicker you get me those five hundred pounds, the quicker you'll be rid of me.'

With a wave of his hand, he turned, and as he walked away, a burst of mocking laughter floated back to her. On legs that felt stiff and not quite part of her body, Alison slowly made her way from Sydney Gardens.

CHAPTER 12

'And after that, the Prince Regent came riding by. He was stark naked and he threw golden guinea pieces to the assembled mob.'

Several seconds passed before Alison at last made a response to this remarkable speech by Meg, who faced her across the breakfast table.

'I knew you weren't paying attention!' Meg frowned in indignation. 'I might as well direct my conversation to the coffee urn.'

'I'm so sorry, Meg.' Alison's cheeks grew pink. 'I'm afraid I was wool-gathering.'

'I should certainly say so! You must have gathered enough today to fashion a carpet. Is there something troubling you, Alison?' asked Meg with sudden concern.

'Oh! Oh, no. That is – no. Do tell me what you were saying. I promise to pay strict attention.'

'I want to know what I should wear to the Kittridges' musicale next week. I should like to look my best – all my particular friends will be there, after all.' She stopped abruptly, blushing adorably.

'I see.' Alison's eyes twinkled. 'Would one of those particular friends be Peter Davenish, by any chance?'

'Pooh.' Meg tossed her head. 'Peter is an infant.'

Alison's heart sank. 'But such an engaging one,' she said, persevering. 'And so good-looking, too. Have you noticed how many languishing glances he has been collecting lately? Why, when we were all out riding in the park the other day, I thought Nancy Farwell would fall out of her carriage when she greeted him.'

Meg's delicate brows flew up. 'Really?'

Alison thought she discerned a note of interest in the girl's voice. At least, she hoped this was the case. She rose purposefully. 'Let us go look at your wardrobe. You know, the white muslin—'

'They're *all* white muslins,' muttered Meg rebelliously.

'. . . with the pale peach overdress,' Alison went on, unheeding, 'is most becoming, and it's very festive. With the addition of gold ribbons to trim it, with more gold ribbon threaded through your curls, it would be simply stunning.'

By this time, they had reached Meg's bedchamber, and the young girl ran to her wardrobe. She pulled out the gown in question and laid it on the bed, a pensive expression crossing her face. 'Do you know, I think you might be right?' She opened a drawer, and after some rummaging, emerged triumphantly with a spray of white blossoms, delicately tinged with peach. 'Perhaps I could wear these in my hair as well and – oh, Alison, what would you think of my gold locket to complete the ensemble? The one March gave me for my birthday last year.'

'Perfect.' Alison moved to the girl and put out a hand to sweep her brown curls atop her head. Standing back to observe the effect, Alison nodded admiringly. 'Yes, lovely. If you will give Finster her head, I am sure she will create something utterly charming. You will be the belle of the evening.'

Meg turned to look in the mirror, her eyes dreamy. 'Mr Crawford mentioned that he will be attending the musicale. Do you think he will like me in peach?'

Alison pulled her hand away abruptly. 'Good Lord, Meg! Jack Crawford is older than I am, and has not a feather to fly with.'

'He is mature, and so much more interesting than the boys I know – and worldly goods do not interest me,' said Meg, the dreamy gaze having changed into one of mulish militancy.

'Thus speaks a young woman who has never wanted for anything in her life,' replied Alison waspishly, and could have bitten her tongue the moment she uttered the words.

Meg glared at her reproachfully. 'I know I am fortunate in my, er, fortune,' she said with exaggerated dignity, 'but I could live in a cottage, if it were furnished with love.'

At this, Alison found herself so out of charity with the girl that she turned with a swish of her skirts and left the room. Back in her own chamber, she had time to repent her action. Dear heaven, how could she have botched matters so badly? She, who fancied herself adept at handling delicate, adolescent sensibilities. She had done what she had taken such care to avoid up till now. She had created a romantic obstacle for Meg to overcome, thus making Jack even more desirable in her eyes than he had been before. With a mental shake, she reminded herself that she couldn't let her problems with Crawford and his blackmail affect her responsibility to Lady Edith.

At least, she thought, she could make amends to Meg for her sharp tongue. Vowing to speak to the girl again before luncheon, she busied herself with some long neglected correspondence until she heard Lady Edith's voice in the corridor.

'I am here, my lady,' she said as she stepped out of her chamber. At the same time, Meg emerged from hers and, seeing Alison, flashed her a smile, half of bravado and half repentance. Relieved, Alison returned the smile and the three ladies descended to the ground floor with Honey bouncing in their wake.

The morning passed swiftly in chatter and plans for the week ahead. It was always a marvel to Alison that Lady Edith and those of her class could while away great chunks of time in the most inconsequential activities, and such was the case now as the old lady and her niece discussed Lady Edith's coming dinner party. The list of those to be invited was discussed with unrelenting thoroughness, and Alison noted with some relief that Jack Crawford's name did not appear on Meg's personal roster.

After lunch, Lady Edith retired for her customary nap, and a group of young misses came to collect Meg for an excursion to Parade Gardens. Alison had barely bid the group good-bye, when her attention was claimed by a thunderous knock on the front door. Masters, hurrying to open it, was nearly thrust to the floor by the sheer volume of several bouquets of flowers that preceded the caller into the house.

121

'My lord!' exclaimed Alison as March finally appeared from behind the blooms.

'Met a flower woman,' he explained tersely, striving to maintain his balance beneath his fragrant burden. 'Never mind,' he said to Masters. 'It will be easier to take them to the kitchen myself than to try to hand them over to you without dropping them all.

'The blasted female was an excellent saleswoman,' March continued as Masters ushered him into a small service room adjacent to the kitchen, where bowls and vases of every size were kept. He let some of the blossoms slip into Alison's hands and laid the rest down on a sturdy wooden table in the center of the room. Masters began pulling containers from cupboards and shelves, until Alison laughingly excused him, promising to call him when the flowers had been satisfactorily arranged.

'And don't bother any of the servants,' she admonished. She turned to March. 'And you call yourself practical?' Her lips curved in an involuntary smile. 'Your punishment for your profligacy is to assist me in arranging its results,' she said, her voice still filled with laughter. 'Goodness, we have enough here to stock our own flower cart.' Brandishing a serviceable pair of scissors, she handed March a like instrument. She frowned. 'I think the best plan of attack would be to sort them by color. Blues here, pinks and lavenders there, and reds and golds in that corner.'

'I am beginning to regret my open-handedness already,' replied the earl with a sigh. 'However, I shall do your bidding, madam. What shade would you call this?' he asked, holding up a newly budded iris. 'It is not blue, but I would not call it purple, either.'

Alison studied him covertly. The unsettling difference in him she had noted earlier seemed to have disappeared. His air was easy and amiable – even a little flirtatious, she noted with a disturbing little flutter in the pit of her stomach.

'With the purples, I think,' she replied, striving to keep her voice calm.

With much laughter and badinage, they completed the sorting

and Alison began filling the bowls and vases provided by Masters. March stood by, observing, loud in his praise of Alison's skill.

'We shall have the place looking like a May bower,' he declared. 'Aunt Edith will be charging admission to the crowds clamoring to see springtime blossoming in Royal Crescent.'

'You may very well be right,' retorted Alison. 'And I hereby appoint you tour guide.'

'I shall be happy to oblige. Ladies and gentlemen, if you will look to your right you will see the largest night-blooming purple fuzzflower in captivity, brought to this sceptered isle by, er, pirates, exhibiting a courage and daring beyond belief so that we might enjoy its beauty and fragrance in the comfort and security of this noble home. And in the library, note the spotted glori-florabunchus, which legend tells us. . . .'

Here, the earl ran out of breath, and Alison paused in her labors to applaud his effort.

'I sincerely hope that you have taken your seat in the House of Lords,' she said, all the warmth of a smiling summer in her eyes. 'It would be a shame to deprive a needful nation of your eloquence.'

March seemed to catch his breath as he looked back at her. His smile, when it finally came, was forced and strained. It had happened again, Alison realized with a pang. The film of ice had returned to transform March's tawny gaze to the color of dead leaves. When he spoke, however, his voice was light.

'Of course I have. It is my duty, after all.'

'Ah yes,' said Alison softly. 'Your duty.'

'I was thinking, however,' continued March, still in that inconsequential tone, 'of joining the circus, for I believe the two careers are not mutually exclusive. Here, let me help you with that.'

He reached to relieve Alison of the heavy bowl she had finished filling with primroses and daffodils, and set it on another table, ready to be carried upstairs. When she drew another container toward her, he moved nearer, handing blossoms to her as she pointed to them.

123

'Have you any idea where all these will be placed?' he asked idly.

Alison forced a laugh. 'Actually, no. Lady Edith always keeps a full complement of freshly cut blooms around the house, and what we are to do with an additional hothouseful is something of a puzzle. However,' she concluded easily, 'my father always used to say there is no such thing as too much beauty in a home, so I'm sure we shall find a place for them.'

March turned to her, and the expression in his eyes puzzled her.

'You loved your father.' It was more of a question than a statement, and Alison lifted her brows.

'Of course. I – I would have felt a great affection for him even if he were not my father and I had known him only as the vicar of Ridstowe. He was an eminently lovable man.'

'I see.' In an almost savage gesture, March drew another pile of flowers toward him, knocking several of them from the table. With a muttered curse, he attempted to catch them against his body, only to find Alison caught against him as she attempted the same thing.

The flowers fell to the floor, forgotten, as March brought his hands to Alison's shoulders. His gaze was hot and golden as it sank into hers, and an unthinking response flowered from deep within her. Without preamble, his mouth came down on hers, hard and urgent and demanding. Alison met his kiss with a fierce acceptance that shocked her. Her lips opened willingly for him, inviting him to plunder at will. When his hands slid down her back, pressing her along the length of him, she arched against him, crying out in her need and raising her arms to pull him even closer. His mouth left hers to press searing kisses on her cheeks, her jaw, and along the line of her throat, leaving a running heat in their wake. Mindlessly, her hands twisted in his hair, and she threw her head back, exulting in the feel of his lips against the pulse that pounded in her throat. She was filled with terrifying emotions she had never known she could experience and she thought she would choke with wanting him.

March's fingers fumbled impatiently with the laces at the neck

124

of her gown and Alison lifted her own to help him. She gasped at the feel of him inside her bodice, but when he pushed aside the thin fabric of her shift to press his hand to her breast, she stilled suddenly. No! A voice cried inside her. This was too much – this was wrong! Terribly wrong. She attempted to pull away, and when he would have stayed her, she cried aloud, jerking from his grasp.

'No! Dear God – I don't know what—' Her eyes were wide and bewildered and cloudy with passion. 'March – please! I – I am not like this! I am not—' She could finish neither her thought nor her sentence, and with another small cry, she turned and fled the room.

Reaching the sanctuary of her chamber, she flung herself across her bed. Dear God, what had she become? She had always thought of herself as a civilized, well-bred female, fully in charge of herself and her emotions at all times. She had heard whispers of other kinds of women, filled with secret desires and cravings – spinsters many of them, such as herself, who in desperate attempts to satisfy their shameful appetites fell victim to men who preyed on their lust and thus brought about their own ruin. Was she one of this depraved sisterhood? Was the shattering response she had experienced at March's touch merely the result of her own long-suppressed urges? She knew a moment of sickening shame at the memory of her body writhing against him – like an animal in heat.

She tried to bring her chaotic thoughts to order. She had been kissed before and never felt the slightest inclination to indulge further. She considered the other men of her acquaintance. Jack Crawford, for example. If Jack were to so much as kiss her cheek, her first instinct would be to hit him with the handiest blunt instrument.

No, it was the man who had prompted her response, not the situation. She rolled over on her back and flung an arm over her eyes. She had returned March's kiss with all the passion in her being. She had wanted to give herself to him wholly. She had wanted. . . .

She groaned and twisted herself into an upright position. Her thoughts were leading her in a direction she feared to pursue. Mayhap she was letting her problems with Crawford overwhelm her usually good judgment? No, she had admitted to herself sometime before that she had come to like March. What she had not realized was that she had come to like him very much. In fact, she very much feared that the explosion of emotion she had felt at his touch could easily be explained by the fact that she had grown to love him.

She groaned again. Damn the man! He had crept into her heart with the ease of a competent second-story man entering an empty house. And in her blissful idiocy, she had let it happen. Of all the men in the world whose presence in her life, let alone in her heart, spelled disaster, it was Anthony Brent, the Earl of Marchford, who was the most dangerous, and it was he who had breached her defenses with practiced ease.

For him, she was sure, the embrace they had just shared was the merest dalliance. Though she rather thought March was above the casual seduction practiced by most men of his class, he would surely regard his aunt's drab companion as fair game for a bit of tickle and squeeze. The fact that she had participated so willingly in that embrace would merely confirm that assumption.

Her mind flicked back to that other embrace, shared in the glittering darkness of Sydney Gardens. Remembering her response then, she squirmed. Lord, he must think her endowed with the morals of a Covent Garden nun.

She had not thought much about love since the days of her abortive come-out. At that time, she had thought to marry someday. Not to one of the uninterested young lordlings to whom she was presented with persistent frequency. But surely there must be someone to whom she would represent a heart's desire. Someone of her own station in life, who did not require a large dowry and an exalted background to make him happy. Surely, there was a man somewhere who would love her for herself alone, and upon whom she could bestow her affection.

Of course, her disastrous sojourn in London had dashed any dreams she might have had for a proper marriage, and in the ensuing years she had come to view love as an unrealistic fantasy, to be indulged in only by the very young or the very respectable. She was, of course, neither.

She sat on the edge of her bed, her fists clenched. She had lived without a man's love, and managed very well, thank you. She had Lady Edith's love and her own plans for a self-sufficient life. She needed no more. What she felt for Lord Marchford was a temporary, painful flowering, which in time, without nourishment, would wither and die. Her lips curved in a bitter smile. Given her susceptibility to his presence, she would simply have to make sure that she would not be alone with him again for the remainder of his time in Bath.

In her mind's eye, she saw again the strong curve of his jaw bent close to her, his lion's eyes piercing her peace. Please God he would return to London soon.

CHAPTER 13

A few days later, Alison, with Lady Edith and March, stood once more in the doorway of the Upper Assembly Rooms. As before, Lady Edith waved the two young people into the ballroom and took a seat among friends attending the gathering. This time, however, Alison immediately swung away from the earl and made her way with an air of determination to a far corner of the room to converse with another group.

March followed her with his gaze, his expression stony. He suppressed an urge to hasten after her, to grasp her arm, to ask her why she was treating him as though he had suddenly contracted leprosy. He uttered a short laugh. He knew the answer to that well enough, he supposed.

My God, he had fallen on her like a starving wolf on a helpless doe. He had never lost himself so completely. He had come to his aunt's house prepared to lull Lissa Reynard with a sprightly, flirtatious manner. Then, when she'd spoken of her love for her father, he had known a terrible flash of anger. How dare she pretend to possess sentiments he knew well she was incapable of feeling? Before he knew what he was about, he had grasped her, intending to vent his fury by shaking her until that dark hair tumbled about her shoulders.

His mistake, he supposed, had been in allowing himself to look into those fathomless, sky-colored eyes, for at that instant, he had been lost. His control had evaporated like snow flung into a fire, transforming his rage into a brutal kiss that had seared him to the core of his being. To his astonishment and unwelcome delight, she had responded with a ferocity that had matched his own, and the heat of her mouth had fired his own passion until he thought he might die of it.

He snorted inwardly. What fanciful, womanish nonsense. As though he would be likely to turn up his toes over an interlude of dalliance – an interlude, admittedly, that had gotten sorely out of hand. Again, he had found himself wanting to punish her, but when her mouth had clung to his with such incandescent sweetness, he had wished only to plunder the warmth within. It was as though she had turned to molten flame at his touch, and he had been consumed in her fire. His rage had turned to need, and the taste of her had stirred him to a frenzy of wanting.

Who would have thought such a furnace could blaze beneath her cool exterior? If he didn't know better, he would have sworn her passion was genuine, and that it sprang from a desire as innocent as it was new to her. And he would also have sworn that she was genuinely dismayed at her response. Her eyes, when she'd finally pulled away from him, had been anguished.

And now, she avoided his touch as though it would contaminate her. That was well and good, he told himself. He had no desire to become emotionally embroiled with the female. He had wished only to gain her confidence and her good will. Unfortunately, it was quite clear that he'd botched his campaign irretrievably.

His only hope of regaining his lost ground was to maintain an air of friendly courtesy with her until she was comfortable with him again. There would be no more embraces in secluded pathways or kisses stolen in a servants' pantry. In the future, he would be all that was correct with Miss Alison Fox – at least, until he was ready to seek his vengeance from Lissa Reynard. He still had not determined what form that vengeance would take, but when she was more at ease with him he would learn what drove her. His path would be made clear.

His eyes narrowed as he watched Alison's progress along the perimeter of the ballroom. She had stopped to talk to – yes, it was Jack Crawford. His insides clenched as Jack placed a possessive hand on her arm. Alison looked up swiftly and whispered something that caused him to flush and jerk his hand back. In a few moments, Alison turned away.

To March's surprise, she moved toward the card room, and he followed at a leisurely pace. He was struck by the rigidity of her demeanor as she moved, and when she turned briefly to face him, he was shocked at the expression in her eyes. They were wide and staring and dark as a winter midnight, like those of a sleeper trapped in a walking nightmare. Just in time, he checked an involuntary motion toward her and stepped back to watch her unobserved. In the card room she was greeted by old Lady Melksham, who invited her to join her and the others at the table. March settled himself against a pillar, hidden from Alison's direct view, and watched events unfold. He was puzzled for a few moments by her seemingly willing participation in a pastime for which she had so little aptitude, but a bitter smile twisted his lips as he realized that he had, for an instant, confused Alison Fox with her skilled alter ego. What was Lissa Reynard up to? he wondered, in sudden apprehension.

A scant hour later, her reticule bulging with the money she had won at whist, Alison rose from the table and moved to another part of the room, where she was again hailed by an acquaintance. My God, March thought, he had just watched his nemesis cheat his aunt's best friend out of what looked like a large sum of money. Swallowing his rage, he continued to watch as Alison, her eyes glittering with brittle laughter, played for another hour. The pile of counters before her grew steadily. When at last she left the card table, the reticule could hold no more.

March suddenly became aware that someone else had taken an interest in Alison's activities. Across the room, a figure emerged from the shadows and approached Alison as she moved gracefully toward the exit. Crawford had to hurry to catch up with her, touching her shoulder in a familiar manner when he finally did so. Alison whirled, and without speaking, transferred the paper notes and coins from her reticule to Crawford. It was as he suspected, March thought. Jack Crawford was – or had been – Alison's lover. They were obviously still co-conspirators. Crawford must have come to Bath with the express purpose of resuming his affair with his erstwhile doxy. And who could blame him? The woman was a veritable gold mine.

The two murmured a few words to each other, then, with a mocking smile, Crawford bowed and hurried away, leaving Alison alone, and, reflected March grimly, looking pitifully vulnerable.

He squelched the thought and strolled toward her.

'Been trying your hand at the tables?' he asked casually.

Alison paled visibly, but she raised her chin and answered calmly. 'Yes, Lady Melksham asked me to join her party.'

'I hope your efforts met with some success this evening.' There was nothing beyond courteous interest in the earl's tone, but Alison's laughter was forced.

'As opposed to last time? Yes, my lord, I am pleased and somewhat astonished to inform you that I won quite handily.'

March's brows lifted in surprise at her admission. Of course, he concluded almost immediately, a lie in that direction would be exposed the very next time his aunt and Lady Melksham came together for one of their gossips. A frown creased his forehead. What was he going to do about Aunt Edith? If the Fox woman was gearing up for another go at the coffers of the *haut monde*, the old lady must be informed. It would hurt her terribly, and at her age, he was not sure how she would deal with such an emotional upheaval. March cursed inwardly, but his smile was bland as he solicited Alison's hand for a country dance. As they moved mechanically through the figures, March's expression gradually lightened, and when he came together with Alison for the last flourish, the smile he bestowed on her was quite genuine. A plan had sprung into his mind, full blown, for the ruin of Miss Alison Fox.

The evening had been the longest of her life, reflected Alison as she sank down on her bed some hours later. She sat for several long moments, simply staring in front of her before she rose again and began making weary preparations for bed. At least, she thought tiredly, the whole ugly business should not take long. She had given Jack over fifty pounds tonight. A few evenings more at the tables would see the fulfillment of their wretched bargain.

She sat down before her dressing table, frowning as a new problem raised its head. Her unexpected winnings had been the cause of much surprised hilarity and speculation this evening. The next time she won, the other players would not be so amused. She was well known to all the people from whom she had won money tonight and, what was worse, so was Lady Edith. Her newfound skill would be commented on. Lord Marchford would be sure to hear of it. Then what?

Then she would be in the suds. March, she was sure, would immediately make the connection between the sudden acquired talent of Alison Fox and the phenomenal skill of Lissa Reynard. No, somehow she must keep March from learning of her success at the tables.

She flung down the brush with which she had been stroking her hair and climbed into bed, where she lay, wide-eyed, staring at the ceiling. It was unfortunate that Bath was such a close-knit little community, where everyone's doings were everyone's business.

No. Wait. . . . She had for so long been a member of the tight little group that was high society in Bath that she had forgotten there was another layer of existence here. Below the light frosting of nobility lay a solid, middle-class wedge of citizenry who, though not possessed of the vast wealth of their betters, still enjoyed taking part in the gambling frenzy that made up life in the Regent's England.

Those with money enough to rub shoulders with the *ton* played in the Upper Rooms or at select card parties. Others confined themselves to less exalted venues, such as the increasingly shabby Lower Rooms in Terrace Walk, or at other, less savory establishments. It would not do for Alison Fox, Lady Edith's favored companion, to be seen in such locales, but if she were to don her wig and tinted glasses and make a few other slight alterations, she would be unrecognizable. She could not visit these places alone, of course. An unattended woman in the seamier sections of Bath would be fair game for its denizens.

However, she had little doubt she could prevail upon Jack to escort her there.

Her main problem would be getting out of the house. Fortunately, Lady Edith usually retired early. Meg had formed the habit of indulging in late-night *tête-à-têtes* with Alison, but she should have no difficulty in discouraging the girl with pretenses of a headache. It would be a simple matter to slip out of the house when all was still.

She wished she could confide in Lady Edith, but it would not be fair to burden her with this new crisis in her life. When it was all over and Jack had wended his profligate way back to London, then, perhaps, she could divulge what she had done.

As for my lord Marchford, she would simply stay out of his way. She would find chores for herself elsewhere when he came to visit his aunt, and find excuses to stay home when he suggested outings for the ladies of Royal Crescent. Please God, he would go home soon, for surely, once he was back in his own milieu, her life would return to its normal, placid routine. She would forget him – eventually – and if she were to see him again, he would be married, with several tokens of his wife's affection in his nursery.

Having settled her immediate future to her satisfaction, she closed her eyes and folded her hands over her coverlet, and proceeded to stare at the ceiling for several more hours before she finally fell into a restless sleep. Her dreams were disturbed by visions of a glittering lion, with great, golden eyes, and claws whose touch did not draw blood, but instead left fiery trails of longing on her skin.

Three days after Alison's appearance in the Upper Rooms, the Earl of Marchford hurried to answer a knock on the door of his chamber in York House.

'Come in,' he said impatiently. 'Come in, Pilcher.'

The little detective stepped inside the room with an apprehensive glance at the earl. He had been traveling steadily since he had received his summons the day before. What, he wondered, could have happened to have so exercised his lordship?

'I have found Lissa Reynard,' March said baldly, relishing Pitcher's gasp of astonishment. 'Sit down – please.'

He ordered a second breakfast for Pilcher, and detailed his discovery while the grateful detective, who had missed breakfast in his haste to reach his destination, dug into a repast of eggs, York ham, kidneys, and buttered toast. When finished, the detective asked diffidently, 'I'm happy that you have at last found your quarry, my lord. But what has this to do with me? If you have located the woman, surely you do not require my services.'

'Oh, but I do.' Lord Marchford's smile was not reassuring, thought Jonas Pilcher. In fact, it was downright frightening. He sincerely hoped he wasn't going to be asked to commit murder. 'I intend to ruin Alison Fox, and I need your help to do so.'

Mr Pilcher gaped at the earl. 'Ruin?' he asked, his nose quivering in distress.

'I should say, rather, that I am going to let her ruin herself.' He shrugged at his employee's look of incomprehension. 'The woman is a cheat, Pilcher. That is how she makes what I am sure is an extremely comfortable living. I am merely going to ensure that she can no longer do so. I believe I have spent enough time at the gaming tables of London to spot her methods – and it was you I hired originally to find the woman because it is my understanding that you make a specialty of unmasking card cheats.'

'That is true, my lord, if I do say so. I'm up to all the rigs and rows, and if you want her scuppered, why, whether the lady chooses to fuzz the cards or tip the double, Jonas Pilcher is your man.'

The earl rubbed his hands together. 'Very good. Now then, it will be necessary for you to watch my aunt's house, where the Fox woman is living now. I do not want her to leave the place to buy so much as a length of lace without my knowing about it. She has an accomplice, as well, and I shall want to know every time they meet.'

'What do you want me to do when I spy her doing something crooked?' asked the detective.

March once again flashed an unpleasant smile. 'Why, simply

signal to me – for I shall be close by.'

For a moment, Mr Pilcher said nothing. Then, apparently gathering up his courage, he asked, 'If I might ask, my lord, what do you intend to do at that point? I believe you would experience some difficulty in having her arrested for cheating.'

'I am aware of that, Pilcher. I do not need to see Miss Fox in jail. No, when we have ascertained her method of cheating, I shall simply expose her on the spot. With any luck, a good number of my aunt's set will be on hand.'

Jonas Pilcher's confusion was evident, as his moustaches trembled and his small, beady eyes peered anxiously at the earl in an effort to fathom his meaning.

The earl raised his hand irritably. 'Don't you see? My aunt will discharge Miss Fox on the spot, and I should imagine the news will travel with the usual lightning speed of titillating gossip. The woman will have no hope of acquiring a position in any other genteel household. Thus, she will lose her entrée into the homes of the plump pigeons she had previously plucked with abandon. Moreover, once having been identified as a cheat, she will have great difficulty in getting up so much as a table of silver loo in London's gaming hells. In short, Alison Fox will find herself very much alone – penniless and friendless. A just fate, I think, for one who has caused such tragedy for others.'

As he spoke, a picture rose before his eyes of Alison, as he had seen her three nights ago. The lost, terrified expression in her eyes had stayed with him for some time after he had left Royal Crescent that evening, and he had spent many hours convincing himself that he had been mistaken in what he had seen. His expression hardened. There was no reason why he should feel a sudden wrench of compassion for this slender witch. She deserved the fate that awaited her, and he would take great satisfaction in bringing about her downfall.

'I see,' was Mr Pilcher's only response. He wiped from his lips the last traces of eggs and ham, and rose from the table. He favored the earl with a mournful stare. 'I shall make arrangements to have the house watched,' he said. 'I'll need an assistant or two, but that will take a very little time to sort out, for I've a couple of acquaintances here in Bath – sharp, young lads, who've helped me before. We'll have the place under round-the-clock surveillance by the end of the day, and shall notify you anytime Miss Fox leaves the premises.'

March nodded curtly, and remained seated before the fire long after the detective had departed, staring at the dying embers in the hearth.

CHAPTER 14

'But, Alison-nn-nn!' The words came out in a wail. 'If you don't go, the whole day will be ruined!' Meg threw her hands out before her in a dramatic gesture, nearly knocking over a vase of flowers set on an occasional table in the drawing room.

'Sally's brother was to accompany us tomorrow, but now he cannot go, and Charlotte's older sister, who was also to go, sprained her ankle yesterday. Rosamund's mother declares she is still too weak from the effects of the influenza she suffered last week. Jane's governess is visiting relatives, and no one else has anyone who could chaperon. We have been planning the ride to the Oaks for weeks! Peter has promised to show me how to shoot a bow and arrow, and James Arbuthnot wishes to take us all to lunch in the village.'

'But, Meg—' Alison interjected weakly.

'Oh, *please*, Alison!'

'I thought you said Lord Marchford had agreed to be one of your party.'

'He has – but if he is the only older person there, he will very likely change his mind. If you come, his presence will be assured, and then all will be unexceptionable. I know Aunt Edith will want you to come with us.' Meg plumped down on a damask-covered armchair and watched expectantly.

Avoiding her beseeching stare, Alison let her gaze fall to the carpet. To think that just yesterday she considered that her world had brightened considerably. It had been precisely two weeks since she had set out to win five hundred pounds for Jack Crawford, and yesterday she had reached her goal. She had thrust the money into Jack's hands, informing him tersely that she hoped never to set eyes on him again. He had laughed as he accepted the heavy bundle of cash, and depositing her cheerfully on her doorstep in the wee hours of the morning, tipped his hat and strode off, whistling.

And now, she most assuredly did not want to join Lord Marchford – damn and blast the man, why had he not taken himself back to London by now? – in an expedition in which they would be thrown together as allies amid a party of youngsters. On the other hand, she was sure that Lady Edith, once apprised of the proposed journey, would not only grant Alison permission, but would insist that she take part.

She sighed deeply. So much for her determination to avoid Lord Marchford's company. She would just have to plan the day carefully, assuring that she never strayed more than an arm's length from her charges.

Meg evidently read capitulation in her demeanor, for she threw her arms around Alison and drew her into a rollicking waltz around the room. Despite herself, Alison laughed, until the dance ended abruptly in a collision with a large, masculine form near the drawing room's entrance.

'Oh!' gasped Alison, finding herself clutched in an impromptu embrace against March's chest. Blushing hotly, she disengaged herself with as much dignity as she could command and retired hastily to the other side of the drawing room.

'March!' cried Meg, not in the least discommoded at finding herself in a similar position. Indeed, she twisted about to plant a noisy kiss on her brother's cheek. 'Alison has consented to join us tomorrow for our ride to the Oaks!'

If the earl's response to this information was less than enthusiastic, Meg appeared not to notice. 'We are going to have a marvelous time!' Meg continued, still bubbling happily. 'I have not been out on horseback for ever so long. The weather promises to be fine, and Sally's mother's cook is going to pack good things for us to eat.'

'I thought we were going to lunch in Step Walford,' remarked the earl.

'Oh, we are, but we shall need something to sustain us till then – we shall be starting out right after breakfast, after all.'

'Of course,' murmured her brother. He shot an involuntary glance at Alison, brimful of amusement, before turning back to Meg. 'We can't have you fainting from starvation a whole three or four hours after your last meal.'

Alison's eyes twinkled in response before she caught herself and looked away abruptly. March, too, stiffened and moved into the room to seat himself. Lady Edith joined them a few minutes later, and the conversation continued with plans for the next day's outing.

That night, sitting in his rooms at York House, March tried to prepare for whatever tomorrow's outing might bring; he never knew what to expect anymore, for that damned witch kept him constantly on edge. He acknowledged ruefully that his unsettled mental climate was perhaps not surprising, since he had spent the last two weeks in a constant state of frustrated anticipation. Alison Fox had displayed an inexplicable reluctance to participate in the doings of Bath Society. How, the earl had fumed, did she plan to carry on her nefarious deeds, when she refused to accompany him and his aunt to a single assembly? She had even pled a headache the evening they were to appear at a select card party, at which a liberal sprinkling of the wealthiest persons in the west of England were guaranteed to be present.

All was explained the morning Jonas Pilcher had appeared at York House to report strange goings-on in Royal Crescent.

'The Fox female,' reported the little detective, thumbing through a tattered notebook, 'hasn't set foot out of the house for three days, according to my agents. However,' he added meaningfully, 'every night, after the house is dark and silent, a woman has crept from the servants' door. She meets a tall, thinnish gent and the two of them set off for the town center. My man didn't follow them, since he perceived his duty to stay at the house.'

'My God!' exclaimed the earl. 'Of course. She knows she would be inviting disaster if, after carefully crafting a reputation as a dim-witted gambler, she starts winning money by the potful from Aunt Edith's friends. She's been going elsewhere to ply her trade. The Lower Rooms for a start, I'd wager. And I'd also be prepared to wager my strawberry leaves that the thinnish gent is Jack Crawford.'

After that, Alison's nightly forays were carefully monitored. Once or twice March joined Pilcher, who had taken over his operative's shift, in a journey to the Lower Rooms and watched from a distance as an odd-looking female with muddy brown hair and tinted glasses proceeded to relieve Mister Lindsey's customers of substantial sums of money. She did not win every hand, but her losses were minimal, and at the end of every evening, she turned money over to Jack Crawford. Strangely, her face bore the same haunted look March had observed on that other night, at the Upper Rooms.

March, of course, was unable to observe Alison at close range, particularly when she and her partner abandoned the Lower Rooms for seedier establishments in Avon and Kingsmead Streets. After a few nights of watching from behind posts and doorways, his sense of anger and betrayal becoming nearly uncontainable, he had forced himself to await Pilcher's reports in the confines of his chambers at York House.

It had been obvious, from their last meeting, that the gentleman was growing increasingly perplexed.

'I've watched her for over a week now,' Pilcher had said, paging through a notebook now nearly falling to shreds. 'Right at her elbow, I've been, and she never twigged I was there, neither.'

'And. . . ?'

The little man's shoulders sagged. 'I've seen the best, my lord, from the fuzzers to the sleeve men to the eyes in the sky, and I can't figure out how she's doing it.'

'But she must—'

'Oh, yes, I'm sure she cheats, right enough. She wins too steadily. But the how is a mystery. I've examined the cards she uses, and cased the place for an accomplice – that Crawford is usually in another room, not that I see him as a gigger. She wears long sleeves, but they're always buttoned tight and if she brings a scarf or anything else big enough to conceal an ace or two, it's always kept well out of the playing area.' Pilcher frowned, looking even more like an apprehensive rodent. 'It's a puzzlement, my lord.'

'Does she always play the same game?'

'No. She seems to favor piquet, but I've seen her take a hand at whist and even écarté. Whatever game holds the highest stakes in the room, there she is. Every night.'

'Damn!' The expletive burst from March's lips. 'I wish I could get her back to the Upper Rooms – perhaps even play with her myself. Although, I suppose in that event, she would take great care to lose, and I would learn nothing.' He sighed heavily. 'Damn,' he repeated, in a softer, duller voice.

Some nights later, after March had accompanied Alison and his aunt to yet another social function, this time an intimate dinner party with neighbors, Alison bade a hurried good night and whisked herself up the stairs before March could suggest a late evening libation.

'Goodness,' commented his aunt, 'Alison certainly had the wind up tonight. Whatever have you done to her?'

'I?' March said, infusing the word with surprised indignation.

'Well, you must have done something,' replied his aunt austerely. 'The girl hardly said boo to you all night. I had hoped that you two had become friends. After a somewhat rocky start, I might add. You were not very nice to her at first.'

'No, I was not.' Friends! March would have laughed aloud were he not so conscious of an urge to howl his hurt and rage into the candlelit darkness of the sleeping house. He led Lady Edith to the library, where a small fire crackled comfortably in the grate. Settling her on a striped satin settee, he took a seat near her. 'Aunt,' he began hesitantly, 'as I believe you have already guessed, the reason for my flying visit to Bath was to discover what I could about Alison Fox. Eleanor thought—'

'Yes, I know what Eleanor thought. Of course, I knew why you had come, but I was sure that by now you had come to see Alison for what she is – a lovely, kindhearted young woman – who is truly devoted to me – as I am to her.'

'Well,' March responded slowly, 'you were right. She had me convinced she is precisely what she appears to be: a gently bred, quietly proper lady's companion. But now...' He hesitated, uncertain of how much he should reveal to this very dear old lady. 'Certain things have come to my attention—'

'Things?' Lady Edith sat up very straight on the settee. 'What things? What nonsense are you talking now, March? If you—'

Observing the signs of growing agitation on his aunt's face, March hastily covered her hand with his own. 'I am not talking nonsense, Aunt,' he continued, his voice gentle, 'but I cannot speak of what I know just yet. I just wanted to prepare you for the... revelation that Miss Fox is... not what she appears.'

'Rubbish!' cried Lady Edith. 'You are still trying to separate her from me, aren't you?' Her voice cracking with tremulous anguish, she wrenched her hand away from her nephew's. 'Well, let me tell you, Anthony Brent, there is nothing you can say to me that will diminish my affection for Alison by so much as a whit.'

Recalling the whole disastrous episode, March uttered a sigh that seemed to spring directly from the ache that lay within him like a wound. He shook his head, wondering when all this would end. With a heavy heart, he reached once more for the decanter at his side.

Alison stood before her mirror, giving a last-minute twitch to the skirt of her riding habit. She knew the ensemble of mulberry merino became her. Indeed, she considered it rather daring and would never have purchased it if Lady Edith had not been with her.

'Yes, I quite agree,' the older woman had said. 'It is extremely dashing. Rakish, even, with all that military braid, and it will suit you admirably. Buy it.'

Alison adjusted the tight-fitting bodice and smoothed the superbly tailored skirt over her hips. Placing the matching shako hat atop dark curls arranged in a glossy swirl, she brushed the feather adorning it into place along the curve of her cheek.

She paused once more to look in the mirror, even though she

knew that by now the others were awaiting her. Aware that Lord Marchford was expected for breakfast, she had elected to skip that meal, settling for tea and toast in her room. She had then spent an inordinate amount of time in mindless drifting, unable to tear her thoughts from that very irksome gentleman. How had she come to fall in love with him? she wondered desperately for the hundredth time. One usually does not become enamored of those who wish one nothing but ill. On the other hand, how could she not love him? Despite his arrogance and, yes, a certain rigidity in his view of the world, he was everything she had ever dreamed of in a life mate. His strength was almost palpable, yet he could be gentle and sensitive with those he loved. The arrogance was leavened with humor – why, he could even laugh at himself. He was intelligent without being pompous – most of the time – and he treated her like a person instead of his aunt's employee. Added to that, of course, were those mesmerizing, brandy-colored eyes and a smile that turned her knees to soup.

She shook herself. It mattered not one whit *why* she had fallen in love with him. It was important only that she maintain a neutral, courteous attitude toward him for another few days. For surely by then he would be gone and she could begin the long struggle to forget him. Surely there would cone a time when she would no longer feel that part of her was missing because he was not beside her. Her arms would eventually forget how it had felt to press his body against hers, and her mouth would no longer ache for the touch of his lips against them.

Oh, for Heaven's sake! Giving the feather one more twitch, she whirled and ran from the room. She was breathless by the time she reached the bottom of the stairs, and she gasped apologetically as she flew headlong into a tall, slender figure waiting there. She looked up and nearly reeled from shock.

'Jack! Jack Crawford! What in the world are you doing here?'

'Oh, didn't I tell you?' said Meg, peering at Alison from around Jack's shoulder. 'I ran into Mr Crawford yesterday and, when he heard of our outing today, he agreed to join us. Isn't that wonderful?' Her tone was casual, her expression ingenuous.

'Wonderful,' replied Alison through gritted teeth. The earl entered the hall from the dining parlor just then, and it was obvious from his expression that he was no happier to see Jack than she had been.

Indeed, March was on the dangerous side of furious. When Crawford had been ushered into the dining parlor he had been sure, despite Meg's crows of delight, that Alison had engineered his appearance.

Now, he watched Alison chatting amiably with Crawford and Meg. To his intense displeasure, his attention was promptly caught by the very becoming ensemble she wore. The need to sweep that lithe, lovely body into his arms was almost overpowering, and the remembered feel of her burned through him. He turned away before his churning emotions could be detected.

At that point, a vigorous knock on the door signaled the arrival of more members of the riding expedition. When an hour or so later, the party finally swept out of Royal Crescent and into the fields on the outskirts of Bath, it was a merry group, indeed, with two notable exceptions. When the group at last spied the silver ribbon that was the River Avon, they gave free rein to their mounts for a race over the green, rolling hills that sloped down to the water's edge.

'You are an excellent rider, Miss Fox.'

Alison, who had joined the throng in their exhilarating gallop, nearly dropped her reins as the voice sounded at her elbow.

'And my aunt has mounted you well.' The words were spoken in a neutral tone, but Alison bridled instantly.

'Yes, Caprice is delightful, with the softest mouth imaginable. I enjoy her company any time I am able.'

'When you can fit a few minutes into your busy schedule,' March concluded, and this time there was a definite edge to his voice.

'Yes, I do keep busy, my lord. I have many duties – one of them being to chaperon Lady Meg and her friends this afternoon. If you will excuse me. . . .' Clapping her heels against the little mare's side, she trotted over to where Meg's mount walked side by side with that of Jack Crawford. The two were so deep in conversation that Meg jumped a little at Alison's approach.

'Oh – Alison,' she said a little consciously. 'Ja – Mr Crawford and I were just discussing my London Season.'

'Oh?' Alison's tone was not encouraging.

'Yes, indeed.' Jack's smile bore a hint of mockery as he turned to Alison. 'I was just telling Lady Meg the names of some of the young men she will likely meet. And who,' he added roguishly, 'will no doubt be sending her flowers and poems by the cart-fuls.'

Meg blushed and Alison felt a surge of annoyance. She bestowed a brilliant smile on young Peter Davenish, who rode with Sally Pargeter some twenty yards ahead. As she had hoped, the two fell back, and Peter challenged the two girls to a race, leaving Alison and Jack by themselves.

'Ah, impetuous youth,' Jack said, his charming smile very much in evidence. Alison was not impressed.

'Jack, I told you to leave Meg alone,' she said peremptorily. The smile remained fixed in place, undiminished.

'I don't know what you're talking about, Alison. I was merely exchanging idle chatter with the girl. My dear,' he continued, 'believe me, I have no interest in unformed damsels. I prefer women of . . . more experience.'

So meaningful was the glow in his gaze that Alison momentarily recoiled. Unthinking, she glanced about to discover March some distance ahead with young James Holiwell, laughing easily over some piece of nonsense, and apparently oblivious to Alison and Jack, who had come to a complete standstill.

In this assumption, Alison was mistaken. March had been aware of Alison's position in the group every second of the journey so far, and for some minutes now, the prattle of the young man next to him had faded wholly from his attention. What the devil was the vixen up to now? God – look at Crawford, laughing with his tart while the two of them left ruin and heartache in their midst. A haze of red clouded March's vision as he watched Jack lift a hand to caress the feather that lay along Alison's cheek, lingering on the soft flesh beneath it. He would give all he possessed to gallop across the meadow and knock the blackguard from his saddle in a satisfying explosion of blood and teeth and tissue.

'Jack, stop that!' Alison jerked away from his touch.

'You are being very tetchy this morning,' replied Jack, his mouth turning down mournfully. His eyes, however, retained their mischievous sparkle. 'I am merely trying to display a little of the affection I feel for you, my dear.'

'And don't try turning me up sweet,' Alison snapped. 'I am the last person in the world to be cozened by your endearments. Come, let us join the others.'

Jack, however, laid a hand on her bridle. 'Not so fast, love. This may be the only chance I'll have all day to be private with you, and I have something of importance to say to you.'

'Well?' asked Alison impatiently.

'You're making this very difficult. I merely wish to say that I think we should marry.'

For some minutes, Alison merely gaped at him.

CHAPTER 15

'Jack, have you gone mad?' Alison blurted the words harshly.
He merely laughed. 'On the contrary. I think marrying you
would be the smartest thing I could do right now.'

Alison began to breathe again. Obviously, Jack was merely
indulging in another of his mad starts. 'Well, I think it would be
the stupidest thing either one of us could do, right now or ever,'
she replied tartly. 'I have no wish to see you again after today, let
alone spend the rest of my life with you.'

'Do but consider,' said Jack, undeterred. 'You have a truly
remarkable talent that has gone for too long unexploited. With
me at your side, you would have entrée to gambling establishments all over the country. We would make a fortune.'

Alison laughed uncertainly. 'Jack, be serious. You are not
going to tell me you have developed a *tendre* for me.'

'No, although I am not at all sure that I would not lose my
heart to you eventually – you are quite lovely, you know. But, I
am perfectly serious.' His face suddenly lost its laughter, and his
eyes narrowed. Alison felt a frisson of alarm skitter down her
spine. He drew closer. 'Listen to me, Alison. I need more money.
Not very much – less than a hundred pounds,' he continued
hastily at her choked protest. 'I was put on to a good thing at the
races – which turned out, unfortunately, to be not such a good
thing after all.' He laughed unrepentantly. 'I thought that, in
addition, you could see your way clear to winning a little extra.
You could provide me with a real stake, you know.'

'I have no interest in providing you with so much as a cup of
tea, let alone a stake,' said Alison through gritted teeth. 'Don't

you understand, Jack? I want no more to do with you. You have the worst case of gaming fever I have ever seen, and there is no doubt in my mind that you will end up at point-non-plus some-day. I will not allow you to drag me down to the gutter with you. I want you out of my life, Jack Crawford, once and for all!'

Jack did not take his eyes from Alison's face throughout this diatribe. When she paused to take a breath, he gripped her wrist and shook her ungently, after first looking around to make sure he was unobserved.

'Have you forgotten the hold I have over you?' He glanced meaningfully at Lord Marchford, who by now was some distance away. His expression softened as his eyes returned to Alison. 'I truly do not wish to coerce you, my dear, but I have no choice. You see . . .' He hesitated, as though uncertain how to proceed. 'I told you that I had come to Bath to seek you out. What I did not mention was that my journey here was at the behest of . . . of those persons I told you about – in London. They were about to become very unpleasant over the money I owed them, and it was only when I explained that I had an ace in the hole, so to speak, here in this little haven, that they granted me some breathing space.

'Giles Morganton, the man with whom I am staying, is hand in glove with some of the most powerful men in the London underworld. He was most impressed by the speed with which you obtained the money I asked of you. He relayed the news of your success to his friends, and now . . . well, now, they want to use your services on a regular basis. If I do not secure those services – permanently – they will be very displeased with me.'

It felt to Alison as though the lovely April day had turned to bitter November. 'You are serious, are you not?' she asked in astonished dismay. When Jack made no reply, but continued to gaze at her, unsmiling, she drew herself up and pulled away from him. 'You may as well forget this whole mad idea, Jack. I will not go to London with you as your wife, or in any other capacity. Even your threat to go to Lord Marchford will not sway me. I will go to him myself rather than place myself in thrall to you and your despicable associates.'

Her words possessed more bravado than she felt as she

returned his stare straightly. His gaze was skeptical, but he was the first to look away. He sighed heavily. 'I will give you a few days to think this over, Alison. In the meantime, I want you to play at the tables for me. If you do not agree,' he continued, observing the rising fury in her eyes, 'I shall tell Marchford everything right now.'

After a long moment, Alison nodded her head. During Jack's revelations, she had realized with blinding clarity that Lady Edith had been right all along; she had made a dreadful mistake in not revealing herself to Lord Marchford long ago. A sick sensation stirred in the pit of her stomach. Perhaps he would have believed that she was innocent of wrongdoing if she had gone to him when Lady Edith had urged her to do so. Was it too late now? If only Jack had not come to Bath to force her to the tables again. March would never be convinced of her innocence now. Nevertheless, she would tell him everything – at the right time. She must choose carefully the moment to speak to him. She could not risk Jack blurting out her story just now. 'Very well,' she said tightly. 'But this is the last time, Jack. And let me tell you that a few days will not cause me to change my mind in regard to haring off to London with you.'

'We shall see.' Bringing a hand to the brim of his hat in a mock salute, Jack slapped his reins against his horse's neck and cantered ahead to join some of the younger members of the party who had stopped to admire the view from the hills above the Avon.

That evening, thinking back on the day, Alison discovered that she could not remember a single event that had taken place after her conversation with Jack. She was aware that she had played badminton with Peter at the Oaks, a lovely old Tudor manor. Luncheon at the Dog and Cart in the village of Step Walford was a blur, as was the ride back to Bath amid the youthful badinage of Meg and her friends. At least, she reflected wearily, she had managed to stay away from Lord Marchford for the most part, and had successfully avoided Jack for the rest of the day as well.

The next day proved uneventful, but after dinner, Lady Edith decided on the spur of the moment to attend the Wednesday night assembly at the Upper Rooms, and now Alison stood before her mirror, checking her appearance. She reflected with grim satisfaction that no one could guess her state of mind by looking at her. Her robe of deep pink, under a net tunic of a paler shade gave her cheeks a false glow, and her eyes sparkled with the tears that lay just below the surface.

The earl, of course, would be present tonight. Lord, did the man not have any social life of his own? She squelched this patently unfair thought – after all, the stated purpose of his presence in Bath was to devote time to his aunt.

She sighed. At any rate, she had become adept at playing least in sight. She would be spending most of the evening in the card room – again.

Unfortunately for her plans, Lord Marchford proved himself to be remarkably adhesive. Looking impossibly compelling in meticulous evening dress, he took her hand in his as they entered the octagonal connecting chamber and, in Lady Edith's hearing, bespoke a dance immediately in such smoothly courteous terms that she could scarcely refuse him. Alison's peace of mind further shattered when March's fingers closed over hers as he led her to the dance floor.

'Did you enjoy the outing yesterday afternoon, Miss Fox?' March's voice was cool and bland, but it seemed to carry a hidden meaning that Alison found herself unwilling to fathom. As before, she was intensely conscious of the warmth of his hand at her waist, and the nearness of his lips as he spoke caused her heart to thud uncontrollably.

'The outing? Oh. Yes. It was most enjoyable,' she replied, her voice thin and reedy.

'How nice that you and Mr Crawford at last had an opportunity to renew your acquaintance.'

'I – I beg your pardon?' The thudding of Alison's heart increased a hundred fold.

'I noticed that you were in conversation with him for some time on your way to The Oaks.'

'Oh,' she repeated. She looked up at him for the first time, her eyes wary. 'Yes, we did speak a little. The merest commonplace, I assure you.'

'But, you need assure me of nothing, Miss Fox.'

150

March gazed down into the blue eyes, shuttered against him. What, he asked himself, was he hoping to accomplish with this exchange. Did he wish to discomfit her? If so, he was succeeding admirably. But, no, that wasn't it, was it? It came as an unpleasant shock to realize that what he wanted was for Alison to confess her perfidy to him. He wanted her to explain why she had selected his family to victimize. He ached for her to. . . . To what? Apologize? The idea was ludicrous. Even if she were to tell him of her misdeeds, to reveal all she had done, what could she possibly say in exculpation?

He was conscious of the pain that lay deep within him, imparting a sense that he had lost something precious. If only. . . .

He straightened suddenly, aware that the music had stopped. Alison murmured something incomprehensible and turned away toward the card room. Moving briskly after her, March managed to stay on her heels as they entered the card room, and when she seated herself at a table at the invitation of two acquaintances, he adroitly slipped into the remaining vacant seat.

Oh, Lord, it needed but this, thought Alison in dismay. She simply could not play successfully in the presence of the Earl of Marchford. Was it her imagination, or was there a special significance in the glance he sent her? Good God, surely he could not have heard of the swath she had cut among the gamblers elsewhere in town. No, of course not. She had been in disguise and had used yet another fictitious name.

From under deceptively drooping lids, March watched Alison. Would she pit her skill against him? Would she be tempted to relieve him of his wealth, even though she had already taken pains to display herself before him as a veritable idiot with the pasteboards? Ah, he concluded in bitter satisfaction, it was as he had surmised; she was going into her inept gambler mode. Look at her – her eyes filled with bewilderment, her delicate hands fluttering as she carefully arranged her hand. Her demeanor was that of a child brought down from the nursery to join the grown-ups at dinner. A wave of bitterness swept over him. When she found herself exposed in the near future, and unable to support herself at the tables, she could well consider a career on the boards.

The game progressed in fits and starts, as Alison made one blunder after another, always followed by profuse apologies to her partner. With March so close by her side, Alison thought wretchedly, it wasn't the least bit difficult to make a show of total confusion.

'Oh, dear,' she choked, after she led a heart and promptly lost the trick to George Maltham, one of the other players. She turned to the earl. 'I was sure you had the king.'

Maltham snorted. 'Did you not see me play the king of hearts early in the hand?'

'Oh my, no. Did you?' She peered apprehensively at Mr Maltham and then at the earl. 'How very stupid of me, to be sure. I am so sorry. But, you know how it is with me.'

'Yes, Miss Fox, I know exactly how it is with you,' returned March coolly, his voice cutting through Mr Maltham's derisive laughter. 'Now, now, George,' he continued, 'we cannot all be expert gamesters. Have a little consideration for Miss Fox's feelings.'

Alison, who had started at March's first words, relaxed a little as he spoke to Mr Maltham. Really, she must cease this ridiculous trembling every time Lord March uttered the most commonplace of remarks. The man was not a mind reader, after all, and there was no way he could be cognizant of her masquerade.

Somehow, she was not reassured by these thoughts, and when the game ended, and the other two players left to repair to the refreshment room, she rose as well, feeling inestimably relieved. March's next words drove her heart back into its now seemingly customary position in her throat.

'This has been such a pleasant interlude, surely it doesn't have to end just yet. I challenge you to a game of piquet, Miss Fox.'

'I think not, my lord,' she replied, her voice betraying only the merest quiver. 'I am quite weary of cards.'

'But over the last few evenings, you seem to have enjoyed yourself at the tables. Can it be that you simply do not wish to play with me?'

Alison felt the floor heave beneath her feet. 'What a ridiculous notion, my lord.' She knew her laugh sounded forced, and she hurried on. 'I was merely offering you a chance to seek out a more skilled player. For you must admit I am no challenge at all.'

March smiled, and to Alison's fevered senses, he was all glittering eyes and sharp teeth. 'Ah, but you must let me be the judge of that, Miss Fox.' He gestured to a passing attendant and requested that a piquet deck be brought. Alison sank back into her chair, feeling very much like a Christian martyr being circled by a large, handsome, and noticeably hungry lion.

'If it is all right with you, Miss Fox, we shall play for chicken stakes, so that neither of us need be concerned about bankruptcy. A penny a point, shall we say?'

Alison nodded numbly, trying to control the trembling of her hands as she picked up the cards dealt casually by her opponent. Unthinking, she discarded her full allowance of five cards and selected their replacements from the stockpile.

'Did I do so badly by you, then?' asked March, laughter in his tone.

'Dreadfully,' replied Alison, pleased that her voice remained steady. 'I feel quite ill-used – particularly,' she added with a crooked little smile as March threw down a single card, 'since you apparently fared much better. In addition' – she displayed her cards and turned over her previous discard for March to view – 'I have drawn a blank. Not a royal face in sight.'

'Ah, *pauvre petite*. At least your misfortune will net you ten points. Not that that will save you, dear lady.' He twirled an imaginary mustache, sneering evilly.

His badinage warmed her, but she found it impossible to join in. She could only force an inane laugh as she returned her attention to her cards.

The next hour passed with agonizing slowness. Alison, recalling that March had seen her win fairly handily on at least two occasions recently, attempted to ameliorate her wretched performance at whist. She discovered, however, that try as she might, she was unable to defeat her opponent. Whether this was due to his obvious skill at the game or to her own inability to concentrate on anything beyond his golden gaze and his predatory

153

smile, she was unwilling to contemplate.

'I am quite destitute, my lord!' she declared at last, as March swept the last of her coins into the pile in front of him. 'And I am perishing for a glass of something cool.' She rose once more, determined this time that the earl would not coerce her into another game. He made no attempt to do so, however, merely offering to accompany her to the tearoom, where they encountered Lady Edith. Immediately after enjoying a revivifying dish of bohea with the ladies, March left to speak with a group of acquaintances just leaving the room.

'You do not look as though you are enjoying yourself, my dear,' Lady Edith observed. 'I did not see you dancing.'

'No, I have been in the card room.' When Alison had nothing further to say, Lady Edith peered up into her face anxiously. 'What is it? Has something happened to overset you?'

'No – not exactly. I played a few hands of piquet with your nephew, and. . . .'

'You need say no more,' interrupted Lady Edith with some asperity. 'You are still afraid of him, aren't you?'

'No, I am not. Truly. I fear his condemnation only, for I have decided to take your advice.'

'You are going to tell him that you are Lissa Reynard?' Lady Edith's brows flew into her hairline.

'Yes. You were right. I should have done it a long time ago. However, I must – oh dear Lord!' Alison's eyes widened in alarm as she gazed across the room. 'It's Jack! I did not know he would be here tonight.'

'Hmpfh!' sniffed Lady Edith. 'From all reports, he's here every evening the place is open. Apparently, he wishes to speak to you. Shall we go into the Little Octagon?'

'No,' said Alison with a sigh. 'He will not be put off. I shall go to him – but I'll return immediately.' Assuring herself that Lord Marchford was nowhere in sight, she moved toward Jack, who immediately drew her into a corner.

'You have been hard at work, I see,' he said with his facile smile. 'Do you have something for me?' The smile broadened in anticipation.

'No, I'm afraid not, Jack,' Alison replied coolly. 'I lost all the money I came with.'

'But how can this be? I saw you with Lord Marchford, and he always plays for high stakes.'

'Not tonight. We played for chicken stakes, and I lost.'

Jack's mouth turned down in a petulant curve. 'We cannot afford to waste an opportunity like this, Alison.'

'We?' Alison's voice was glacial, and she suppressed an urge to rake his cheek with the nails that were biting into her palms.

Jack had the grace to flush, and he continued hurriedly. 'That isn't what I wished to speak to you about. I have come to help you, actually.'

'You could help me by leaving Bath early tomorrow morning, never to return again.'

He chose to take her remark as a pleasantry and snickered accordingly. 'You may sheathe your pretty claws, my dear. I have a present for you.' From his waistcoat he brought out a small velvet pouch from which he shook a boxed deck of cards. Alison stared at him in bewilderment.

'But – but I do not need cards. They are readily available anywhere I wish to play.'

'Ah, but not cards like these.' He lifted one of her hands and curled her fingers around the deck. 'These are very special cards, for they will assure that you will win every hand in which you partake.'

Alison, jerking her hand as though the little packet had bitten her, allowed the cards to fall to the floor. 'Jack! Are these—?'

Bending, he scooped them up. 'Yes. They've been fuzzed. I want you to use them from now on. Just look at them!' he continued eagerly, as Alison stared at him in blank horror. 'If you didn't know what to look for, you'd never know they're marked. See? In the design! The swirls in the upper left-hand corner have been shaded ever so faintly on the face cards. You will be able to tell instantly what each player has been dealt.'

'No, I will not, Jack.' Alison's breath came in harsh gasps. 'For I have no intention of using these cards. My God, have you no shred of decency left? I have been doing very well for you using the talent God gave me – though why He should wish to saddle me with something so unwanted . . .' she cried in rising hysteria. With an effort, she brought herself under control. 'I have acquiesced to all your demands, but I will not cheat for you.'

'My dear, you're making too much of this. I'm not asking you to rob anyone at gunpoint, after all. Look around you. These people are rolling in the stuff – they won't miss the paltry sums we will take.' His eyes were wide and unfocused in their febrile greed. 'Very soon, Alison, you and I are going to be very, very rich.'

'Jack, I will not do this. I—' But Jack merely shook his head and patted her hands as though she were a recalcitrant child. She was struck by the undesirability of quarreling with him in this very public place, and, taking the cards from him, thrust them into her reticule.

'Good evening, Jack.' She turned and walked swiftly from the room.

March watched the interlude from the gallery above the tea-room, and stared after Alison long after she had left the chamber. When he finally moved away through the crowds of pleasure seekers, his shoulders sagged as though he walked under the weight of a heavy burden.

A short time later, when he joined his aunt and Alison in the ballroom, Lady Edith declared herself weary of the evening's entertainments and asked to be taken home. As soon as the little party reached the house in Royal Crescent, Alison, pleading a very real headache, bade Lady Edith and her nephew a hurried good evening. As she turned to ascend the staircase, she met March's glance, and nearly gasped at the pain and bitterness she encountered there. What could have happened to cause him such anguish? she wondered dully as she made her way to her room. It was as though she had looked into a mirror of her own soul, for her own reflections were equally painful. Was this how he would look when she confessed her perfidy to him? Wearily, she disrobed and climbed into bed, only to stare, sleepless, at the ceiling.

CHAPTER 16

Downstairs, Lady Edith gazed up anxiously into her nephew's face.

'Are you all right, March?' she asked. 'You look—'

March's answering smile was not wholly successful. 'I am merely a little tired, Aunt. I must be shuffling into middle age, for a few late nights begin to tell on me.'

'Oh, dear. Alison seemed somewhat out of sorts, too. Perhaps you are both sickening for something.'

'Very possibly,' answered March dryly.

Lady Edith glanced sharply at him. 'You still do not trust Alison, do you?'

March sighed. 'I'm afraid I find it impossible to do so, Aunt. No,' he continued as his aunt bristled. 'I shall say no more on that head, but ... Aunt, I'd prepare myself, if I were you, for some rather unpleasant revelations in the near future concerning that female.'

Tipping his hat, he hastened from the house before his aunt could respond. As he walked away from Royal Crescent, he looked back and saw that candles were lit in one of the bed-chambers. He knew it was not that of his aunt. Was Alison still awake? He smiled grimly. Were her reflections as unpleasant as his own?

An unexpected vision rose before his eyes of Alison, garbed in her night rail, her hair tumbling in an ebony cloud about her shoulders. He wished ... God help him, he wished he were standing in that room with her, pulling her toward him so that he could bury his face in those dark, silken tresses. He could

157

almost feel her lithe body against his, feel himself sinking into the molten cobalt of her eyes.

His mouth twisted bitterly. He supposed he was not the first man to be seduced by the physical attributes of a vicious temptress. It was unfortunate that men were so susceptible to the curve of a breast, or the smoky enchantment in a pair of vivid eyes.

He paused suddenly, gripped by a wave of anguish that nearly overcame him. Dear God, it wasn't the sway of her hips or the creaminess of her flesh that had drawn him to her. It was the seeming warmth of her smile, her wit and intelligence, the genuine goodness he'd thought he perceived, the indefinable sense of rightness when he was with her and the feeling of loss when he was not, that had combined to steal his heart, and seemingly his soul.

He laughed, but it was a sound without joy. What a fool he was! The moment he had anticipated for so long was nearly at hand, but his triumph had already turned to ashes. God help him, he was in love with Alison Fox!

No, he reminded himself harshly. He did not love Alison Fox, but rather a dream, unreal, and as insubstantial as the night mist that swirled about his feet.

He thought he must be going mad. How could a man yearn for a fantasy – a vision that did not exist? The dazzling warmth of her smile hid a heart of sculptured stone; her kindness to Lady Edith was false and empty. He accepted this now as a fact, yet, Aunt Edith, and even his little sister had fallen under her spell. He reviewed what he knew of Alison Fox, and a flicker of something like hope rose within him. Was it possible that Alison was blameless in the deaths of Susannah and William? Could he have been so wrong in his assumptions about her? He longed to believe in her innocence, as a sinner cries out for redemption. But what had she been doing in the gaming hells of London, if not fleecing unsuspecting prey? And more recently, he had watched her scoop in a great deal of money in some extremely unsavory establishments. Impossible to consider that she could win such sums honestly – and had he not seen her accept those cards from Jack Crawford?

No, he was grasping at straws. No matter what his heart told him, he could not ignore the evidence. She was undoubtedly the scheming harpy he had known her to be from the start, and he might as well learn to live with the pain this knowledge would bring him for the rest of his life.

By the time he reached York House, his reflections had become almost unbearably anguished and as he prepared for bed he realized that he had never felt so unutterably weary. He fell almost immediately into a troubled sleep from which he awakened early and unrefreshed.

Upon rising, his first act was to send round for Jonas Pilcher.

Alison awoke with a headache and the feeling she'd never really slept. Heavy-eyed, she responded mechanically to Meg's breakfast sallies and sipped a cup of coffee while she crumbled toast on her plate. Honey prowled about their ankles, hinting pointedly for largesse.

Meg expatiated at length about her plans for the morning, which included yet another shopping expedition in Milsom Street. 'Wouldn't you like to join us, Alison?' asked the girl, bending to tuck a piece of ham into the spaniel's mouth.

'Go with you?' responded Alison after several seconds. 'Oh. No, I'm sure Mrs Pargeter will be company enough for you. And, Meg,' she added automatically, 'you know Lady Edith does not like Honey to be fed at table.'

'Then we must be sure not to tell her,' Meg replied promptly, her brown eyes brimming with laughter. When Alison failed to rise to the bait, the girl glanced at her quizzically. 'You seem a bit blue-deviled this morning.'

Alison forced a laugh. 'No, not at all. I . . . I am just reviewing all that needs to be done for Lady Edith's dinner party.'

To their surprise, the lady herself entered the room at that moment.

'Aunt! You are down early this morning,' said Meg, smiling. She ran to pull out a chair for the older woman, while Alison poured her a cup of coffee. Lady Edith accepted their ministrations without enthusiasm and bade Meg to run along. 'For, I know you will change your gown four times before you are ready to set out,' she finished fretfully.

Exchanging a mystified glanced with Alison, Meg dropped a kiss on her aunt's cheek and hurried from the room. Lady Edith intercepted the look, and shifted uncomfortably in her chair. 'I expect I was a bit testy with the gel,' she said apologetically. 'Sometimes I push the prerogatives of old age too far, I fear.'

'Nonsense,' replied Alison, smiling. 'We are all entitled to our crotchets now and then. Particularly,' she added with a twinkle, 'when one decides to face the world two hours earlier than usual.' Alison peered at her employer closely and her expression grew cloudy. 'Are you all right, my lady?'

Lady Edith sighed. 'I did not sleep well.' She raised her eyes to Alison. 'Marchford will be here today. I invited him for luncheon. Meg will be gone for most of the day, so you will have an opportunity to speak to him.'

Alison felt her heart stop. 'Oh! That is – I did not plan. . . . It is too soon! I thought – later, perhaps. After your dinner party. . . . He mentioned something about going back to London then.'

Lady Edith drew herself up. 'Alison,' she said, her voice stem, 'the time has come for you to clear things up with March. You have placed me in an untenable situation with my own nephew, and I simply cannot maintain the deception you – we – have perpetrated.' Observing Alison's stricken look, her expression softened. 'If there were any benefit to be gained by putting off your . . . confrontation, I would not speak so, but you must see that things are coming to a head between you two.'

Dear God, thought Alison. How could she have been so selfish? So caught up was she in her determination that Lord Marchford never penetrated her wretched secret that she had given little or no thought to the pain it must have caused Lady Edith to deceive one whom she held in such strong affection.

'I'm so sorry, my lady,' she whispered, tears glittering in her eyes. 'That I should be a cause of hurt for you. . . .'

'Yes, well never mind all that.' Lady Edith fluttered her hands in distress. 'Just make sure that this ridiculous charade does not

continue a moment longer than necessary. Talk to him, Alison –
talk to him today.'

Alison swallowed. 'Very well.'

For the rest of the morning, Alison busied herself with inconsequential duties, her thoughts a chaotic jumble of emotion. At
one point, her hands stilled in her work as she realized to her
surprise that the fear that had been her constant companion for
so long was strangely absent. The next instant, she was almost
overcome with a sudden wave of pure anger! Of course, she
thought almost dazedly. She had done nothing wrong! She had
known this all along, but she had always harbored a faint sense
of guilt, as though her actions in London had somehow
contributed to Susannah Brent's tragedy, but this was nonsense,
as Lady Edith had assured her so many times. She might regret
Susannah's death, but she was not to blame. *She was not to blame.*
She drew a deep breath. She had cowered in fear of the Earl of
Marchford for four years, and for the last two weeks, she had
almost withered and died at the thought of his contempt. Well,
by God, she would set him straight this afternoon. She loved
him – there was nothing she could do about that, but if he chose
to disbelieve what she was about to tell him, then so be it. She no
longer feared his retribution, for she knew him now. He was not
evil, and his anger at her supposed perfidy would only take him
so far. She did not feel herself in danger of transportation, or of
being tarred and feathered or of any of the other dread punishments that had haunted her imagination for so long.

As for the other – his hatred and contempt – she would be
devastated at losing his friendship, but she had already resigned
herself to living her life without his love. She would warm
herself in Lady Edith's affection, and when that wonderful
woman was gone, there would be the school to occupy her fully.

As she concluded her task at hand, her lips curved into what
might almost be called a smile. No, she was no longer in a quake
over the coming interview. Indeed, she assured herself, she
almost looked forward to it.

As it turned out, however, private speech with Lord
Marchford became an impossibility. When Alison descended to

the drawing room shortly before luncheon, the earl was there before her. To her intense annoyance, her heart lifted at the sight of him, and she lowered her gaze to hide her feelings. Lady Edith was also present in the drawing room and after a prosaic exchange of pleasantries, the little group moved to the dining room. Conversation at table, of course, was cordial. At least, that would have been the impression a stranger might have received. Lady Edith detailed in a high-pitched voice scraps of gossip that might have escaped March and Alison, while March responded with absent courtesy. All the while, his eyes remained determinedly averted from Alison, who, despite her best efforts, found herself unable to contribute to the brittle conversation that flowed around her like icy currents from a window opened to a January blizzard.

She found it impossible to eat, and pushed salad and cold meat about her plate in endless circles. At the end of the meal, she noticed that March had scarcely touched his own food, and Lady Edith's remained virtually uneaten as well.

The three filed out of the dining parlor, and in the hall, Lady Edith announced her intention of going to her rooms to rest.

Her pulse hammering, Alison accepted March's invitation to join him in the library. His eyes, she had noted, were impenetrable, their tawny brightness dimmed by the film of ice she had observed before. Her heart sank. Despite her brave resolutions of the morning, in a secret corner of her heart she had hoped against hope that he would accept her explanation of her actions and that they could still be friends, but watching him as he gestured her silently to a chair and took one himself, she knew that the next minutes would be even more difficult than she had envisioned. She jerked to attention as the earl spoke.

'Did you have something in particular that you wished to speak to me about, Miss Fox?' His expression was quizzical and, she thought, guarded. Drawing a deep breath, she opened her mouth to reply, but at that moment a commotion rose out in the hall. At the sound of Meg's stifled sob, Alison and March jumped up simultaneously and ran out of the room.

There they found the girl seated on a small bench near the

front door, surrounded by her friends and – good God – Jack Crawford! Meg sat, pale and whimpering, with both hands clutched to her stomach.

'What is it?' said March, glaring at Jack. 'What has happened?'

An expression of alarm crossed Jack's features as he observed March's clenched fists, and he spoke hastily. 'I was in my friend's town carriage, when I came across the young ladies in Poultney Street. Lady Margaret appeared ill, so I took it upon myself to bring them—'

Mrs Pargeter, who had also come into the house, interrupted. 'We had scarcely begun our little expedition this morning, when Meg began to feel unwell. By the time we had completed only half our shopping, she was quite sick. She is feverish, I am afraid, and I wonder if she mightn't be coming down with the influenza.'

'Oh dear,' said Alison, going immediately to Meg. 'You spent a great deal of time with Rosamund Pinchot when her mother was so ill. I'm so sorry your outing was spoiled,' she added to the group at large, ignoring Jack. She assisted Meg to rise and assisted her up the stairs. 'We must get you to bed at once. I know your friends will excuse you.'

Meg waved wanly to the group below, and soon, dressed in her night rail, she was tucked solicitously into bed. Being one of those persons who is rarely ill but suffers inordinately when sickness does strike, she felt perfectly wretched. Promptly expelling the contents of her stomach, Meg lay against her pillows moaning and complaining that her head hurt and that she felt as though she had been kicked by a team of horses. The doctor was sent for, and that gentleman arrived just as Lady Edith emerged from her room.

By the time Alison had explained to the older woman what was afoot, the doctor, a tall, thin man with a harassed air, had finished his examination.

'No, no, it's nothing serious at all,' he hastened to declare. 'She has only a slight fever; I do not think it is the influenza, just a slight upset. She will no doubt feel quite ill for a while.' He cast a mischievous glance at his patient, snuggled under her comforter. 'She will think she is about to expire, but such is far from the case. I shall leave some drops to make her a little more comfortable, and she'll be fine as fivepence before the cat can lick her ear.'

So saying, he made his farewells and took himself off in a bustle of advice and reassurances.

March, assured that his little sister was in no real danger, left the house in the wake of the doctor. It was only later that Alison had time to consider that by failing to reveal herself to Lord March, she was still in thrall to Jack and was obliged to set out for yet another excursion to the unsavory environs of Avon Street.

Thus, having satisfied herself that Meg was not seriously ill and slept soundly under the effects of Dr. Bentham's medication, Alison crept from the house after everyone was abed. Jack was waiting for her at the corner of Royal Crescent and Brock Street and together they made their way through the center of town to a certain high stakes establishment in Avon Street.

Observing her clandestine departure from the house, and the meeting with Jack, March followed at a discreet distance. By the time he entered the High Flyer, a notorious gambling hall, where the play was known to be deep and dangerous, Alison was already seated at a faro table. Jack stood some distance away, watching. Jonas Pilcher, March noted with grim satisfaction, stood almost directly behind Alison.

Lord, she was lovely, he thought with a tightening of his throat. Even garbed as she was, in an outmoded ensemble of dark muslin, her face half-hidden under a drooping brown wig and a large, feathered hat, the purity of her features was still evident. In this pit of greed and debauchery, she managed to convey the pristine beauty of a Renaissance angel.

A servant brought a fresh deck of cards to the faro table, and March observed with a sinking sensation that they appeared to be identical to those given to Alison by Crawford the night before. Just then, a loud crash jerked his attention across the room, where he saw that Jack had apparently bumped into a waiter, causing him to drop a tray loaded with glasses. Realizing with a smothered curse that he had just witnessed an attempt at diversion, his gaze returned instantly to Alison. He could observe no difference in the cards that lay on the table near Alison's hand, but he sucked in his breath as the man to Alison's right picked them up and began dealing.

March gripped the handle of his walking stick with painful intensity, his eyes fastened now on Jonas Pilcher. The minutes crawled by with agonizing slowness until at last the little detective raised his head. His eyes searched the room until he found March and, his expression grim, he gave an almost imperceptible nod.

March nearly gasped as the sure knowledge of her duplicity stabbed through him. He had not realized how great had been his hope that, despite what he had learned, he would be proven wrong in his assumptions about Alison Fox. He could not believe that he was watching the woman whom, despite his best efforts, he had come to love, sitting at a grimy table in a den of thieves, cheating at cards! God, how could he want her so, knowing his original assessment of her character had been proven so painfully?

He grew cold with the realization of what was to come. His direction to Jonas had been to allow her to accrue a small pile of winnings. Then he was to exclaim in a loud voice that the cards were marked, following which, he would snatch hat, wig, and glasses from her. Among the gamblers here tonight were several men of his acquaintance who would recognize her instantly. Their wives traveled in the same circles as his aunt. By tomorrow, every lady of quality in Bath would be prepared to give Alison the cut direct. Aunt Edith would be devastated, but she would be at last brought to a realization of Alison's true character and she would no doubt turn her off without a character.

His revenge would be complete.

He had known for days now that her ruin would bring him nothing but anguish, but he had not anticipated the full extent of the hurt he now experienced. In fascinated horror, he watched the unfolding of events at the faro table.

CHAPTER 17

So focused was March's attention on the scene he had planned so meticulously, that when a cry sounded at the table, he knew an instant's disorientation, as though the scene before him had fragmented into whirling kaleidoscope pieces.

He shook his head in momentary bewilderment, his gaze narrowing as one of the players abruptly rose from his seat.

'Oy!' he cried, holding up the hand he had been dealt. 'These 'ere cards 'as been fuzzed!'

March's gaze flew to Alison, who stared at the man in apparent bewilderment. The gambler caught her glance and he paused for a moment before flinging out a hand in accusation. 'It was 'er!' he continued loudly. 'The mort! I saw 'er messin' with the pasteboards just before the deal. She switched decks!'

At this, Alison rose from her seat, her eyes wide in denial. Another man, seated next to her, grasped her wrist. 'I thought there was somethin' funny about 'er,' he snarled, reaching for her hat. 'Let's see what you look like, then.'

With one hand he wrenched the large hat from her head, nearly dislodging the wig, and, ignoring her frightened cry, he swept off the tinted glasses with the other.

Acting without volition, March ran to Alison's side. With a single blow, he felled the man who had assaulted her. As the other players at the table stood paralyzed by surprise, he picked Alison up bodily and, gesturing to a befuddled Jonas Pilcher to follow, he ran through the room toward the exit, pushing past patrons craning their necks toward the now actively belligerent faro players.

166

Outside, he did not pause, but raced for the curricle he had left nearby in the care of Toby, his tiger. The boy leaped to attention and betrayed by not so much as a hair any surprise he might have felt at his master's unorthodox behavior. He merely assisted in wedging the unresisting female into the front seat of the curricle next to the earl.

In truth, Alison was laboring under severe shock. She had been stunned at the faro player's accusations, and when March had appeared from nowhere to snatch her from what appeared to be imminent danger, she had slipped into a sort of twilight of incomprehension. She knew she should protest the earl's highhanded treatment of her, but she seemed without will or volition.

It was not until March climbed into the driver's seat, after issuing a few brief instructions to Jonas Pilcher, that Alison came to herself.

'What. . . ?' She twisted in her seat beside March. 'What. . . ?' she repeated breathlessly, furious at her own inability to form a coherent sentence.

'Never mind!' shouted March, and Alison recoiled from the savagery in his tone. 'We will talk very soon, you and I, but not just now, I think.'

Slapping the reins on the horses' backs, March guided the curricle through the silent streets of Bath. He drove at a shocking pace. They would surely overturn at any moment, thought Alison. She clenched her hands in her lap to keep from crying out. Her fear, however, lay blurry and formless at the edge of her consciousness as her mind struggled with the events that had just occurred. How could that man have accused her of cheating? She had done nothing to the cards. Had Jack somehow. . . ? And how had March appeared so suddenly? In her terror, she had breathed his name in a mindless prayer for succor, and like a genie from a bottle, he had appeared at her side. A hysterical chuckle burst from her. If she closed her eyes and wished this night away, would she awake to find herself safe in bed in Royal Crescent?

She cast a sidelong glance at the man next to her. She thought

167

she had already seen the earl at his most forbidding, but now, with jaw clenched and golden eyes glittering in rage, he was truly frightening.

When they clattered up to the house in Royal Crescent, however, Alison found herself still mired in a panicky daze. She made no move to descend from the curricle, and gasped in shock when she was pulled unceremoniously from the vehicle. Grasping her arm roughly, March virtually dragged her into the house. He did not release her until they were in the library, where, he thrust her into the nearest chair. He moved to close the door before returning to stand above her.

'Now, Miss Fox – or Miss Reynard – or whatever your real name happens to be, we will have our little talk.'

March almost trembled in his fury. His carefully crafted plan had crumbled before his eyes onto the grimy floor of the High Flyer. The moment for which he had waited so long had come and gone, and instead of relishing the triumph of Alison Fox's exposure, he had saved her from it! Everything he had worked for was undone, and he had no one to blame but himself for the ruination of his grand design.

He felt sick with self-loathing. At the last minute he had been unable to watch Alison's downfall. He could not bear that she should be shamed before those men, to say nothing of the danger she faced, so it was he who had been ruined – for love of a woman who deserved his undying hatred.

He observed almost with detachment the torment in her face. Her lovely blue eyes were wide with shock as she lifted one hand to him in petition. She was really very good, he thought tiredly. He waited for the tears he was sure would brim over at any second. Instead, to his surprise, a spark of anger lit her amethyst gaze. Her voice, as she replied, was husky but calm.

'Yes, my lord, a talk between us is long overdue. Please be seated, and I will tell you everything you want to know.'

Once more, rage boiled within him. He remained standing, so that she was obliged to twist her neck upward to look at him. 'I have already discovered everything I need to know about you,' he grated. 'I know that you are the harpy who is responsible for the deaths of my brother and his wife.'

Alison recoiled as though he had struck her. She gripped the arms of her chair and after a moment, continued tonelessly. 'You are quite wrong, my lord. I am in no way to blame for their deaths. My only misdeed was in keeping my part in their tragedy from you for so long. I should have come to you imme-diately after ... after Susannah ... I should have tried to explain—'

'Explain!' The word exploded in a hiss of outrage. 'What explanation can you possibly offer for what you did? You came skulking into London in disguise and bled Susannah white. When you had wrung her dry, you crept away again like the she-snake you are, leaving her to face her desperation alone.

Alison uttered a small moan, and her hands fluttered in her lap. 'That is not the way it happened!'

March's lips curved in a contemptuous sneer. 'Then, do tell me, Miss Fox/Reynard – God, how fortuitously you are named, for you are an unprincipled vixen – how, precisely did it happen?'

Alison stared at him. Once more March observed a flush of anger rise to tinge her cheeks as she rose and moved to face him. 'If,' she repeated in a voice of steel, 'you will be seated, I shall tell you everything.'

Despite himself, March sank into a nearby chair. He said noth-ing, merely staring at her with empty eyes.

'My name,' began Alison, 'really is Alison Fox.' A ghost of a smile played about her lips. 'You are not the first to call me vixen, although I am used to hearing the word as a term of affec-tion.'

March said nothing, his stony stare unsoftened.

'Everything I told you about my background is true,' she continued. 'It is because of Jack Crawford that I set out for London four years ago.'

'Ah,' interjected March savagely, 'I thought we eventually would come to Mr Crawford.'

Alison's fingers curled into fists, but she continued as though she had not heard. 'As you know, Jack was married to one of my best friends. Beth came to me at my home in Ridstowe to tell me that Jack was in terrible trouble.' She bent her head to scrutinize her hands. 'He is much addicted to gambling. He had lost a great deal of money and had stolen to cover his debt. The theft was discovered, and, according to Beth, Jack would be hauled off to prison if the money were not returned in three months' time.'

'And how much money are we speaking of?' asked March harshly.

'Four thousand pounds.'

'Four thousand. . . . My God!'

'Yes.' Once more, Alison permitted herself a small smile. 'That's what I said, too.' As March stiffened, she continued hastily. 'At any rate, Beth, knowing of my skill at cards—'

'Skill! Is that what you call it?'

'Yes, my lord, for that is what it is. I do not cheat. I have never cheated, and would never do so.'

At this, March stood again. 'Listen to you!' he snarled. 'One would think you virtuous as a nun. How can you face me and tell me that you don't cheat?'

'Because it is the truth,' Alison replied quietly. 'My uncle taught me to play cards, and, unlikely as it might seem in someone of my background, I was an apt pupil.'

March snorted. 'To wrap it in clean linen! All the world knows you cheated Susannah. You cannot deny it!'

'I can and I do!' cried Alison. 'It was Susannah who spread that lie after I left London. Although, even if I had been present to defend myself, no one would have listened.'

'And why should anyone listen to a fraud with no past?'

'But, I could not gamble under my own identity! Don't you see? It would have broken my father's heart.'

'How commendable,' replied March, sneering. 'Instead, you broke the heart of another old man – *my* father.'

Alison bowed her head. 'I . . . I am truly sorry for that – and for Susannah and her husband, as well. If I had known the outcome of my association with Susannah Brent, I would never have sat down to the tables with her.'

'Do you really expect me to believe that you were able to win thousands of pounds from Susannah without cheating? You're a female, for God's sake!'

'I see.' Once again Alison's mouth twisted into a smile. 'A man might have such a skill, but not a woman?'

March dropped his gaze. 'You must admit it is very unlikely.'

'Quite so. But I do possess that skill. I discovered in myself the ability to remember every card dealt and played in any given hand, and the knack of estimating the odds in my head. I also have what might be termed a gift for reading faces and the thoughts behind them. In addition,' she concluded, 'I rarely drink spirituous liquors and then only sparingly. I was usually the only sober player at table, which I found to be rather an advantage.'

When March made no response, she continued hesitantly. 'I can understand why you find it difficult to believe what I'm telling you, for you have only the reports of me spread by your sister-in-law.' She ignored the growl that issued from him. 'That is why I did not come to you long before this. You must admit, the way you were shouting threats from the rooftops—'

'I was not—'

'Yes, you were!' Alison could feel the heat rise to her cheeks, but she could not control her indignation. 'It was perhaps under-standable, given the depth of your grief, but you vowed revenges too horrible to name against me. Why, Molly told me—'

'Molly?'

Alison dropped her eyes again. 'The Viscountess Callander. She and Beth and I were best friends in school.'

'Oh, my God!' cried March, incensed. 'Of course. She knew all the time, didn't she? Please give her my congratulations. Her acting ability almost outshines your own.'

'Please, my lord, you must believe that neither of us enjoyed deceiving you. Well,' she amended, 'perhaps Molly enjoyed it just a little. She was always somewhat of a scapegrace, and she was determined that you would not ruin me.'

'You are fortunate in your friends, Miss Fox. Not only do they contrive appropriate nicknames for you, but they lie nearly as cleverly as you do. However, we are straying from the point.

171

Even if I were to believe your ludicrous assertions of innocence in the matter of cheating Susannah, what possible excuse can you offer for separating her from every guinea she possessed? Had you no compunction about ruining her? Or did you view our family as a bottomless pit from which to assuage your greed?'

Alison's lips tightened.

'I won three hundred pounds from Susannah Brent. It seemed a great deal to me, but I believed the sum was not beyond her means.'

March simply stared, his mouth a thin slash, his eyes opaque and mud-colored. 'Of course, it was not beyond her. Her pin money would easily have covered that amount – but I do not believe you.'

Alison felt suddenly weary, as though her life's blood were draining from her.

'I do not know why I am wasting your time and mine telling you all this,' she said tonelessly. 'You obviously do not believe a word I've said – and I suppose that's understandable. You've been nurturing your hatred for so long, it must be well nigh impossible to let go of it.'

'Spare me your insight, Miss Fox. And no, I do not feel my time is being wasted. I am keenly interested in what you have told me, and even more so in what is to come. For example, we have not even touched on Jack Crawford's fortuitous appearance in Bath.'

'You must know by now his arrival was planned,' snapped Alison. 'He came to Bath in search of me, so that he could avail himself once more of my . . . services.'

'And you were only too happy to oblige. You must have felt yourself sadly constrained as Lady Edith's companion. Allow me to compliment you on your performance at the Dunsaneys' card party, by the by. No one would have guessed you to be anything other than a helpless widgeon at the card table. To continue, however, with Jack's help, you were able to don yet another of your knacky disguises so that you could prey at will on the less fortunate citizens of this fair city.'

Outraged, Alison had to resist the urge to slap that sneering smile from his face. 'Of course I did not wish to help him! I was completely at his mercy. He had only to suggest that he would tell you everything, and I was just so much clay in his hands.'

'And it did not occur to you at that point that you would be better off coming to me yourself than to accede to Jack's request?'

Alison suddenly found herself at a loss for words. She could not tell March of the feeling for him that had caused her reluctance to confess. If he were to learn how much she had dreaded to see the look of contempt in his eyes that would surely follow such a confession, he would realize that she loved him. She could not bear that.

'I wanted to come to you, but I was afraid,' she said haltingly. 'I had come to know you, and, though I no longer believed that you would have me transported – or any of the other dreadful punishments I had envisioned over the years – I knew you would be terribly angry, and rightfully so, and I had come to look on you as a friend. I—'

'Oh, my god!' March's voice was a harsh rasp. 'Cut line. You do not know what the word "friend" means. It is useless for you to deny that you were in a conspiracy with Jack Crawford – or that you intended to cheat the other players tonight at the faro table.'

'No!' The cry seemed to burn her throat. 'I had no idea. . . ! You cannot believe that I marked those cards!'

'Of course, you did not!' he spat. 'Your good friend arranged that for you. My dear Miss Fox, I saw you accept those cards from Crawford last night at the Upper Rooms.'

Alison stared at him in horror, a tide of deep red flooding her cheeks. Very slowly, she rose from her seat. She moved with difficulty, as though she had been mortally wounded, to a small table near the window. Turning to the earl, she whispered, 'Yes, I did take those cards from Jack, but I never had any intention of using them. I thrust them in my reticule and forgot about them until I started to leave the house tonight. When I descended the stairs, I became aware of their weight.' Opening a drawer in the

173

table, she pulled out a small packet and thrust it at the earl. 'Here, my lord, are the cards I received from Jack last night.'

March gazed at the packet, speechless. His gaze lifted to meet Alison's, and still he could say nothing. When he finally spoke, his voice was loud and uncertain. 'I suppose you left an extra deck in there. You must have several of them, after all. I wish you would cease trying to cozen me.'

Despite the warmth of the May evening, and the small fire burning cheerfully in the hearth, Alison felt numb with cold. For a long moment, she listened to the silence of the room, broken only by the crackling of the little blaze and the ticking of a clock somewhere behind her.

With an almost unbearable effort, she looked into March's eyes. 'Then there is no more to be said, my lord, except for you to tell me what you plan to do now.'

March shifted his shoulders heavily. 'I must tell my aunt, of course. After that, your fate is in her hands. I cannot imagine that after tomorrow morning, she will retain you in her employ, but that is for her to say. In all likelihood, you will very shortly find yourself out of a position and out of this house.'

A terrible trembling began deep within Alison. He was serious! He would actually see her turned into the street without a character, with no way to earn an honest living. She had known in her mind that his anger would be painful, but in her heart she had not believed he would be so utterly vindictive. She could only stare at him, unbelieving.

March turned to pace the carpet for a moment before swinging back to her. Abruptly, he said, 'I wish I could believe you, Alison. Truth to tell, I do not bear you the animosity I once felt. In fact,' he added casually, 'I have been considering placing you under my protection after you leave my aunt. You are quite lovely, you know.' He placed a hand under her chin. 'Would you like to live in a fine house in London?'

March listened in astonishment to the careless cruelty of his own words. Good God, what had possessed him to say such a thing? Make Alison his mistress? Something unholy in him stirred in response at the thought. For a small eternity he found himself hoping she would agree, even as the shame of what he'd asked overwhelmed him. Her face was perfectly white. She swayed, and, unthinking, he put out a hand to her. The next moment, however, she steadied, and her tone when she spoke a few moments later was prosaic.

'I think not, my lord.' Her mouth twisted in a credible imitation of a smile. 'My future is quite secure. I have had a similar offer from Jack, you see, who promises me I shall be quite useful to him. It is so pleasant to feel useful, don't you think? And to occupy oneself in something one is good at.' She moved with careful precision toward the door. 'Now, if you will excuse me, my lord, I shall retire. Tomorrow promises to be a busy day.'

March put out a hand to her. 'Alison. . . .' he whispered. But she was gone.

CHAPTER 18

'You know?' The question burst from March as though expelled by a blow to his gut. He faced Lady Edith in the small room adjacent to her bedchamber that she used as a study. Morning sun streamed through the window, tinting cream-colored hangings to rose. 'You *know* Alison Fox is really Lissa Reynard? I don't understand. How. . . .'

'She told me shortly after she came to me. I happened to mention your name one day, and I thought she was going to faint. When I asked her what was troubling her, the whole story came tumbling out.'

'And you didn't tell me?' March's face was a mask of agonized bewilderment. '*Why*? You knew I'd been searching for her!' He let his gaze stray over her countenance, observing the weariness in her eyes and the unhealthy flush in her thin cheeks. He had found it more difficult than he could have anticipated to break the news of Alison's perfidy to his aunt. Now, told that she'd known all along, he felt betrayed anew.

'Because I knew you would react precisely as you are doing,' she replied calmly. 'And because I promised Alison I would not. It took a great deal of courage for her to confide in me, you know. She expected to be turned out on her ear, or handed to you on a salver.'

'And why wasn't she? Turned out on her ear. My God, Aunt, did the deaths of William and Susannah mean nothing to you? And my father. . . ?'

'Of course, they did,' Lady Edith snapped. 'As for your father – I remind you he was my brother, and his pain was my own.'

She seemed to shrink physically into the damask armchair in which she was seated. After a moment, she continued in a milder tone, though her veined hands remained clenched in her lap.

'Sit down, my dear. It is time you were told a few home truths about William and Susannah – and perhaps yourself.'

Almost without volition, March did as he was told, staring at his aunt as though she had drawn a pistol from the folds of her skirt and pointed it at him.

'March,' she began, 'how well did you know Susannah?'

'What?' he responded blankly. 'Quite well, of course. That is . . . well, I saw quite a bit of her during her first Season, when she became betrothed to Will.'

'But did you ever really talk to her?'

'Well, of course I did.' March paused, frowning. 'N-no,' he continued slowly, 'I guess I didn't. Not really. I only saw her with Will, or with a number of other people. Why do you ask?'

'What was your impression of Susannah?'

March lifted an impatient hand. 'She seemed a good enough girl. A little flighty – spoiled – somewhat self-centered. Aunt. . . ?'

Lady Edith inclined her head in a frail gesture. 'I promise you I have a reason for all this, my dear. Were you very close to William in your growing up years?' At his uncomprehending nod, she continued quietly. 'And what is your assessment of his character?'

March stared at his aunt, and it was several moments before he responded to her question. 'I suppose,' he said slowly, 'he was a great deal like Susannah. I loved him dearly, but there is no denying he was a care-for-nobody – as was I at the time, truth to be told. He was basically decent, but wild to a fault, indulging in all the vices of a young man about town – cards, women, the bottle. But after he married' – his gaze sharpened – 'I left for the continent shortly after they married, but surely he settled down – did he not?' He frowned again, remembering his father's fretful letters.

'No, he did not, March. He left his young wife completely

177

alone while he continued his carousing – and his philandering. Susannah was terribly hurt by his neglect, and she was devastated by his womanizing. As you say, she had been spoiled all her life, and she did not suffer his slights in silence.

'She treated him to public tantrums to no effect, and then fell in with a set of persons who might have been created for the sole purpose of ruining her. Her name became a byword, and it was rumored that she changed lovers as she would her slippers. I do not know if this is true. I do know she became addicted to gambling in its worst forms. At every fashionable event, she arrived alone and would disappear immediately into the card room, emerging in the small hours of the morning, her purse disastrously lighter than when she came in.'

'My God,' whispered March, stunned, 'didn't Will make any effort to stop her?'

'He apparently did not care what she did until her losses became too large to ignore. She dipped deeply into her own funds, and when those were exhausted, she began selling family jewels and stealing money from her husband's purse. I was not privy to their discussions on the subject, of course, but your father told me of late-night quarrels filled with loud recriminations and vituperative insults – on both sides.

'I cannot say I knew nothing of this.' March's face was gray. 'Father begged me to stay home, and I would not. I was so damned anxious to escape the duties of a peer's son ... He wrote something of Susannah's escapades and mentioned Will's ruinous behavior, but I thought he was exaggerating, with the purpose of bringing me home. Or, at least, that's what I told myself. God, I should have listened. I should have come home.'

'What could you have done?' asked Lady Edith gently. 'Was William in the habit of listening to you?'

'Of course he was,' came the instant response. Then, March paused. 'Well, actually he usually came to me for advice after he was already in trouble. The few times I tried to counsel him against some piece of folly, he just laughed at me, saying it would be like a toper taking advice from the village drunkard.'

'Well then, if William would not listen to his father, was it likely that he would have paid attention to your strictures?'

'Perhaps not, but . . .' He shook his head. 'No wonder Susannah fell prey so easily to Lissa Reynard.'

The signs of fatigue on Lady Edith's lined face were obvious, but she straightened in her chair. 'It is my firm belief that Susannah was not Miss Reynard's prey, March. After her death, I spoke at some length with Susannah's maid and with some of the other servants of her household. At any rate, by now, Susannah was in dire straits. She began to frequent all the notorious hells in town, and before long, put herself deeply in debt. From what I have been able to determine, in order to excuse her excesses, she spread it about that the Reynard woman had cheated her out of thousands of pounds. At last William came to a sense of his duty, and prepared to bundle Susannah away to the park—'

March grimaced. 'But none of the family lived there at the time.'

'No. William hired a companion. A sour old woman, big as a navvy, who was obviously chosen to act as jailer.'

'I suppose Susannah was not happy about this state of affairs.'

Lady Edith's mouth turned up in a ghastly smile. 'No. She ran away with one of her lovers – or she was all set to do so, but her plan was discovered before she could put it into effect. That was when Will said he would accompany her himself to Marchford Park.'

Her veined hands shaking, the old woman put a hand to her head. 'A storm came up shortly after they set out, and it was still raining by the time they reached the river. Susannah's maid, who had accompanied her mistress, reported later that Susannah had worked herself into a fit of hysterics by then. Just as they reached the bridge outside Little Marchbeck, she wrenched open the carriage door and leapt out into the night. She scrambled up the bridge's stone railing and turned to scream something at William. I truly believe she was only trying to scare him, but when William went after her, she stepped back out of his reach. The next moment, she had disappeared over the side of the bridge. To his credit, William did not hesitate a

179

moment, but jumped into the swollen stream after her. That was the last time they were seen alive.' Lady Edith's voice was a rasping whisper as she finished.

'And all this time, I was busying myself with the affairs of the world,' said March, his eyes empty. 'I should have been here.'

'But you were not,' replied his aunt. 'You were living your own life, as you had every right to do.'

March rose abruptly. 'Be that as it may, if I had followed Father's behest, I could at least have spared Susannah the machinations of such as Lissa Reynard.'

At this, Lady Edith rose to her feet. She tipped her snowy head back to stare belligerently at her nephew. 'I am about to lose patience with you, March. You are so blinded by your own guilt, so eager to find a scapegrace for the deaths of William and Susannah – and your father – that you have lost the power to see reason.'

March whitened. 'You are very dear to me, Aunt,' he said stiffly. 'But, I will allow no one to talk like that to me.'

'Then, it's time you did,' snapped the old woman. Trembling visibly, she walked to the door, where she turned to add querulously, 'You are making a grave mistake in thinking her guilty of the deaths of Susannah and William. She is innocent of wrongdoing – as are you.'

After she had left the room, March listened to the soft sound of her receding footsteps. He stood for some moments, staring sightlessly at the carpet, before striding out of the room and into the silent corridor. In a mindless daze, he collected hat, cane, and gloves when he reached the hall, and exited the house.

He crossed the street and, striding away from Royal Crescent, he plunged into the parkland and fields bordering the city. He did not stop until he flung himself, exhausted, to the ground beneath a tree overlooking the village of Little Weston.

He felt as though the world had exploded beneath him, leaving him adrift in a midnight void. The vendetta he had nursed to his bosom with such persistence was dissolving in his grasp. Alison denied all, and his aunt, whom he knew to be a woman of great perspicacity, believed her implicitly. Believed her as he so desperately wanted to do.

He thought back to his aunt's words. His guilt? Was that really why he had pursued Lissa Reynard with such driven perseverance? Beneath his rage at what had been done to his family, was there an underlying theme that had tortured him all this time? He had admitted long ago that he was partly to blame for the tragedy that had befallen his family, but had he sought an additional scapegoat? Had he singled out Lissa Reynard for vengeance in order to ease his own conscience?

Even if that were the case, it surely did not excuse Alison's part in all of it. But just what was her part? He stared blindly at the columns of smoke issuing from chimneys in the village below him. That was the nub of the problem, wasn't it? If Alison was telling the truth, his house of cards was even now tumbling about him in ruins. Everything in him cried out that of course she was telling the truth. Her sincerity had proclaimed itself in her every word, gesture, and action. To be sure, the facts about her as he knew them had not changed. She had gone to London to gamble. She had won money from his sister-in-law, and she had covered up her activities by fleeing the city. Everything else he wanted to believe about her would have to be taken on faith.

He drew a deep breath. He had put away the follies of his youth and had spent the last four years of his life living as an eminently practical, dutiful man. He had grown cynical and worldly, and he had almost become affianced to a woman who would drive him to screaming boredom inside of a fortnight. Had all this been an overreaction to his previous carelessness, which he believed had cost the lives of three people?

Now, another life had opened up for him. He had been given the opportunity to release himself from the guilt that had caged him for four years.

He loved Alison Fox. At last he was able to answer this thought, for he now realized with blinding clarity that she was worthy of all the love a man could give her, and any man that could win her heart was blessed beyond measure.

Another thought struck him, one not nearly so pleasant. Unfortunately, that man would not be him. She had gone in

181

terror of him for a long time, and she had opened herself to him last night, only to be insulted and, in the end, crudely propositioned. He still could not believe he had invited her to be his mistress – and in such a manner, as though he had only to crook his finger and she would hurl herself with becoming gratitude into the dubious haven of his protection. She had mentioned friendship. God, he wanted that from her and so much more. He wanted to be her friend, her lover, and most of all her husband. His thoughts drifted into a rosy fantasy of early mornings with her hair spread out on the pillow next to him, of late-night wine sipped by the fire, of intimate murmurings on long walks at Marchford Park.

He shook himself abruptly. Lord, he must be going round the bend. Friendship had been all he could ever have hoped for from her, and now he had ruined even that possibility. She had not even deigned to tell him that she had no need to consider his despicable offer, that her position with his aunt was secure. He had not even been given a chance to recant his threat – to tell her that he had no intention of seeing her thrown into the street. Would she believe him now if he told her that even if his aunt was prepared to act on his words, he would persuade her not to discharge Alison? Would it make any difference to her? He shook his head, and the next moment his breath caught in sudden memory. What was it she had said about Jack Crawford? He, too, had made her an offer? The taste of bile rose in his throat, which, he conceded a moment later, was clearly ludicrous. If Jack had, in fact, made her an indecent proposal, it was no more than he had done himself. And, surely, it was no more likely to be accepted than the one he had made. It was clear she held Jack Crawford in as much disfavor as she did the Earl of Marchford. God, what a mull he had made of everything.

What was he to do now? He must apologize, of course. Perhaps, for Aunt Edith's sake, she would listen to him. He would go back to Royal Crescent that afternoon. He would speak to her then, and to his aunt, offering his apology and his assurances of support in the future. Then he would announce his departure from Bath the next day. He would, in all probability, never see Alison Fox again. He grunted involuntarily at the stab of anguish this prospect caused him, but it was probably all to the good.

He would return to Marchford Park. He realized suddenly that he was weary to death of London and all that living there entailed – the stuffy parties at which he was obliged to appear, the duty visits, the obligatory appearances at the theater and the opera. And Frances.

March sighed heavily. He would have to marry eventually, for the closest heir to the title at present was a ne'er-do-well cousin living in the Indies. However, he would do himself a favor and pass on Frances Milford. It had only been his exaggerated sense of duty that had forced him to dance attendance on her. No, he rather thought he would hie himself to Almack's and pluck some seventeen-year-old bud from next year's crop of eager debutantes – a biddable miss, who could be counted on to present him with the requisite heir 'and one to spare,' and to leave him to his own devices.

Contemplating this laudable course of action with the most profound depression, he hauled himself to his feet. The morning sun was now high in the sky, but, as he retraced his steps with dragging feet, he took little comfort in its warmth.

In Royal Crescent, the sunlight streamed through the window of Meg's bedchamber. That young lady lay propped up on a mound of pillows, sipping a cup of broth as she expostulated with Alison, who sat at her side.

'But, I feel quite well now,' she said in a martyred tone. 'I'm a little weak, but I believe I am fully recovered. Could I please have something to eat? I mean real food, not this stuff.' She indicated the broth with a disdainful gesture.

'Later,' replied Alison with a smile. 'The doctor said that if you keep the broth down during the day, you may have a light meal this evening.'

Meg sighed into her pillows and said in that case she would take a nap. 'For I am still rather tired,' she admitted.

Alison tucked the quilt about the suffering patient, and, gathering up the empty bowl and a half-finished glass of barley water, tiptoed from the room.

In the hallway, after setting the utensils on a table for later collection by one of the maids, she paused irresolutely. There were a hundred small tasks demanding her attention but she could not seem to focus on a single one of them. She felt curiously hollow inside, as though someone had scooped out her heart with a crude instrument. Last night, after she had left March in the library, she had wept until there were no more tears to cry. Now, she felt detached, and void of emotion.

She glanced at the closed door to Lady Edith's chamber. From her window, she had observed March's departure from the house early this morning and was thus aware that he had returned to divulge his supposedly earth-shaking news to his aunt. The thought of the short shrift he must have received at Lady Edith's hands brought a grim smile to her lips.

She turned to make her way downstairs, but was stayed by the opening of Lady Edith's door. The old lady emerged a moment afterward, looking pale but composed. She nodded good morning to Alison, then gestured for her to come into the room. 'We have a good deal to talk about,' she said somberly.

Alison experienced a chill of apprehension at Lady Edith's demeanor. Was it possible that, after all, March had convinced his aunt that her companion was not fit to reside in her house? Her fears were dispelled a moment later when Lady Edith turned and drew her into a gentle embrace.

'Oh, my dear,' said the old lady in a trembling voice, 'I am so sorry to have brought such trouble upon you.'

'You?' gasped Alison in astonishment. 'My lady, you have been my salvation!'

'Perhaps,' responded the old woman grimly, 'but if it were not for me, my misguided nephew would never have discovered your existence.'

'And a very good thing he did.' Alison was pleased that her voice remained firm. 'Otherwise I never would have cleared the record with Lord Marchford. At least now he has heard my side of the story.'

'Mpf. For all the good it has done him.' She sighed wearily. 'March was always the most reasonable of men – I have never known him to be so intractable.'

'I suppose . . .' began Alison hesitantly. 'I suppose he was still very angry.'

Lady Edith smiled sourly. 'You could say that. Then, when I ruined the grand climax of his plan by telling him that I Knew All, he was like a bear with a thorn in his toe.' The smile faded. 'I had so hoped he would believe you.'

'I did, too,' said Alison, 'but I might have known better.' Her throat lightened again, and Lady Edith, observing the tears glittering in Alison's eyes, placed a hand on her arm.

'There, there, my dear. It is over now. Perhaps when March has cooled down – when he has considered all that he has learned. . . . It is not easy to have one's dearly held convictions turned upside down in the span of a few hours. Given time, I am sure he will come to his senses.'

Alison drew a deep breath, then put her hand over the one that lay on her arm. 'Well,' she said briskly, 'none of it really matters, does it? Your nephew is no doubt a – a fine man, but he means nothing to me, after all. As long as I am still in your good graces, all is well with the world.' She affixed a bright smile to her lips and drew her employer from her chair. 'I heard the postman's whistle a few moments ago. I should imagine he has brought us a clutch of acceptances for your dinner party. Shall we go see?'

Lady Edith eyed the young woman shrewdly, but said nothing, merely allowing herself to be escorted downstairs with good grace.

CHAPTER 19

Alison had managed to hold her anguish at bay for most of the afternoon, but now, as she faced the earl once more, it washed over her in such crushing waves that she thought she must sink to the floor under the weight of it.

It was perhaps fortunate that Meg still lingered in her room, for on his arrival, March had sought an audience with Lady Edith and Alison. In halting phrases, he spoke of his regret over the misunderstanding which had caused him to pursue Alison with such single-minded fury. His apology for having placed her in an untenable position with Jack Crawford was undoubtedly heartfelt, and Alison had no difficulty in accepting his assertions of future goodwill.

She should have been ecstatic. She was free now. Free of the threat of vengeance that had hung over her for so long, and free of Jack's importunities. Certainly, Lady Edith had experienced no difficulty in accepting March's apology.

'Nonsense, my dear boy,' said the old lady, her eyes shining in relief and happiness. 'I have already told you that your anger was completely understandable – and I'm sure Alison feels the same way. After all' – she shot a glance at Alison – 'if the naughty girl had gone to you at the very beginning, all this – unpleasantness might have been avoided.' Alison bent her head stiffly in a nod of agreement. 'There,' continued Lady Edith joyfully. 'We need not thrash it over anymore, then, for we are all friends again.'

But there was so much more, cried Alison silently. She stared at the man seated before her in Lady Edith's drawing room. Had it really been only a fortnight since she had faced him for the first time, telling herself that he was a perfectly ordinary man? Even then, she had been drawn into those golden eyes. She loved him. He was no doubt the only man she would ever love, yet last night she had listened as he expressed his complete indifference to what was to become of her. And, in his disgust of her, he had made a contemptible proposal.

'Will you pour us some wine, March?' Lady Edith spoke in the high, pleased voice of a little girl. 'I think we have something to celebrate.' She stopped, gazing questioningly at her nephew.

March's eyes had not left Alison for some moments, but now he looked at Lady Edith.

'Aunt,' he said softly, 'may I be private with Miss Fox for a few moments? There is still something I must say to her.'

Lady Edith's hand flew to her mouth. 'Oh, dear. I don't—' She shot a glance at Alison, who hesitated before nodding once more in acquiescence. 'Very well. But don't be long. Meg will be coming down soon, and. . . .' She did not finish the sentence, but left the room with a single backward look and closed the door quietly behind her.

'Please,' said March. 'Sit down.'

Alison, who had risen with Lady Edith, dropped back into her chair, her body rigid. March seated himself nearby, but rose almost immediately to pace the carpet before her. After a moment, he turned to face her. He looked, thought Alison, as though he had not slept well. Sharp lines were drawn along his cheeks and the square jaw that had so caught her attention was tense and rigid.

'I'm a little at a loss as to how to proceed,' he said, smiling uncertainly, 'for I am about to ask you to forgive me for the unforgivable.'

Alison stiffened and drew about her the cloak of indifference she was beginning to discover was the best defense against the pain of her feelings for the earl. She lifted her brows and said nothing.

March began again. 'First of all, let me say again that I am truly sorry for the anguish I have put you through for the past four years.

187

Alison answered coolly. (Really, she thought, pleased, she was getting very good at this.) 'My lord, if all that you suspected of me had been true, you had every right to be angry.'

'But to pursue you with such rage, to vow vengeance against you—'

'I am sure it was understandable under the circumstances,' she replied hastily. Dear Lord, why could he just not leave it be? 'If I suspected you of driving someone I loved to his or her death, I might have reacted in the same fashion.'

'Perhaps, but I doubt it, for you lack my single-minded vindictiveness.' The irony in his tone was plain, and Alison was in no danger of mistaking his meaning. 'In addition, you do not know quite all of it. You see, I did not plan to divulge your identity to my aunt. Oh no,' he continued sourly, observing the surprise in her eyes, 'my original plan was to see you revealed before that crowd of lovelies last night as a card cheat. There were enough "gentlemen" in the room so that I was sure the tale would reach Aunt Edith's ears in a matter of hours.'

The torment in March's gaze sparked a corresponding ache within her breast. 'Yes, my hatred burned that strongly. Yet, I had come to consider you my friend. I know in my heart you were not the harpy I had thought you, and when I saw you, standing alone and defenseless among that scum, I could not allow you to be so demeaned.'

Alison leaned forward. 'Tell me something, my lord. If you had not come to know me, would you still have abandoned me to my fate at the High Flyer?'

The air about them seem to change imperceptibly, as though the atmosphere had become charged with electricity. The intensity of March's gaze was almost unbearable.

'At this point,' he answered slowly, 'I like to think that I would not, but I don't know. I just . . . don't know.'

Alison sat back, distantly pleased at his honesty. He had called her 'friend.' Friendship – with March? Oh yes, she remembered. Once she had thought she could be satisfied with being his friend. She clenched her hands in her lap.

'I have already told you, my lord, there is nothing to forgive.

That is not to say the . . . the episode was not most unpleasant, but Lady Edith is quite correct in calling it a misunderstanding – a most unfortunate misunderstanding.'

'And my insult to you last night?' March ran his fingers through his hair. 'Please forgive me, Alison, when I tell you that I had no intention of allowing you to be turned out of my aunt's employ. As for my offer to make you my . . . that is, to take you under my protection, came as much as a surprise to me as it no doubt did to you. Again, it was my hatred talking. Oh, God, Alison' – he flung himself into the chair next to her and took her hand in his – 'I had come to admire you – and to respect you. I liked you! Then to discover that you were in reality the woman I loathed most in the world . . . I felt betrayed.'

Alison stirred, forcing herself to ignore the warmth of March's hand and the swirl of sensation that emanated from the spot where his thumb absently stroked her flesh. She spoke through dry lips. 'I am . . . very sorry about that deception, my lord. I had come to like you as well.' Lord, what a pallid turn of phrase, she thought despairingly. 'I deeply regretted the lie I lived, but, as I said. . . .' She wrenched her hand from his and he stood once more, as though she had struck him.

'Yes,' he said quietly. 'So you said. You were afraid.' He moved to the window and looked blindly out at the traffic moving along Royal Crescent. After a moment, he turned back to her, a twisted smile making its way over his lips.

'Then, as you also said last night, there is no more to be said. Except—' he hesitated and swallowed hard, 'if at any time in the future, you need a friend, please remember me. I will be here for you.' He paused again and the air once more shimmered about them, almost crackling with something Alison dared not put a name to. March continued at last. 'I shall be leaving Bath tomorrow.' His voice was brisk and prosaic except for the slight crack that could be heard in its depths. 'In all likelihood I shall not see you again.' When she lifted her hand, he took a quick step forward. 'What is it?' he asked, in a tone that seemed strangely hopeful.

'Your aunt . . . she is expecting you at her dinner party in two

189

days' time. She is holding it just for you, you know, and has invited her closest friends.' Alison smiled, albeit rather painfully. 'She wants to show you off.'

'Oh, God. In that case, I suppose I'll have to stay. Will you mind terribly?'

Alison shook her head mutely. Another lie. She would mind. Terribly. She needed to get the Earl of Marchford out of her life before he created any more chaos. Even more, she needed to get on with her mundane existence, to forget him completely – to erase from her heart for all time his warmth and his intelligence and his decency, not to mention those magnetic, sleepy-lion eyes.

March took her hand once more, for the merest moment. He bent to press a brief kiss on her fingertips, and then he was gone. Alison resisted the urge to move to the window to watch his retreating figure, and stood for some moments in the center of the room, her fingers pressed to her lips.

Some hours later, Alison sat with Lady Edith in the drawing room. Her friend, thought Alison, looked ten years younger than she had at this time the day before. She hummed happily over her embroidery, pausing every now and again to issue a suggestion for the upcoming dinner party. Abruptly, she set her work aside and beamed at her companion.

'Alison, I must say it again. I am so pleased that this dreadful matter between you and March is over. What did he say to you after I left – if the matter was not private?'

'Of course not, my lady. The earl merely apologized again for his behavior. He . . . he offered to stand friend for me if I should need one.'

'Oh. Is that all?'

'Why, yes. I thought it most generous of him. Do not you?'

'Um, of course. I had hoped . . . Oh, it's nothing. I am indulging in a silly whim,' she said, laughing, in response to Alison's lifted brows. 'Now, tell me what you plan to wear Thursday night. I believe I shall wear my violet silk with the silver trim, so perhaps you should consider your rose sarcenet.

It's most becoming, although I think the hem could stand another flounce. Meg says—'

She was interrupted by the entrance of a footman, who brought the information that a visitor awaited downstairs.

'It's Mr Crawford, ma'am,' he said. 'He's brought a bouquet for Lady Margaret.'

'What?' gasped Lady Edith and Alison in unison.

'I cannot believe that rogue would have the nerve to show his face here,' said Lady Edith, trembling with indignation. 'Tell him we are not receiving, Blickling.'

'No!' interjected Alison. 'That is,' she continued in a quieter tone, 'I would like to speak with him, my lady. I have much to say to him.'

'I daresay,' said Lady Edith. 'But surely you do not wish to be alone with him. Do you want me to join you?'

'No. Thank you, my lady, but I see no reason why you should be subjected to his presence. What I have to say will not take long, and certainly, there is nothing he can do to me in your home.'

'Very well, my dear. I shall leave you then. Show him up, Blickling.' She hurried from the room, turning at the door to add, 'I shall leave my door ajar, Alison. All you have to do is call.'

Amused despite herself, Alison nodded gravely, and arranged her skirts against the sofa on which she sat. When Jack Crawford was ushered into the room a few moments later, she knew herself to be the picture of assured respectability.

'Alison!' Jack halted at the threshold in surprise. 'You are all right?'

'Yes, quite. Lady Edith is upstairs, and Meg has not left her chamber as yet. I shall give her your flowers.'

'Never mind that,' said Jack, hurrying to seat himself beside her, leaving the flowers lying forgotten on a nearby table. 'It is you I wished to see. Last night ... what in God's name happened?'

'Behold me unmasked,' replied Alison, smiling grimly. 'Tell me, Jack, were those marked cards your doing?'

'Yes, of course. I gave you those cards. Do you not remember?'

Alison gritted her teeth. 'No, Jack. As I told you, I never had any intention of using them. I left the deck you gave me behind. I thought perhaps you had somehow discovered this and slipped in a new deck for me.' She shrugged. 'It must have been one of the other players or perhaps the dealer. I should imagine the High Flyer is not too nice in its methods.'

'Never mind about that,' cried Jack, shrugging with impatience. 'I want to know about Marchford. What was he doing there, and why did he scoop you up in such a fashion?' He stopped suddenly. 'Unmasked? What do you mean, unmasked?'

'Just what I said, Jack. His lordship has known for some time that I am – was – Lissa Reynard.'

Alison watched with detached interest as Jack digested this piece of news. 'But you are still here,' he said in blank bewilderment. 'Did he not—?'

'Punish me? No. We have come to . . . an agreement.' She lifted a hand against the questions she could see writhing on his lips. 'And that is all I propose to say on the matter. I am still in Lady Edith's employ, where I shall probably stay for some time to come.'

Slowly, Jack's narrow gaze made the transition from puzzlement, to comprehension, to alarm. Alison smiled unpleasantly. 'I see you have come to the nub of the situation, Jack. You no longer have any hold over me. It is with great pleasure that I must insist you leave this house, now, and do not return.'

'But, Alison – you promised! What am I to do?'

'I promised nothing. I gave in to your coercion, and now I am no longer obliged to do so. For Beth's sake, my offer of a loan still stands, but that is as far as I am prepared to go. I advise you to take my hundred pounds and leave the country.' She rose, preparing to usher him from the room. Instead, Jack sprang to face her, grasping her by the shoulders.

'Don't you understand, you stupid little—?' He drew a deep breath. 'Alison, I must have that money. My life won't be worth a tinker's damn if I don't pony up. You've got to help me!'

Alison disengaged herself from Jack's grip. 'I have already offered to help you, Jack,' she said coldly. 'If you choose not to avail yourself of my offer, that is your own doing. Frankly, any sympathy I might have had for your plight dissolved quite some time ago. Now, will you leave, or must I summon a footman to assist you in your departure?'

For an instant, Jack did not move, and Alison knew a moment of alarm at the ugliness that flared in his pale gaze. Then, he flung her away from him and stepped back, his face whiter than his modish shirtpoints. His eyes glittered malevolently.

'No,' he said in a choked whisper. 'You need not call anyone. I will leave, and may God damn you to hell, Alison Fox!'

He whirled and lurched unsteadily through the door. Numb with shock, Alison moved toward the door herself, feeling a need to assure herself that he was really departing.

'Why, Mr Crawford, I did not know you had come to visit!'

Alison listened in horror to Meg's laughing welcome. She hurried into the corridor to see Meg crossing the floor to intercept Jack. For one terrifying moment, Alison thought he would strike the girl in his mindless rage, but to her astonishment, he halted, his contorted features transforming themselves instantly into a charming smile.

'Lady Meg! You are up and about. I expected to be told you were still abed with the collywobbles, but I see the roses have returned to your cheeks. This is good news, indeed!'

To Alison's annoyance, Meg's roses deepened perceptibly as she dropped a self-conscious curtsy to Jack.

'Yes, I am much better, thank you, Mr Crawford. I am so glad you are here, for I wanted to thank you for coming to my rescue yesterday.'

'It was my pleasure.' Jack's leg came forward in a sweeping bow. 'Rescuing damsels in distress is my specialty.'

Meg giggled adorably. 'But you are not leaving? Did Alison offer you tea?'

'Mr Crawford has an engagement,' interrupted Alison tersely. 'He must be on his way.'

Meg's face fell. 'Oh, that is too bad. But perhaps you will return another time?'

Before Jack could respond to this artless invitation, Alison put a hand on his arm and, pinching it meaningfully, urged him down the stairs and out of the house. Jack turned to wave laughingly at Meg. 'Yes, indeed – another time!'

'Really, Alison,' said Meg after he had left, 'you were almost rude to Mr Crawford!'

'He had already informed me he was in a hurry. He left flowers for you,' Alison added reluctantly. She gestured to the drawing room.

'Ooh!' Meg hurried away, returning in a moment with the blossoms in her arms. 'How very thoughtful of him, to be sure. I have never received flowers from a gentleman before.'

And you still have not, breathed Alison to herself. Meg continued to burble on, unheeding. 'I expect he will return soon, don't you?'

'I rather think not. Mr Crawford informed me he has many matters demanding his attention just now.'

Meg merely smiled knowingly and skipped down the stairs. Alison hurried away to inform Masters that under no circumstances was Jack Crawford to be admitted again to the house.

As Jack strode away from Royal Crescent toward his lodgings with Giles Morganton in the Paragon Buildings, he was in something of a taking. Giles was not going to be pleased with the events that had just taken place. In fact, he dreaded facing Giles, and as he walked along George Street, his pace slowed. Thus, it was perhaps not surprising that the gentleman standing in a window in York House noted Mr Crawford dawdling in front of the hostelry.

A few moments later, Jack's attention was claimed by a voice behind him, and turning, he beheld the Earl of Marchford. He knew a moment's panic and was obliged to suppress a strong desire to take himself elsewhere with all possible speed, but the earl's voice held only cordiality as he invited Jack to join him in a heavy wet. Every instinct urged him to refuse, but his reluctance to return to his abode overcame his unease, and it was with a reasonable show of nonchalance that he followed the earl into the dark interior of the York House taproom. The few customers ensconced in the inn's comfortable chairs did not lift their heads as the two men passed.

Jack settled warily into a seat opposite the earl. Neither man spoke until two sweating tankards of ale had been set before them.

'I understand you'll be leaving Bath soon, Mr Crawford,' said March in his blandest voice.

'What? Leaving Bath? Well, I don't know – I hadn't planned. . . .'

'I'd start planning, if I were you.' The blandness had left March's tone, and Jack sat up very straight. 'Your presence in this city,' continued the earl, and in his quiet voice Jack heard death, 'seems extremely detrimental to the well-being of a friend of mine, and I do not want to see her disturbed any further.'

Jack took refuge in bluster. 'I can't think what you are talking about,' he said, shifting uncomfortably in his seat. 'Nor do I intend to be dictated to.'

'Then you are very unwise,' replied March silkily. His demeanor changed abruptly. 'Crawford, you are a toad, and I will not have you trouble Alison Fox's peace of mind for so much as another instant. If you are not out of Bath by tomorrow evening, several critical portions of your anatomy will come in for severe disrepair. Do I make myself clear?'

Jack, not to put too fine a point on it, simply sat back in his chair and goggled.

'B-but, I thought. I mean – I would think you'd be busy destroying Alison Fox, now that you've found out she's really—'

'My relationship with Miss Fox is none of your concern,' March interrupted coldly. 'I asked if I had made myself clear, and since you have not answered, perhaps I should be more plain.'

With a swift motion, he reached across the table and, grasping Jack's cravat, lifted him out of his chair. He twisted his fist into Jack's throat, and the young man's face crumpled like a pricked balloon.

'*Urk*!' he uttered. '*Gtchchch*!' He sank back into his chair, gasping as March released him with a contemptuous shake. His eyes bulged, froglike, as he put a hand to his throat. 'Y-yes,' he half sobbed. 'Yes, you have m-made yourself clear.'

'Good.' Rising, March nodded pleasantly. 'In that case, I shall bid you good afternoon.' In the next moment, he was gone, leaving Jack to stare after him, his expression a blend of fear and hatred.

CHAPTER 20

March stood in the center of his sitting room at York House gazing pensively at the fireplace. The interview with Jack Crawford had provided him with some degree of satisfaction, though not as much, he reflected with fingers bunched into fists, as if he had ground Crawford's face into the wooden table and then knocked him to the floor.

The next moment he shrugged. What right had he to punish Crawford, when the snake had done no more damage to Alison Fox than he himself had accomplished. His mouth twisted in an ironic smile. Of course, his own motives had been pure, so that made everything all right, did it not?

He flung himself into a chair. Alison had forgiven him – so she said – but that did not relieve his conscience, or the ache that continued to grow in him at the knowledge that he loved a woman he could never have. He would be very fortunate if she would so much as allow him to be her friend. God, he was coming to hate that word.

What was she doing now? he wondered idly. Something for somebody else, he'd wager. Making arrangements for Aunt Edith's dinner party, or accompanying Meg on a shopping trip. He pictured her in bonnet and pelisse, swinging through the streets of Bath, her cheeks flushed and those great blue eyes sparkling with enjoyment. Lord, would he ever get over wanting her? He shook his head. It was like wondering if he would get over needing to breathe.

He toyed briefly with the idea of strolling to the Pump Room later in the day in the hope of encountering her. No. He had promised to stay out of her way. He would just have to contain himself until Thursday evening. She would undoubtedly be fully occupied at the famous dinner party in ensuring the comfort and pleasure of his aunt's guests, but if he was lucky, and very persistent, he might be able to take her away from her duties for a few moments. A few moments that would have to see him through the rest of his life.

Thursday seemed a long way off.

As it happened, Alison was engaged in a somewhat less enjoyable task than shopping. She was seated at the dining parlor table with Mrs Hopgood, Lady Edith's plump, capable housekeeper. Glancing for a last time over the menu the two had devised, she rose and stretched. 'Well, I believe that does it. The house looks beautiful, Mrs H. You've had the staff busy, and it shows. My, if the chandelier lusters were polished any higher, they'd blind our guests.'

Mrs Hopgood straightened, blossoming from the praise, then rose from the table with a murmur of thanks and departed the room.

Alison remained behind for a moment, her thoughts turning to Thursday's engagement. Try as she might, she pictured one guest in this room above all others. March would, as always, look magnificent in evening dress, and the candlelight would turn his brandy-colored eyes to gold. Would those eyes seek her out? She tried to suppress the idea, for she knew her salvation lay in staying clear of March on Thursday night. Thank God he would be gone soon, she repeated for the hundredth time. Lady Edith would undoubtedly travel to London for his wedding, but Alison was determined not to accompany her.

Another, even more terrible idea occurred to her. Please God, March would not bring his bride on a duty call to his aunt. She did not think she could stand that. She must simply make it her business to avoid March on Thursday night. In fact, it would be better not to speak to him at all before he left.

But she knew she would be unable to follow her own advice. She wanted desperately to see him once more . . . to say good-bye to him with her heart.

She wished it were not so long until Thursday.

Even a two-day eternity must eventually pass, and after only a year or so, Thursday dawned, clear and sunny and warm. Alison found herself heavily occupied even before breakfast, and just before luncheon she was summoned to fill bowls and containers with flowers delivered moments before.

Meg had offered her assistance in the day's tasks, but since that young woman's help consisted mostly of a great deal of bustle with very little accomplished, Alison had encouraged her to go along when friends called to whisk her off to a visit with a friend living in Bailbrook, on the London Road. The party had left some two hours earlier in great good spirits.

Alison glanced down at the blossoms lying on the table in the little service room off the kitchen, and her eyes grew dreamy. She drew her fingers over iris and daffodil, reliving the moment days before when March had swept flowers from that same table and taken her in his arms. Now, shivering anew at the memory of his touch, of the heat of his lips on hers, she pressed the blooms to her cheek. Her body warmed again in an unthinking response and she was forced to take several long breaths to bring herself back to the present. She bent once more to her task, and had just begun working on the huge arrangement to be placed in the entrance hall when quick footsteps in the corridor caught her attention.

'Finster!' she cried as Meg's maid hurtled into the room. 'Whatever are you doing here? Did you not go with Lady Meg when she left for Bailbrook?'

Finster had taken great pains to avoid her since the night she had assisted her mistress in her clandestine attendance at the masquerade ball, so Alison was doubly surprised when Finster ran to her and clutched her sleeve anxiously.

'Yes, I did leave with Lady Meg, but she is still with her friends – or at least – oh, Miss Fox, I'm so afraid something bad is happening to her!'

The maid now had Alison's undivided attention and she drew her to a nearby chair. 'What is it, Hannah?' she asked quickly, using the maid's first name in an effort to put her at ease. 'Tell me.'

'As you know, ma'am, the young ladies and the mamas of two of them left here in two coaches, and at that it was something of a crunch. Well, we'd not got out of town yet – only to Grosvenor Place – when Miss Pargeter declared that the little tea shop we were just passing sold the best damson tarts in the world. So, nothing would do but we must stop. We had no more got into the shop when in walks Mr Jack Crawford.'

'Jack!' gasped Alison.

'Yes, ma'am, and I know you're not overly fond of him.'

'No,' agreed Alison faintly.

'To make matters worse, he was with another, er, sporting gentleman, and I recognized him, too. Yes,' she said in response to Alison's expression of surprise. 'He ain't – hasn't never been to the house here, but I've seen him hangin' about, asking questions of the younger maids when they were outside polishing the door brass or sweeping the steps. Short little weasel, he is, with squinty eyes.

'Anyway, Mr Crawford was all grinning surprise when he greeted the girls and their mamas, and after a few minutes of him emptying the butter boat over Lady Meg, she invited him to come along on their visit.'

'Oh, no!' *Damn* Jack Crawford! How dare he try to cozen Meg after he had been warned to stay away from her.

'Yes. Well, there wasn't room for him and Giles Something – the squinty-eyed fellow – in either of the coaches, so Mr Crawford says, cool as you please, that he would take Lady Meg up in his curricle. The little minx – begging your pardon, ma'am – was tickled purple at the offer, of course. Now, there was only room for two in the curricle, so Squinty Eyes – Morganton, his name was,' said Hannah in sudden memory, 'Giles Morganton. Anyways, he says, oh, that's all right because he wished to return to town anyway and would hire a rig to take him back.'

'But, I don't understand. Why did you return home as well?' asked Alison with some impatience.

'It was all because,' continued Hannah Finster indignantly, 'of that Mrs Binsham, Mary Binsham's mama. If you don't mind me saying so, ma'am, the woman is fat as one of those hippy-potteruses and she'd been complaining from the start of the journey about me being along. Said she was being squeezed to a thread, and Lady Meg didn't need to be accompanied by her maid anyway, since she and Mrs Featherstone were along.

'I didn't like the idea of Lady Meg traveling in Mr Crawford's company, but I thought it would be all right as long as I would be following in the coach. Well, I had no sooner started to climb up when Mrs Binsham says to Lady Meg, "You may as well send your maid back to Bath with Mr Morganton. That way we can all travel comfortably." '

Alison muttered something unintelligible under her breath.

'Yes,' said Hannah. 'Well, as you might imagine, Lady Meg thought this a brilliant idea, and despite my protests insisted that I return home, and they all clattered off without me. Lady Meg looking like the cat that ate the canary as she tooled off with that Crawford feller.'

'I'm surprised Mr, er, Morganton agreed to this,' said Alison after a moment.

'It's my belief he and Mr Crawford had it all planned out, for they exchanged such a look before they parted. Then – if you can believe it – Morganton turned to me and said he wanted to get a bite to eat before we left, if I didn't mind. Well, I wasn't about t'be outsmarted by the likes of him, so I smiles politely and says I had to use the necessary house and I'd wait for him outside. As soon as he went into the tea shop, I nipped across the road to the livery stable there and hired a gig to bring me home. Luckily I had the needful in my reticule, and I set off that instant.' The little maid drew a deep breath. 'I may be all wrong, ma'am, but it's my belief that Mr Jack Crawford is up to no good with Lady Meg, and that squinty-eyed Giles Morganton is helpin' him.'

Alison did not respond immediately, her thoughts whirling in distress. Jack had been furious at her defection, and frightened as well. Desperate for money and terrified of his creditors, he must have searched frantically in his mind for a solution to his problems. Obviously, it had not taken him long to realize that little Lady Margaret Brent could provide his salvation. Good God, Jack meant to compromise Meg, forcing the wealthy Brent family to accept him as a husband for her! Jack Crawford would be supplied with funds for his immediate needs as well as almost unlimited treasure for future speculation.

Not if Alison could help it.

She whirled around. 'Hannah, you are a godsend! And I think you may have saved Lady Meg from a very sticky situation. Go get one of the footmen and meet me in the stables. We're going after them.'

The maid ran from the room, and Alison, pausing only to scribble a note to Lady Edith, ran from the house. Once in the stables, she made a hurried perusal of the vehicles available. Unfortunately, Lady Edith did not possess a curricle, having no need for a sporting rig. Her town carriage was large and heavy, and the traveling coach even more so.

'We'll take the gig,' said Alison to the bemused head groom. 'We shan't need to bother John Coachman, for – ah, Blickling!' she called to the young footman running toward her with Hannah close behind him. He was tall and sturdy, with yellow hair and round blue eyes that were at present blazing with excitement.

'Hannah explained everything, ma'am,' said the young man, the words tumbling from him. 'We'll find them, never fear.'

Whatley, Lady Edith's head groom, hitched a horse to the rig in bemused silence, shaking his head as the little group clattered from the stable yard.

'I wish,' said Alison rather breathlessly, 'that the gig could be pulled by two horses instead of one, but perhaps since it is so small and light – even more so than a curricle, I think – we shall have the advantage.'

Conversation among the three was minimal as the young footman guided the gig with surprising expertise through the traffic of Bath, soon emerging on the London Road. He let the horse have its head, and it was not long before they left the environs of the city.

It was not for another two hours, however, until they passed

Lambridge, that their pursuit bore fruit.

'Look!' cried Hannah, pointing a finger.

Alison strained to look, and saw two coaches at the side of the road ahead. As they drew nearer, a small group of persons could be seen standing about, chattering excitedly. Alison perceived Sally Pargeter in the group and ordered Blickling to pull up. As she dismounted, Sally separated herself from the group and ran up to the gig.

'Oh, Miss Fox! How fortunate that you are come! We have had an accident!'

Alison, ascertaining that no one in the party was injured, hurriedly questioned the two coachmen, who were laboring at the left rear wheel of one of the vehicles.

'Demmed – beggin' yer pardon, ma'am – dratted thing just up and broke. One of the spokes snapped. Don't understand it, neither. I'd be willin' to swear there warn't nothin' wrong with it when we left. I'da noticed, sure.' The burly man gestured to the wheel, lying in the road near the awkwardly leaning coach. 'Can't be fixed, neither. We was just about t'send t'other coach on ahead for help, but pr'aps y'could send the youngun there instead.' He gestured with a stubby thumb toward Blickling. 'He'd prolly get there sooner.'

'But—' said Alison, looking around, 'did you not send Mr Crawford for help? I do not see his vehicle.'

At this, Mrs Binsham bustled up, her plump face florid with indignation. 'No, nor are you likely to,' she said, puffing noisily. 'We haven't seen hide nor hair of Mr Crawford – or young Miss Meg – for the last ten miles.'

'What?' gasped Alison, her heart lurching in fear.

'Immediately we set out, Mr Crawford slapped his reins and that dashing rig of his spurted ahead of us and was very soon out of sight. Scandalous, I call it!'

Alison turned away without answering and, remounting the gig, ordered Blickling to drive on.

'Wait!' shrieked Mrs Binsham. 'You are not just going to leave us here!'

'I am sorry,' Alison called back as the gig picked up speed. 'I shall send help back when we have caught up with Meg.'

It was not long before they came to the Bailbrook turnoff and Blickling lifted his hands to guide the horse to the left.

'No,' said Alison sharply, 'I do not believe Jack has taken Meg to Bailbrook. I think he will continue on – and so shall we. Keep on the London Road, and we shall soon catch sight of Jack's "dashing rig." '

Please God, thought Alison, let them find the pair soon. With a start of guilt, she realized that, though she was filled with outrage at the thought of what Jack was doing to Meg, her anger was mainly on March's behalf. Was tragedy about to strike his family again? True, Meg stood in no physical danger, but if she were forced to marry Jack, her life would be ruined, and March would feel her pain as his own. With a surge of desperation, Alison knew that, just as with Susannah and William – and the old earl – she was at least indirectly responsible for this latest disaster. For it was through her that Jack had become acquainted with Meg. March would not likely see this as her fault, it would be simply one more reason for him to wish devoutly that Alison Fox had never left the small, safe village of Ridstowe to blunder into his life.

As the miles slipped by with no sign of Jack or his curricle, Alison's hopes sank. Jack would be unable to reach London today, but once he reached Marlborough, he could branch off onto one of several other, less traveled roads leading to the metropolis without much loss of time. It seemed unlikely that he would risk a moment to stop at an inn along the way.

Still, she hastily scanned the yards of every hostelry they passed, and suddenly her breath caught. At the same time, Hannah jerked to attention.

'Look – there!' she exclaimed, pointing. 'Just outside that little posting inn. That girl in the pink dimity! It's Lady Meg!'

CHAPTER 21

'Oh, thank God,' breathed Alison. For Meg, though struggling in Jack's grasp, seemed unharmed. So engrossed were the combatants that they apparently were not aware of the approaching gig. Blickling, who had been apprised by Hannah of the facts regarding Lady Meg's present contretemps, strode up to Jack and placed a purposeful hand on his shoulder.

'What the devil—?' Jack snarled, whirling about. Seeing Alison, he stopped abruptly. Meg caught sight of Alison at the same moment and flung herself upon the young woman.

'Oh, Alison! You'll never guess what happened! This awful man was trying to abduct me!'

At this, Blickling, who apparently felt words at this point were insufficient, threw a punch at Jack and dropped him like a felled tree.

'Oh, my goodness,' breathed Hannah, gazing worshipfully at the young footman.

'Thank you, Blickling,' said Alison unsteadily. 'No, do not hit him again. I think he has been properly subdued.' She turned to Meg, whose face was buried in Alison's bodice and whose shoulders shook with sobs. 'There, there, my dear. It's all right. You are safe now.'

With the point of her toe, Alison nudged Jack, who was beginning to stir. 'You unspeakable blackguard,' she said flatly. 'To think all this time I have been trying so hard to convince myself and others that you are not a truly bad man. Get up.' She prodded him again and Jack rose to his feet with a groan. He turned a baleful glance on Blickling, but made no move to offer retribution for the bruise swelling on his jaw.

'Alison! I can explain. . . .'

'Explain!' shrieked Meg, moving to add her own punishment to that of the redoubtable Blickling. In a swift movement, she administered a stinging slap atop the bruise, prompting an inelegant scream of anguish from Jack. 'I'd like to hear you explain how you tricked me into getting into your curricle, and then, when I pointed out that we had gone past the turnoff to Bailbrook, you spouted some nonsense about taking a shortcut.'

'Yes,' said Alison, her blue eyes turned to steel, 'I should very much like to hear all about this.'

'Ma'am,' interjected Hannah, gesturing to the little crowd of onlookers gathering about them, 'pr'aps we should go inside.'

Alison nodded and swept Meg into the inn, indicating to Blickling her wish that Jack follow. Blickling saw to this by the simple measure of twisting Jack's arm behind his back and lifting him from the ground to propel him forward.

After the landlord had ushered them into a private parlor at the rear of the inn, Alison turned to face Jack.

'Now, Jack, what is this all about?'

'I *told* you what it was about!' wailed Meg before Jack could answer. 'He was abducting me! When I saw that we were actually on our way to London, I pretended to be sick and said he would shortly be very sorry if we didn't stop for a moment.'

'How clever of you, Meg,' said Alison soothingly.

'I wasn't really going to abduct her,' Jack said sullenly, then ducked as Meg rounded on him once more.

'You dreadful man! If you say one more word, I shall—' Meg raised two small fists in a threatening manner, to Blickling's obvious admiration.

'Alison!' Jack's voice held an agonized plea. 'Could we speak privately? Truly, I can explain . . .' He flinched, shooting a wary glance at Meg. 'I will tell you what happened if we could just get out of this commotion for a moment.'

Alison hesitated. She did not trust Jack Crawford any farther than she could throw the sturdy table against which he was leaning, but if he did have an explanation of what he had done. . . .

And, after all, she had Blickling's fierce protection.

'All right, Jack. Meg, do you feel well enough to travel back to Bath?' At Meg's vehement nod, she continued. 'Then, Hannah, will you take Lady Meg outside? Blickling will wait with you. I shall only be a moment.'

The little group, though vociferous in their disapproval of this program, eventually trudged from the room to the front of the inn. Alison turned once more to Jack.

'Now then,' said that gentleman with a nervous chuckle, 'I really had no intention of abducting Meg. At least, not permanently.'

'Of course not,' retorted Alison. 'You merely wished to compromise her. Marriage into the Brent family would solve all your problems, would it not?'

'No, that wasn't it at all,' said Jack in some indignation. 'I did plan to compromise her, but as for marriage. . . . No, all I wanted to do was put Marchford in a position where he would pay a great deal of money for my silence.'

'Good God! You were going to blackmail him?'

Jack shifted uncomfortably and tried out an ingratiating grin. 'Only a little. And, it's not as though Marchford can't afford the blunt.' He perceived the grin was having little effect, and continued hastily. 'Well, what else was I to do? I told you, I am in between the devil and a steep cliff.'

'Would you had chosen the steep cliff,' was Alison's sharp rejoinder. She rose. 'If that is your idea of an explanation, Jack, it needs a great deal of improvement. Now, I am going to join the others, and if I were you, I would make myself extremely scarce for the foreseeable future. When the earl hears of this, I have a feeling he will be on your trail like a burr. And let me tell you, Jack, the Earl of Marchford can be very tenacious.'

Jack merely stared at Alison for a long moment, and a curl of unease stirred inside her. When he finally spoke, his voice was soft, almost tender as he drew closer to her.

'Oh, Alison, why do you have to make things so difficult? If only you had—' His sentence went unfinished as he raised his fist suddenly and caught Alison with a blow to her chin. She fell in a soundless heap, and Jack gathered her up in his arms. Laying her on the floor for a moment, he paused to avail himself of notepaper and pen procured from a small desk set before the window. Quickly, he scribbled a note, which he twisted into a screw and tossed on the table in the center of the room. Then, stepping to the window, he called softly to a short, thick-set young man standing outside in the stable yard. Lifting Alison up once more, he climbed with some effort through the window into the stable yard, where, with the assistance of his companion, he half walked and half carried Alison to his waiting curricle.

Moving quickly, the two bundled the young woman into the vehicle, thrusting her to the floor, where Jack threw a rug over her unconscious form. The few persons in the stable yard, busy with their own concerns, paid no heed to these odd goings-on.

The young man clambered onto the small seat at the rear of the vehicle as Jack took his own place, smiling as he slapped the reins against his horses. The curricle moved at a brisk trot through the gate. Once out of the stable yard, Jack chose a circuitous route, entering the highway some half a mile beyond the entrance to the inn, where Meg and her protectors stood waiting for Alison.

Jack permitted himself a congratulatory chuckle as he gazed down at the motionless rug. 'When the kit bolts from one hole,' he murmured, 'the wise man knows to wait at another for the vixen.' Bursting into a loud laugh at his own wit, Jack slapped the reins once more, and turned his curricle toward London.

March hurried up the steps to the house in Royal Crescent in response to an urgent summons from his aunt. Entering, he found her pacing the marquetry floor of the entrance hall.

'March!' she cried. 'Thank God you've come.'

'I came as soon as I received your message. What is it, Aunt?' Indeed, the old lady looked agitated and most unwell. Her silvery hair was in disarray and her face was pale and drawn.

'It's Alison! She's gone! She's gone after Jack Crawford!'

An unpleasant sensation curled in the pit of March's stomach. 'What? What are you talking about?'

Lady Edith handed him the piece of paper she was waving in one hand. 'She left a note saying that Jack had left town and that she was following him. My God, March, why would she do such a thing?'

March snatched the missive from her and scanned it hastily.

'*Lady Edith,*' Alison had written, '*Jack has left Bath for London. I must go after him. Do not worry, I am taking Blickling with me.*'

'Blickling?' he asked blankly.

'I don't understand that, either. Why would one take a foot-man on an elopement?'

'Elopement,' he echoed stupidly.

'March,' said his aunt in some asperity, 'if you are simply going to repeat everything I say, we shall get nowhere. I cannot believe Alison would run off with Jack Crawford, but why would she want to give that impression?'

'My God.' March perused the note once more. No! She would not do this. He could have sworn that Alison's feelings for Crawford consisted only of contempt and fear. The bastard's precipitate departure from the city had been expected, but why in God's name would Alison follow him?

'This is Alison's handwriting?' he asked, grasping at straws.

'Yes.'

March's jaw tightened as he faced his aunt. 'I'm going after her. I cannot believe she is doing this of her own free will.'

'I quite agree with you, March. I don't know what's going on, but I know Alison. She would never simply pick up and leave like some sort of lightskirt – particularly not with Jack Crawford. Go, my dear.' Her fragile voice trembled. 'And please, bring her back safely.'

March whirled and ran from the house. Mounting his curricle, he flung a brief word of explanation to Toby, who assumed his post with an expression of determination on his gamin features. The next moment, the curricle vanished from Royal Crescent in a whirling cloud of dust.

Grateful for the thinness of the traffic on this midweek morn-ing, March soon turned onto the London Road. Since he did not expect to catch sight of his quarry for some time, his attention

209

was solely on the road and his horses, for he was driving at what could only be called a shocking pace. Thus, it was with some astonishment that upon glancing up at a coach speeding past him in the opposite direction, he beheld his sister's face pressed in a pale 0 against the window. Looking over his shoulder, he saw Meg, her entire upper body thrust from the window of the coach, waving wildly at him.

Perhaps to ignore her – he really had not time for an idle gossip with Meg and her friends – he lifted his hands to slap his reins against the backs of his horses, but was suddenly struck by the distress evident of Meg's face. Cursing, he drew up sharply, barely waiting for his vehicle to stop moving before he leapt to the ground.

'March! Oh, March, thank God!' Meg cried breathlessly as she ran toward him along the side of the road. Flinging herself on him, she burst into tears, and over her shoulder, March observed Sally Pargeter and a varied assortment of unknown damsels and their mamas climbing down from the coach.

'Here, Meg. What the devil—?' He shook her gently. 'What is toward?'

'Oh, March,' gasped Meg again. 'It's Alison! She has run off to London with Jack Crawford.'

Dumbfounded, Jack stared at the young girl. 'What? How – how do you know about this? And what makes you think she has run off with him?'

Meg stared back, openmouthed, her eyes round as coat buttons. '*You* know? How—?'

'Never mind that,' grunted March as the party from the coach caught up with them. Their voices rose in unbridled cacophony until silenced by Mrs Binsham.

'What is the meaning of this?' asked the indignant matron, her several chins quivering with abandon. 'Are you in pursuit of Lady Edith Brent's companion?' At March's curt nod, she exclaimed in virtuous satisfaction. 'I knew it! Well, you may as well save your efforts, my lord, for the little tart is off and away with that Captain Sharp. No better than she should be, that one is, I've always said. That is. . . .' she trailed off, quailing before the undisguised malevolence in March's glare.

'Just what makes you think Ali – Miss Fox is in Mr Crawford's company?' asked March coldly, feeling that the thundering of his heart must be audible to the whole group.

'Why, she left a note!' exclaimed Mrs Binsham, triumphantly proffering a screw of paper to the earl. March took the paper in numb fingers and simply stared at it, his gaze finally transferring to Meg in bewilderment.

'I don't understand how you are involved in this,' he said. 'Any of you,' he concluded, his gaze sweeping over the females.

Meg, perceiving his bewilderment, put her hand on his arm.

'March, it's all very simple. Let me explain.' In a few words she described the circumstances that had led to her presence in the little hostelry a few miles down the road. March's features hardened as he listened to her tale, but he forbore to give Meg the scolding she no doubt richly deserved for haring off with Crawford in his damned curricle to begin with. That, he promised himself, would come later.

'We all went outside, as she told us,' continued Meg, 'and waited in front of the inn for her. And waited, and waited. Finally, we returned to the private parlor only to find both Alison and Ja – Mr Crawford gone, and this note left on the table.' She gestured to the piece of paper in March's hand. 'It's signed by Alison and it says that she has come to the conclusion she would be better off going to London under Jack's protection than she would remaining in Bath and dwindling into a dried-up old prune. Those were her very words,' the girl added hastily. 'But, I don't think for one moment she really wrote it.'

'You are familiar with her handwriting?' asked March.

'No, but—'

'Really, my lord.' It was Mrs Binsham again, her prominent jaw thrust before her like the blade of a plough. 'It's plain as a pikestaff that—'

She was interrupted rudely as Finster thrust herself to the forefront of the little group and grasped March's sleeve.

'What's plain, my lord, is that some people don't have the sense God gave a banty rooster. I'd be willing to swear Miss Fox

211

was ready to do that Crawford murder. She wouldn't any more have run off with him than she would with Old Nick himself.'

Mrs Binsham swelled ominously, and her mouth opened, only to close swiftly as the earl lifted a hand for silence. Quickly, he ran his gaze over the note, written in a thick, awkward scrawl. No, there was no similarity to the delicate hand he had seen on the note given to him earlier by his aunt. Not that he needed any proof to know that if Alison were indeed in Jack Crawford's company, she was not there of her own free will. His trust in Alison, he thought almost exultantly, was unshakable. The next moment, he was almost overcome by a wave of pure rage. He had warned Crawford not to make any more trouble for Alison, and the unspeakable cur had dared try once more to ensnare Alison in his wild plans.

Well, we shall see, he mused murderously. We shall soon see. He turned to Meg. 'Where?'

'At the Horse and Jockey Inn,' replied Meg. 'Just outside Atford. And they must have left there less than an hour ago. Oh, do hurry, March. And I hope you horsewhip that dreadful Mr Crawford!'

Smiling grimly, March dropped a kiss on his sister's forehead and climbed once more into his curricle, which soon receded to a point on the horizon.

'Well!' exclaimed Mrs Binsham, after which, discovering that no one was listening, she clambered aboard the coach.

CHAPTER 22

Alison woke in the darkness beneath the rug to the conviction that her head was cracking in two. Her jaw ached wretchedly, and a vile odor filled her nose. The next moment, she became aware that she had been gagged and bound and that the surface beneath her was moving.

She made an instinctive movement to free herself, to no avail. The only result of her efforts was the sound of soft laughter coming from somewhere above her.

'Awake, are you, Alison? Sorry for my rather rough and ready methods, but you left me no alternative.'

Alison had little difficulty in recognizing Jack's voice, and she realized with alarm that she was in a moving vehicle that was apparently being pulled off to the side of the road. The next instant, the rug was drawn away from her, and she blinked for a moment at the sunlight before glaring balefully at Jack.

Her captor then reached to remove the gag. Alison immediately opened her mouth to scream, but Jack cautioned her gently. 'It will do you no good to make a fuss, love. As you can see, we are in a deserted section of the highway, and there is no one to hear.' He stared with some regret at the ugly bruise he had left. 'I am truly sorry, Alison.'

'You keep saying that,' Alison replied through clenched teeth as she struggled to lift herself upon the seat of the curricle.

Jack's laugh held the merest hint of repentance. 'Yes, I guess that is true, but it is not through my own desire that we keep plunging from one disaster to another. Now, I think it would be unwise to release you, but, if you are very good, I shall not replace the gag. I must warn you, however, that if you so much as squeak during the remainder of our journey, Felcher here will simply hit you over the head.' This last was uttered in such a matter-of-fact tone that Alison had no difficulty in believing him. Alison gaped in surprise at the young man crouched in the tiger's seat. Jack, observing the direction of her stare, chuckled.

'A gentleman does not set out in his curricle without his tiger, my dear. Meet Twist Felcher. If he has another name, neither of us is aware of it.'

Alison sent a pleading glance toward Mr Felcher, who appeared to be barely out of his teens, but received only a surly scowl in response. Desperately, she turned to her captor once more.

'Jack, this is insane. Do you not think we will be pursued? How long do you think the others will have waited before coming back to look for me? When they find I am gone—'

'All taken care of,' he answered with an airy wave of his hand. 'I left a note that I believe will discourage any such interference. By the time anyone should decide to come to your aid, we will be safely tucked away in London, for I plan to stop only briefly – at a snug little hideaway I know of in Foxfield, just off the highway. We'll be on our way again in the morning before cockcrow, and by this time tomorrow we will have reached our destination.'

'Which is?' asked Alison fearfully.

Jack set his curricle in motion again. 'I think I shall not tell you that right now,' he replied pensively. Unceremoniously, he pushed her back to the floor of the vehicle and threw the rug over her head again. 'Time enough for all to be revealed to you when we reach London.'

'But, Jack—' she expostulated, her voice muffled beneath the folds of the rug. She was rewarded with a minatory thump on the head.

'Enough, my dear,' said Jack calmly. 'Remember – not so much as a squeak.'

Subsiding into her musty prison, Alison gave herself up to a frantic evaluation of her position. She must get free of Jack somehow, for once he got her to London, her situation would become desperate. God knew where he was taking her, and even though it was unlikely that he could keep her a prisoner indefinitely, her eventual escape would leave her little better off than before. A woman alone and penniless in London was prey to evils too horrible to contemplate.

At least Jack had taken that filthy rag from her mouth. She had no doubt that he would carry out his threat to render her unconscious again were she to call out. But . . . if she could just put herself out of his reach once they reached a village, perhaps. . . .

She gave an experimental tug on the rope that bound her wrists, and her heart leapt. In his haste, Jack – or his surly young cohort – had not tied them very securely. Trying to keep her movement to a minimum in order to avoid notice, she began to work her hands back and forth. At first her efforts met with little success, but after a small eternity she began to feel a loosening of the rope. At one point, Jack pulled the rug back, and Alison immediately slumped forward, her head drooping to one side as though she were on the verge of fainting.

'Jack, please . . .' she whimpered, and her captor shrugged an apology.

'I'm truly sorry, Alison—' he paused, his mouth twisting in a grimace, 'I do seem to say that to you fairly frequently, don't I? If only you had not been so recalcitrant. You'll see, Alison, that I have only your best interests at heart. Life in London as a wealthy woman will suit you much better than mouldering away in Bath at the beck and call of a crotchety old woman.'

Alison, unable to give vent to even one of the furious responses this ingenuous speech provoked, contented herself with a contemptuous glare. Unheeding, Jack continued. 'We won't have to keep this up for too much longer, my dear. To-morrow, you may sit on the seat beside me, for there will be no one looking for us then. Felcher, of course, will see that you do not do anything foolish.' With what he no doubt considered a reassuring wink, he tossed the rug over her once more.

Another reason she must escape before they reached tonight's destination, Alison thought grimly, working in silent fury at the ropes. To her vast relief, it was not long before she was able to slip one of the coils over her wrists, and the rest soon followed. Thank God! Now, all she needed to do was wait until the curricle slowed for a village – or better yet, a tollgate – and she could—

Her racing thoughts were interrupted by a startled cry from Jack. He cursed fluently, and the curricle swerved violently before picking up speed. Cautiously, her hands still held behind her, Alison wriggled enough so that the rug fell away from her head. Jack's attention was wholly centered on the road ahead, as was that of Felcher, although both glanced frequently over their shoulders.

Risking further movement, Alison twisted so that she, too, could see the road behind the curricle. She discerned a vehicle some distance behind them that seemed to be traveling at a great rate of speed. Was it Blickling? Or – her pulse quickened – could it be March? Jack evidently thought this an all-too-real possibility, for he urged his horses on to breakneck speed. His face was contorted with fear, and he did not so much as glance at Alison as she fought free of the rug.

Behind them, the pursuing vehicle grew closer and closer, until. . . .

'March!' The cry sprang involuntarily from Alison's lips, bringing her immediately to Jack's notice. He raised a hand to strike her, but she twisted away from him. Bringing both hands up, she grabbed at Jack's wrists, thrusting them into an upward position that caused the horses to break stride.

With a snarled curse, Jack swung at her, knocking her back to the floor. Alison was dimly aware that behind her, Felcher was moving toward her and she cowered defensively. The next moment, however, to her astonishment, Jack jerked viciously on the reins.

When the vehicle had stopped, he turned to her and, with a savage growl, struck her once more, nearly rendering her unconscious. Felcher loomed over her as well, with fist upraised.

'No!' Jack's voice cut harshly into the fuzzy haze that surged

216

at the edges of her mind. He reached to shake her shoulder. 'Get out!' he snapped.

'What?' she blurted, echoed by Felcher.

'I said get out,' repeated Jack in a high scream. To Felcher, he shouted, 'The game's up, you fool! We can't outrun Marchford, but if we give him the girl, he'll give up the chase.'

So saying, he shook her again and jerked her upright with a vicious tug. Still momentarily disoriented, she gaped at him before struggling to do his bidding. She did not move quickly enough to suit Felcher, however, and grasping her with both hands, the burly tiger literally threw her from her seat to the side of the road. Without a second look at her, Jack set the curricle once more into violent motion, and within moments was nearly out of sight.

Alison did not watch his progress, but leapt to her feet to fly along the road toward March. The earl, bringing his vehicle to a shuddering halt, ran to her, and the next instant, she found herself caught in his arms. Pressing against the wonderfully solid, safe length of him, she could only repeat his name over and over, murmuring unintelligible endearments into his waistcoat. She wrapped her arms around him, trying to pull herself even closer, as though she might somehow be absorbed into him.

For a moment, March was content just to hold her, exulting in the fact that he had her safe. He drew his hands over the dusty disarray of her hair and down over her shoulders. He pulled back for an instant to look into her face.

'Alison, my dearest girl. Are you all right?' He stiffened as he observed the bruise discoloring her cheek. 'My God! Did that bastard—?'

Shuddering, she nodded, luxuriating in his concern. 'But please,' she cried as she felt his muscles bunch beneath her hands, 'don't go after him!' She could not bear to leave his embrace.

He laughed mirthlessly. 'No, I shan't do that – at least for the present. I believe he's plunging helter-skelter toward a punishment more fitting than any I could contrive for him. There will

217

be some very ugly, angry persons awaiting his return to London.'

Drawing her into his arms again, March led her toward his curricle and assisted her into a seat beside him. Toby, moving to help, beamed a reassuring smile that sat oddly on his elfin features.

'His lordship's been in a real swivet, ma'am, but we've got you safe now, so all's right and tight.'

Right and tight, indeed, Alison thought muzzily, reveling in the warmth of March's smile. In the recesses of her mind, she was aware that his daring rescue was merely an indication of his affection for his aunt – in addition, of course, to his famous sense of duty – but she did not want to consider that right now. It was enough for the moment to know that she was safe and to bathe in March's golden gaze.

March remained oddly silent for the next few miles. Then, straightening as though he had come to a decision, he turned to her. 'I believe we will stop at the next inn. You will want to repair yourself before we reach Bath.'

Startled, Alison put a hand to her hair. Gracious, it felt like a rat's nest! Glancing down at herself, she realized the same might be said of her clothing, which was torn in some places and incredibly dirty.

'Dear me!' she said, blushing. 'You are very right. I don't suppose I can do much for my gown, but if we can procure a clean comb, my hair would benefit, I am sure.'

March grinned at her, but the expression in his eyes was very odd. She could have sworn she beheld a certain possessiveness in their tawny depths, but she must be mistaken. Or, perhaps it was simply the male mentality at work. Rescuing a damsel in distress inevitably granted the rescuer certain prerogatives in arranging the rescuee's life, she supposed. At any rate, when he turned the curricle into the stable yard of the Five Swans at the top of Bower Hill, she gratefully accepted the offer of a bedchamber where she could put herself to rights. Having accomplished as much as she could in this direction, she betook herself downstairs, where she found the earl waiting for her in a private parlor.

She was a little startled at this circumstance, since she had expected March would want them to be on their way as soon as she was presentable. Her brows lifted in mute question as she entered the room.

March rose to greet her, his eyes drinking in the sight of her. Back in the curricle, with her hair straggling down her back and a bruise on her cheek, she had still managed to look breathtakingly beautiful. Now, her appearance only marginally improved, and with her hair swept into a makeshift knot atop her head, she looked like a princess in disguise. He noted the grace with which she moved toward him and the smile that shone in the depths of her blue eyes, and he swallowed spasmodically.

He took a deep breath. The notion that had struck him on the road had seemed brilliant in its clarity and simplicity at the time, and he had made an instant decision to act on it. There had been only a few moments to consider his next move, and now he was uncertain of his wisdom in proceeding. He knew only that if he were to miss this opportunity, he would regret it bitterly for the rest of his life.

'Do sit down, Alison,' he said briskly, indicating a chair near a curtained window. 'May I pour you some wine?' He indicated a tray on a nearby table. 'Or perhaps some lemonade?'

Alison was finding his demeanor curious in the extreme. If she did not know better, she would have said he was nervous. The Earl of Marchford nervous? How perfectly ludicrous, she thought.

'Should we not be getting home?' she asked hesitantly.

'Yes, in due time, but I thought this would be a good time to make our plans before facing my aunt and the rest of Bath society.'

'Plans?'

'Yes, for our wedding.' He spoke in a matter-of-fact tone, and for a moment, Alison thought she could not have heard him aright. Either that, or she was going mad.

'I – I beg your pardon?' she gasped.

'For our wedding,' he repeated slowly. 'I think it best we decide very soon when and where the ceremony should be

219

held.' He cocked his head to one side, putting her very much in mind of a large, expectant cat. 'Don't you?'

'Don't I what?' she asked dazedly.

March reached out to cover his hand with her own. 'I know this must be somewhat confusing to you, my dear, but—'

She snatched her hand away. 'Confusing! My lord, I think it is you who are all about in your head. You – you spoke of marriage!'

'Yes. Now, do you prefer Bath or London? Or perhaps you would like to be married in Ridstowe.'

'My lord!'

'We must be married, you know – and, by the way, I do think it's time you dropped that ridiculous "my lord". You must realize that you are utterly compromised.'

Alison's hand flew to her mouth. 'Oh! Oh, but. . . .'

'You were thought to have run off with Crawford this morning, and that unspeakable Bumshot female will have brayed the tale all over Bath by this afternoon. Whatever possessed you, by the way, to leave a note for Aunt Edith saying you were eloping with Crawford? And, of course, here you are, completely alone with still another man.'

Alison had by now gone perfectly white, and March ached to gather her into his arms. 'I did *not* say I was ... Oh.' Comprehension flooded her face. 'I did not want to mention Meg's name for fear of worrying Lady Edith,' she finished lamely. 'Anyway, you are being perfectly ridiculous!' she cried. 'Do you think I care for what Mrs Binsham' – she pronounced the name with great precision – 'will say? I know I did nothing wrong, and that is all that counts.'

'Really? What about Aunt Edith? Of course, she will stand by you, but at what cost? How many of her friends will be coming to her dinner parties from now on? How many cuts direct do you suppose she will suffer at the Upper Rooms?'

'Oh, dear God,' said Alison, stricken. She rose abruptly to pace the floor before whirling to him once more. 'But to suggest that you are obliged to marry me. . . . You cannot be serious!'

March, too, rose, and stood before her. He placed his hands on her shoulders and drew her toward him. 'I have never been more serious in my life.'

'But—' Her eyes, as she gazed up at him, were like forget-me-nots, fresh from the heart of the forest. 'You cannot *wish* to marry me.'

'Of course not,' he said gravely, bending his head to hers. 'Why should I want to be leg-shackled to a lovely woman whose wit and intelligence warm me and whose smile turns me to jelly.'

The thought flashed through Alison's mind that she must somehow save March from himself. It was, she told herself with great firmness, his stupid, single-minded sense of responsibility talking. She must make it clear that she had no intention of accepting his very kind offer. Indeed, she thought, just before his lips came down on hers, the idea of a marriage of convenience between herself and the Earl of Marchford was unthinkable. Dear God, if only she didn't love him so, were the last words her brain was able to form as she lost herself in the dazzling wonder of his kiss. If only his mouth weren't so warm and firm; if only his touch did not send her into a spiral of wanting.

Breathless, she wrenched herself away from him. 'My lord,' she said in a completely unsuccessful assumption of authority, 'the idea of a marriage of convenience is not at all to my taste. It is very kind of you to offer . . . but, I fear we would not suit.'

'Kind! Is that what you are thinking? Do you really think I would offer for you out of a misguided sense of duty?' His gaze bored into hers. 'Are you saying that you do not care for me?'

'R-really, my lord,' she stammered, 'I am sure I have never given you cause to believe—'

'To believe that your heart is not untouched? I must admit, my very dearest love, that is what I thought until a little while ago. Do you recall your words not an hour hence when you – well, not to put too fine a point on it – you flung yourself into my arms?'

The pallor of Alison's cheeks was replaced by a painful flush, as she put her hands to her face. 'Oh! Oh, noo-oo,' she wailed. 'You heard? I did not think – that is . . .' she backed away from him. 'It is not gentlemanly to throw words spoken in – in distress in my face.'

March's laughter was gentle as he gathered her into his arms once more. 'No, it is not, my very dearest love, but I have grown so tired of being the perfect gentleman.' He paused to gaze down into her face, and his own grew serious. 'Alison, I have wasted a great deal of time in my vengeful pursuit of one I considered a heartless vixen. Now, I have discovered that a vixen – one with midnight hair and eyes the color of heaven – is precisely what I need in my life.' Alison shivered as she beheld the gold fire in his eyes. 'Oh, Alison, I have contrived probably the most idiotic proposal in the history of mankind, but I have not been thinking clearly of late, and desperation does call for strong measures. I have allowed myself to hope that you love me . . . but, in truth, I will not force you. If you wish to proceed to Bath unbetrothed, I will stand with you against the world. But, oh, my love, I would so much rather stand with you before the world as your husband.'

There was a long silence, broken only by the sound of the breeze that sighed through the window, ruffling the curtains. At last, with a little cry, Alison moved once more into the circle of March's arms.

'Then, I think you had better kiss me again,' she whispered brokenly. 'I do not think I am compromised nearly enough.'

It was many moments before Alison was again capable of speech. Somehow, she found herself in March's lap, with her stained gown in even more disarray than it had been after her escape from Jack Crawford's curricle. 'March!' she gasped tremulously. 'We must stop!'

'Urn?' murmured March thickly, his lips against the silky skin at the base of her throat. His hands stilled at the point of undoing the last of the buttons that trooped down from her collar. 'Oh, my God,' he groaned, raising his head at last.

'I suppose you are right,' he continued, his voice husky. 'It would not do for us to be late for Aunt Edith's party.'

'The dinner party! Oh, good heavens, I had forgotten!'

'And after you have gone to such trouble on it?' An unholy

gleam sprang into his eyes. 'Aunt will be in alt at the fruition of her plans, I should think. Did you not guess?' he asked, observing the quizzical lift of Alison's brow. 'If I am not very much mistaken, it was her intention from the moment I set foot in Royal Crescent that we would wed.'

Alison uttered a little crow of laughter. 'I shouldn't wonder if you are right. I caught her perusing a display of wedding gowns in *La Belle Assemblée* the other day. She said she was looking ahead to Meg's nuptials, but she was blushing furiously. Immediately afterward she sat me down for a chronicle of your virtues.'

'You poor dear,' March murmured, gathering her to him again. 'It must have taken hours.' Following this statement, of course, March found it necessary to stifle Alison's laughing protest by the most expedient means at hand. 'By the by,' he continued some moments later, lifting his head with reluctance, 'do you recall if Aunt's party is to be graced by the presence of Mrs Bagjaw?'

'That's Mrs Binsham,' said Alison severely. 'As a matter of fact, she will indeed be there. Why?'

'I was just thinking, if we tell her our news right away, she should have the word spread about the country inside of a week. Just think of the savings in wedding announcements.'

'I do love a practical man,' whispered Alison, drawing his face to hers once more, and for some time thereafter, the only sound to be heard in the private parlor of the Five Swans was the rustle of the curtains in the spring breeze.

Also by Ann Barbour
and soon to be published:
A RAKE'S REFORM

THE RAKE AND THE REBEL

Lord Charles Trent was as infuriating, and as handsome, as Hester Blayne expected him to be – and more. He made no secret of his scandalous love life as leading rake in the realm, or of his scorn of anyone who would censor him.

For her part, Hester was as enraging as Lord Trent had heard – a firebrand of discontent whose eyes sparked with passion and whose writings inflamed women to stand up to men's power and proclaim their independence.

But when Hester tried to teach Trent the error of his immoral ways . . . and Trent set out to show Hester the folly of a female defying male might . . . both the unbending lord and the unbowed lady discovered how little they knew about each other—and about their own hidden yearnings and secret hearts. . . .